Other Books by

BRIDGET ANDERSON

Soul Mates
Lost to Love
Rendezvous
Reunited
All Because of You
Hot Summer Nights
Hotel Paradise

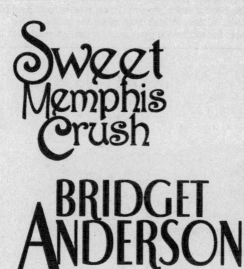

Sweet Memphis Crush

BRIDGET ANDERSON

ARABESQUE®

SWEET MEMPHIS CRUSH

An Arabesque novel

ISBN-13: 978-0-373-83003-9
ISBN-10:   0-373-83003-3

Copyright © 2007 by Bridget Anderson

www.kimanipress.com

Printed in U.S.A.

To my family and friends for all their support.

Chapter 1

"It's basketball, baby, not ballroom dancing." William Duncan sat across from Vince Harper, a local assistant coach, talking about one of Will's favorite subjects— sports. "The Grizzlies need a strong big man, not a bunch of little guys dancing around the court."

Vince laughed at Will's comment. "They already have a big man. What he needs to do is put some numbers on the board and average more than ten points a game."

"Okay, we'd better watch out before we get into trouble with the Grizzlies." With that said, Will turned and faced the camera.

"Well folks, this is William Duncan from *The Memphis Zone*, and that's it this week in Southern sports. I'd like to thank my guest tonight, Coach Vince Harper, who's with the Melrose High School Golden

Wildcats." He turned toward the coach. "Thanks for coming out, coach."

Vince smiled and nodded. "Not a problem, Will. Thanks for having me, I had a blast."

Will turned back to the camera. "I'll see you next week when my guest will be Gary Rankin, head coach for the Riverdale Warriors football team. So remember," Will said, holding up two fingers toward the camera. "Where can you get the inside scoop on local sports? Right here on *The Memphis Zone*."

The camera panned out, the lights rose, and Will unhooked his mike. He now had show number twenty-two successfully under his belt. He stood up and extended his hand to Vince. "Thanks again for coming down, man, I appreciate it."

"Sure man, anytime. And if you ever decide you need a cohost include me on that list. I like sitting around talking sports." Vince gave Will's hand a firm shake.

"I'll keep that in mind," Will said with a chuckle. He knew Coach Harper wasn't about to give up being on the field for sitting in a studio. Besides, he didn't want to crush his fantasy by revealing all the work that went into a weekly sports show. Somebody had to plan the show, book the guest, and write the script; and right now that somebody was Will.

"Vince, before you run off I wanted to invite you to bring some of the guys down to the studio sometime. I'd like to have them on the show. Or, we can come out and film a show from the gym."

Vince nodded. "I'll talk to Coach and get back to you."

"Thanks." Will made a mental note to call Vince in a couple of weeks.

Larry Stone, the executive producer of Gator Productions, and his sidekick, Manny, walked into the studio and over to the set, which consisted of a basic black laminated coffee table and two comfortable dark-brown cracked leather chairs. A mural of athletes in action completed the backdrop. As they crossed the room, the lights turned up full blast.

Larry was a short, stocky guy with the presence of a much larger man, which is why almost everyone called him Stone instead of Larry. He gave Will a thumbs-up.

"Great show," he said, before extending his hand and looking up at Vince. "Thanks for coming down, Vince, you're a natural on camera."

"Yeah right," Vince laughed. "But, I'll come back anytime you want me, just ask."

"I'm gonna hold you to that," Larry said, pointing at Vince. Then he turned and motioned for Manny to take a note. "Write that down. When the Wildcats win the state championship this year we'll call that marker in."

The men laughed and strolled off the set. An intern escorted Vince out while Will headed for his office.

Manny stopped short of running into his boss when Larry stopped and snapped his fingers. "Will, hold up. I've solved our little problem." He glanced back at Manny as he walked up to catch Will. "You got the résumés?"

"Right here, boss." Manny held up a manila folder.

"Give it to him."

Manny handed the folder to Will. "Mr. Stone wants

you to look those over and give him the green light on one. His preference is noted."

Larry's cell phone rang, and he gave Manny a sarcastic look. "I'm standing right here," he said flipping the phone open. "You were supposed to tell him that if I was gone." He rolled his eyes and mumbled something under his breath before answering the phone.

Eyes bulging, Manny rested a hand on his hip, and pulled his chin in. "Pardon me, but I'm performing my duties as assigned," he said, in a fake French accent.

Will shook his head, trying not to laugh as he turned his attention to the folder. This week Manny's a Frenchman; last week he was British. Will couldn't keep up with his changing accents and mannerisms. The love-hate relationship between Manny and Larry amazed Will. Manny took his job as office manager as seriously as he took his acting career. He never missed a beat. Larry recognized that but was homophobic, which kept things in the studio interesting.

Will didn't care one way or another about Manny's sexual preference, as long as it didn't affect any of his shows.

"Anyway," Manny said, turning back to Will.

The name on the first résumé caught Will's attention. He couldn't believe his eyes. He blinked and read it again. *It can't be.*

"Is everything okay?" Manny asked. "Your eyebrows are practically touching."

"When were these candidates interviewed?" Will asked, without looking up from the folder.

"Larry conducted phone interviews with them last

week. He's worked with one of them before, and I think his uncle Mack recommended the other one."

Will focused on the details in the résumé. Was this the Jodie Dickerson he knew? The age seemed about right. There was no high school or any other telltale information on the résumé, but somehow he knew this was his Jodie.

"You have this glazed-over look in your eyes." Manny waved his hand in Will's face. "Is something wrong?" he asked.

Will shook his head, clearing the images running through his mind's eye. It might not be her, he told himself. "No, everything's fine. I'll look these over in my office and get them back to you. When does he need an answer?" Will asked, gesturing with the folder toward Larry who was still on his cell phone.

"ASAP. In other words, I go home at four today and he wants your answer before then."

Will checked his watch. Eleven-twenty. "I'll let you know something in a few." He left the two of them standing in the hallway and walked down to his office.

Once inside, he sat down, took off his tie and leaned back in his chair. He propped his heels up on the corner of the desk, and pulled Jodie Dickerson's résumé from the folder. He read through the two pages carefully, noting all of her television experience, and longing for the days when personal information topped your résumé. Her employment history started at *The Clifton Reader* in Clifton, Tennessee. Bingo! The Jodie he knew worked at the hometown paper after he left for college. Stapled to the résumé was a business card that included her e-mail address and a Memphis phone number. The corners of his lips curled up.

"You're looking at the new producer of *Today's New Bride,* a show for the gal who's tired of the traditional and wants to jazz it up a bit."

Jodie Dickerson took out her last hot roller and glared at the imposter looking back at her in the mirror as she finger-combed her hair.

Her new roommate, Tracy, poked her head out from the bathroom at the other end of the hallway and laughed. "What do you know about brides or weddings? You've never been a bridesmaid or even in a wedding for that matter, unless something happened in Atlanta that you didn't tell me about."

"No, but I know how to produce a show, and I've been reading through a stack of bridal magazines. Plus, they'll have a production assistant to help research everything, anyway. That's the sort of stuff I did when I was a P.A." Jodie thought for a second and bit her lip. "I hope the company's not so small they don't have a P.A."

"I still can't get over the fact that you left Atlanta to come up here and produce a show about some country bumpkin brides."

Jodie heard Tracy's voice drawing closer. "That's okay, I got a promotion out of the deal. I might not have made producer at CNN for a couple more years. When I interviewed with Gator House Productions, he said I'd have an opportunity to work on multiple shows, which will propel me into a producer spot at one of the major networks in a couple of years or so."

"But Memphis isn't as exciting as Atlanta. Do you think you'll last a couple of years?"

Jodie looked up at her friend now standing in the doorway dressed in a light blue cocktail dress with matching shoes. Her unruly red mane had been brushed up into a ponytail.

Jodie shrugged as she slipped on a pair of black sandals. "I'll have to." Tracy knew why she was in Memphis. "Coming here serves two purposes."

"Speaking of which, have you seen him yet?" Tracy asked, hesitating a bit.

Jodie shook her head. "Not yet. I've only been in town two days. I need to settle in first."

"Right, so I guess you haven't seen Roz yet either?"

"What! And ruin my weekend. I think not." Jodie stood up, dressed and ready to go.

Tracy folded her arms and gave her friend a skeptical look. "You know, everybody has to go home and face the music some time."

The music in Tracy's home had been quite different from the music at Jodie's. Had her friend forgotten that? "Tracy, I came here to help my little brother, so I plan to see him, but I don't have to see Roz in order to do that. At least not right away. Besides, I stand a better chance of having him open up to me if she doesn't know I'm in town."

Tracy shrugged and twisted her lips. "Yeah, but she's still your mother."

Jodie gently grabbed Tracy by the shoulders, turned her around, and headed down the hall. "Yes, ma'am, I'll give her a call in due time. It's just like you to keep me straight. So, where is this wedding? We're going to be late if you don't stop drilling me."

Minutes later, with the windows down and a cool March breeze blowing in the car, they whizzed through Memphis in Tracy's Prelude passing popular spots from Jodie's past. Growing up everything exciting happened in Memphis. Clifton was over fifty miles away and dullsville.

"Remember when we used to sneak out on weekends and drive down to Memphis and hang out on Beale Street?" Tracy asked.

Jodie laughed. "Yeah, and stand around outside because we weren't clever enough to get fake IDs."

"Boy, were we country," Tracy said laughing.

"Yeah…and luckily we never got arrested for driving without a license."

"Man, I forgot about that," Tracy replied, and they laughed together.

Jodie remembered all the good times, and unfortunately, the bad ones as well. They had been friends since the sixth grade, so she was sure Tracy remembered her dysfunctional upbringing, but she was nice enough not to bring it up.

Before Jodie knew it Tracy whipped into the parking lot of a massive redbrick church that resembled one of the Roman cathedrals she'd seen on television. A selection of high-end luxury cars filled the lot.

"Who's Caroline marrying again?" Jodie asked, barely able to remember the details Tracy shared about the wedding.

"Walter Oats, and his family's filthy rich. They're

philanthropists who support every local arts project and charity for the poor that happens in this town. Tax write-offs, you know."

"Yeah." Jodie laughed and shook her head.

"But Walter's actually a pretty nice guy. He's helped with a couple of things I've been involved with. He's a rich sweetheart, but he's a sweetheart."

In high school Caroline hung with the *in* crowd that Jodie was all too aware of, but never a part of. Caroline grew up in Clifton a few blocks from Jodie, but moved to the other side of town once her mother remarried. Her new father gave them a fresh start. She started talking proper, wore different clothes, and found more important friends. Somehow, the three of them had remained friends over the years. That is, when Jodie could stomach her.

As they exited the car, Tracy kept talking. "That's how Caroline met Walter anyway, at one of his family's fund-raisers."

"And he's a white guy?"

"Yep, but nobody's told Caroline she's black yet."

An older white man slowed between two parked cars to let them walk by ahead of him. "Good afternoon, ladies."

"Good afternoon." They exchanged greetings.

"Nice day for a wedding, isn't it?" he commented, falling in step behind them.

"It sure is," Tracy answered.

"You gals must be friends of the bride?"

Jodie glanced back at him and smiled. "No, we're old girlfriends of the groom's."

The look on the old man's face was priceless.

The doors to the church were open and scores of beautiful people, black and white, flocked inside. Flowers draped the church and the strong fragrance of lilies filled Jodie's nostrils.

As they were escorted down the aisle Jodie whispered to Tracy, "So this is how the other half lives?"

"Must be nice," Tracy whispered back.

The who's-who of Memphis, Tennessee had come out this afternoon, Jodie noticed. Several black faces dotted the audience dressed to the nines and iced down. There were so many women dripping in diamonds in the church that Jodie felt naked in nothing but her small diamond studs—a gift from an old lover.

After everyone was seated and the music began, Caroline started down the aisle. Jodie remembered how when they were children Caroline always wanted to be a princess. She'd finally gotten her wish. She looked like a black Cinderella.

The ceremony lasted longer than Jodie thought it would. Walter was Catholic, but there were some traditional African touches included in the ceremony. Jodie would have bet money that Caroline couldn't find Africa on a map, but the African touches made the ceremony look exotic and the local newspaper photographers would no doubt have great shots for the metro or community section of the paper, if not the front page.

After the ceremony, husband and wife descended the aisle all smiles at a pace that suited all the flashbulbs going off in their faces.

"Champagne time?" Tracy whispered, as she snapped a few pictures with her disposable camera.

During the slow steady crawl out of the church and into the reception hall next door, Tracy introduced Jodie to some of Caroline's new friends. Out of the corner of her eye Jodie thought she glimpsed a familiar face, but when she turned around she didn't see anyone she recognized.

The receiving line was long and tiresome. By the time Jodie reached the bride and groom her stomach was grumbling. Caroline greeted Jodie with a huge smile, a "don't touch the dress" hug, and an air kiss.

"Jodie, I'm so glad you could make it. We can't seem to get you out of Atlanta these days."

"Yeah, well, I'm back." Jodie faked a happy smile, surprised to hear a Southern drawl in Caroline's voice that she didn't remember. "I live in Memphis now."

"That's wonderful. We're going to have to get together and talk about old times." She turned to her husband who'd been listening to every word. "Walter, Jodie is one of my oldest and dearest friends from Clifton."

Dark hair, a tanned complexion, and perfect white teeth offset Walter's lack of height. He couldn't have been an inch taller than Jodie's five feet and seven inches.

He took Jodie's hand. "So glad you could attend, and it's a pleasure to meet you."

"You too," Jodie said, peering into his baby-blue eyes and wondering if he knew what he was getting himself into. Caroline was a handful. She was born a diva and she'd probably die a diva.

Caroline turned and smiled at Tracy. "Call me sweetie. We'll all do lunch."

Tracy smiled and agreed to give the little princess a call as a woman standing next to the groom thanked them and ushered them away so as to keep the line moving.

Food, champagne and music were plentiful. After the bride and groom took the dance floor, Jodie headed back to the buffet table.

She turned around and spotted Tracy on the dance floor batting her eyes up at her groomsman dance partner. Big flirt, Jodie thought with a smile. She stuffed a mushroom cap filled with crabmeat into her mouth.

"You always were a big eater." A male voice boomed from behind her.

The hairs on the back of her neck stood up and she almost swallowed the mushroom whole. She hadn't been seeing things after all. That voice matched the face she only thought she'd glimpsed earlier. Jodie slowly turned around.

Chapter 2

"When you were eleven you ate a whole pepperoni pizza by yourself, extra cheese and all. I was impressed."

The smile on his face was apprehensive, as if he were waiting on Jodie to smile before he unleashed a set of pearly whites that used to make her blush.

"William Duncan," she said, out of the side of her mouth, as she chewed and swallowed her mushroom. An old familiar flutter began in the pit of her stomach that she never could control around him.

"Jodie, how've you been?" he asked.

"Great," she said. "And you?" Not that she had to ask; he looked like a million bucks. He had the solid body of a linebacker with a clean-shaven, groomed-to-perfection face.

"I'm doing good," he answered with a slow nod. "How's your family?" he asked, in all sincerity.

"Wonderful," she lied, with a straight face.

"I'm glad to hear that. I see Keenan's burning up the basketball courts."

She nodded. "I haven't caught one of his games lately, but that's what I hear, too."

"He's got talent, and a great future ahead of him."

"Hopefully his luck will be better than Corey's." A chill ran through her body and she regretted that smart-ass comment the minute it left her lips.

Will responded by dropping his head and clearing his throat. "Yeah…I'm sure it will be."

When he looked at Jodie his eyes had softened and she felt like a first-class heel. He hadn't forgotten about Corey, and he probably never would. After all, they'd been best friends.

"Hey, Will." Tracy bounded into their space as if she were at the party of all parties. Then she stopped, and glanced between Jodie and Will. "I'm sorry, am I disturbing something?"

"We were just saying hello," Will responded. He diverted his attention to Tracy. "I haven't seen you around lately. Where've you been hiding?"

Jodie popped another mushroom cap into her mouth while the two of them exchanged pleasantries.

"Busy working like a dog as usual. By the way, I enjoyed that article you wrote on the upcoming draft."

"You follow sports?" Will looked surprised.

"Not actually. My coworker has a nephew being drafted and she showed me the article."

"Yeah, what's his name?"

They talked basketball while Jodie checked Will out. He was taller and even more handsome than she remembered. After noticing how impeccably groomed he was, she glanced down at his large hands for a wedding band. *Good Lord,* why was she checking out his ring finger? She had no interest whatsoever in this man anymore.

She glanced up and caught Will staring at her.

"Are you a friend of Walter's?" Tracy asked him.

"You might say that. He's one of the sponsors of my foundation. I work with troubled high school athletes."

Jodie lowered her eyes to his feet and almost choked on her mushrooms. He had the largest shoes she'd ever seen. Fourteen, fifteen maybe, she didn't know. Whatever, he had to have a big…foot.

Tracy glanced over at Jodie who shrugged. "Now that's what I call giving back. You work with all the high school athletes?"

"No," he laughed. "Just the ones that need mentoring. Most of them don't have a good support system at home."

Unable to follow their conversation, Jodie glanced up at Will's face again and their eyes locked. His tongue peeked out to lick his full pink lips and she wanted to scream. She'd spent most of her teenage years dreaming of him putting those lips all over her innocent young body. For Christ's sake, she'd learned to pleasure herself fantasizing about him.

"I see. You're a mentor?" Tracy yapped on. "That's kind of why Jodie moved back."

"Tracy!" Jodie reeled her wandering mind in and back to their conversation. "If you don't mind, I'm ready to leave." She set her plate down and gave her roommate a hard stare. Her personal business wasn't any of his business.

"What?" Tracy looked down at her watch. "It's still early," she said, before she caught the icy stare Jodie didn't bother hiding. Then she said to Will, "You know, she's right, we'd better be going. We've got some…stuff to do. It was good seeing you again, Will."

"Same here. Jodie…" He stepped closer before she could turn and run away. "It's good seeing you again too." He held out his hand.

Hair tossed back, chin held high, Jodie placed her little hand in his and gave him a firm, businesslike handshake. "Yeah, same here. Goodbye, Will." She turned and walked away.

"I'll see you around," he said to her back.

Like hell, she thought, and kept walking.

As soon as they cleared the church stairs, Jodie turned and let Tracy have it. "Why didn't you tell me he'd be here?"

Tracy's mouth fell open. "Like I knew. I wasn't privy to the guest list. If I had any clue I would have told you."

Jodie marched the rest of the way to the car, mad but not sure why.

"Come on now, you used to have a thing for him didn't you?"

"Not since the accident."

Tracy stopped before opening the car door and smacked her palm to her forehead. "Oh my God! Jodie, I forgot. Girl, forgive me for acting like a butt back there. I completely forgot."

Jodie took a deep breath and glanced around the lot of fading luxury cars. "Tracy…let's just get in the car."

They climbed in the car and Tracy started the engine.

Jodie's head fell back against the headrest and she took a deep breath. "Of all the people I could have run into, I run into William Duncan."

"Sounds like you're still mad at him," Tracy commented.

"Wouldn't you be?"

Tracy pulled out of the church lot and drove down the street. "I don't know, I guess so, but… But are you sure you want to be mad at him? I mean, it was such a long time ago and he looks better now than he ever did in high school. I remember seeing pictures of him in the paper when he was in college. He looks better now than then, too."

"Oh, he looks good until you remember… He's a killer."

Will stared out the window as Jodie climbed in the car. Seconds later, it pulled away.

All legs and curves, Jodie looked damned good and Will was happy to see her. Unfortunately, she wasn't too happy to see him. But then again he hadn't expected an overly warm greeting.

"What's out there?" A soft feminine voice came from behind him.

He turned as Allyson Pendleton walked into the room.

"Nothing," he responded, turning away from the window.

Tall, tanned, and dressed in a sexy blue dress that

would have accentuated her breasts or ass, if she had either, she'd been following him around like some puppy ever since he arrived.

"Hey, after the reception is over a group of us are going out to the country club." She sashayed closer to him. "I thought you'd like to join us for a drink or two…that is, if you don't have plans for the evening."

She stood so close Will could smell the overpowering flowery fragrance of her perfume. Fake red fingernails reached out and stroked the lapel of his jacket.

"What do you say? Come spend some time with me," she purred.

Cackles of laughter came from the hallway as several women passed down the hall.

Will reached for Allyson's hand, and gently removed it from his jacket. He'd been out with her on a few dates, but the last thing he wanted was her clinging to him. "I'm afraid I'll have to pass. I do have plans for this evening."

Her ruby-red lips turned down as she batted her big brown eyes up at him. "They wouldn't be with that woman you were talking to earlier, would they?"

He squared his shoulders. "I've been talking to several women, including you." He took a step back.

"You know, that black woman with the long hair, and the big dimples that you couldn't take your eyes off."

"You must mean Jodie, and I'm afraid not."

Allyson took a step back with hands propped at her hips as she smiled at Will. "You like her don't you?"

"She's one of Gator House's new producers." He led the way out of the room with Allyson beside him.

"Oh really. Will she be working on your show?"

He thought about it for a moment, now realizing Jodie probably had no idea his show was produced by Gator House Productions, if she was even aware of his show. "I think so. I'll be seeing a whole lot of her."

They descended the stairs from the second-floor room, back down to the main hall.

"Why, I'm jealous," Allyson said in a playful tone.

Will laughed. "Don't be. She may not be too happy about it."

Even with a bright March sun in her eyes, Jodie recognized Keenan a mile away. He had a long narrow head like their father Lou, and the infamous Dickerson swagger when he walked. He'd grown since the last time she'd seen him, and he'd lost too much weight. Aside from the weight loss, he had dark bags under his eyes, and his hair looked as if he'd stopped combing it weeks ago.

All she'd intended to do was drive by her mother's house in order to build up the courage to stop by later. But on the way she spotted a crowd at the park and stopped. She'd been sitting across from the basketball court for over thirty minutes now, biting her nails, unable to get out of the car.

For the last two years she'd volunteered to work Thanksgiving and Christmas, the only times of the year she usually returned to Clifton. So, she hadn't seen Keenan in a couple of years. The last time she tried to talk to him, he hung up on her.

But, she couldn't stay in Atlanta and let him destroy himself thinking she didn't care about him. Keenan was the only brother Jodie had left, and she'd do everything in her power to help him kick whatever drug habit he'd developed.

After taking a deep breath, she opened the car door and stepped out. She crossed the street, her pace slowing as she approached the court.

Keenan bent down and pulled a towel from a large black gym bag. He wiped his face and stared right into Jodie's eyes as he lowered the towel.

For an instant, she noticed a flicker of excitement in his eyes. The way he used to look at her when she came home during the Christmas holidays. But that look was quickly replaced with a *what the hell does she want* expression. He shoved the towel back into the bag, and slung the bag across his chest, before walking toward her.

Jodie's heartbeat quickened. With her hands clasped behind her back, she smiled up at him. "Hey there. How you doing?"

He looked at her with dead, emotionless eyes and sniffled. "What you doin' here, it's not Christmas?"

She lowered her head. Okay, so she deserved that. Then she looked up, puffed out her chest, and took a deep breath. "Can a big sister get a hug?" she asked, holding out her arms.

Keenan chuckled and strolled past her. "Now you trippin'." He started across the grass walking away from her.

Jodie told herself to suck it up, as she followed him. "Keenan, I know I haven't been much of a sister, but—"

He spun around and continued walking backwards. "But what? You'd like to make up for lost time by coming in town and taking a brother to dinner, or maybe you want to take me to the mall and buy me a pair of expensive sneakers." He stopped and glared at her. "Whatever you're selling, I'm not buying. I don't need you Jodie."

His words, sharp like a knife, stabbed her in the chest. Whoever said sticks and stones can break your bones, but words will never hurt you, lied. She opened her mouth in a feeble attempt to say something, but he turned and jogged away. Jodie stood there with her hands clasped behind her back on the verge of tears.

She walked back to her car and sat there crying and gripping the steering wheel. Her baby brother didn't look like himself. It pained her to see how he'd deteriorated over the last couple of years. At that very moment she thought about Corey lying dead in the ground because of a drug—alcohol.

Fueled by her anger she started the car. Roz lived several blocks from the park, and if Jodie hurried she could cut Keenan off before he reached the house and let it slip that she was in town.

A few blocks from his house she found Keenan standing on the corner in front of a small restaurant talking with several older men. She pulled up and lowered the passenger side window and called out his name. "Keenan." When he saw her he turned to go inside.

"Keenan," she called out again.

One of the men grabbed Keenan's arm thinking he hadn't seen her, and pointed toward the car. "Hey man, somebody's calling you."

Keenan turned around with a disgusted look on his face, and rolled his eyes.

Her heart sank. But, no matter how unpleasant, she could take it. "Can I speak to you a minute?"

He approached the car with the gym bag still slung across his chest, and squatted until they were eye level.

"What do you want?"

"Get in," she said, unlocking the doors.

He stood up and laughed a little snort, shaking his head.

"We need to talk. Come, go to Smoothie King with me. I'll buy you a smoothie. It's not a pair of expensive sneakers, or dinner, but I live here now so we can schedule that for later."

He took a step back and peered down into the car. "You live in Memphis?" he asked, as if in disbelief.

"Yes. Now come on and get in."

He hesitated a few minutes, and then pulled the bag over his head holding it by the strap. He glanced over his shoulder at the men on the corner. "I'll catch y'all later."

"All right, dog, take it easy," one man said.

"Hey, you not gonna introduce your lady friend?" another man yelled out.

"Yeah, yeah." Keenan waved him off as he opened the car door and climbed in. He adjusted his seat all the way back and cocked his head at Jodie.

The minute he closed the car door she let out a sigh of relief, and pulled away.

"You sick or something?" he asked.

"No, why did you ask that?"

"Because I thought this was the last place on earth you wanted to live. I didn't figure you'd ever move back this way." He shifted uncomfortably in his seat. "Or is somebody else sick and they sent you to tell me? How's Dad?"

She changed lanes trying to remember where the Smoothie King was. "Nobody's sick, and he's fine as far as I know. It wasn't Tennessee that I wanted to get away from it was Roz. She and Lou seemed to get off on making my life miserable." If anyone understood what coming back to Tennessee meant for her, Keenan should have. All he'd seen growing up was her fighting with her parents.

"So, what have you been doing?" she asked, when she noticed he'd stopped talking and started staring out the window.

"Playing ball."

"I heard you made the all-star team this year. Excited about the game?"

"Why, you coming?" he asked with a chuckle, still staring out the window.

"Keenan, I'm sorry I know I've missed most of your career." No excuse was good enough, and she knew it. Guilt consumed her for even trying to come up with a lame excuse.

She turned into the Smoothie King and parked.

"There's a drive through, you know," he commented, pointing toward the side of the building.

"I thought we'd sit down and talk for a little while."

He turned to face her with cold hard eyes. "We already did that."

Jodie ignored him and turned off the engine. She pulled her wallet from her purse and climbed out of the car. He took a deep breath and did the same, throwing his gym bag into the backseat.

"Is that where you live?" he asked, pointing to the pile of clothes, shoes and assortment of junk in her backseat.

She punched the remote and locked the doors. "Of course not. Give me a break, I just moved and haven't had time to clean the car out yet."

"You must be in a constant state of movement then, because it looked like that the last time you were here. You sure somebody isn't living back there?"

For the first time he grinned just a little bit, and then looked away. A surge of excitement flowed through Jodie and she felt as if she'd taken the first step toward communicating with her brother.

He even opened the door for her as they entered the small shop. They ordered and sat outside on the patio. Jodie loved smoothies, and sipped slowly so she wouldn't get brain freeze like she used to when they were little. Keenan sat across from her with his long legs stretched beyond their table. Without his gym bag strapped to him she had a better look at his pencil-thin body.

"Lost some weight, haven't you?" she asked, risking a backlash.

"Nope," he replied.

"You're thinner than the last time I saw you."

"When was that? 1998, 1999, I was about eleven years old."

"Keenan, I've seen you since then. But, I didn't come here to talk about the last time I was home. I came to talk about you."

He sat his drink down and started laughing. "What about me?"

When he laughed he resembled Corey so much she momentarily lost her train of thought. Both of them had Lou's pudgy nose and full lips, only Keenan had more hollow cheeks. A sign of his overconsuming lifestyle, she assumed.

"I heard you've been drinking a lot, and smoking dope." She laid it all out on the table.

"You heard wrong. Who told you that? Roz?"

"Keenan, have you been doing drugs?"

He shook his head and sipped his smoothie. "I said no. And I know you don't believe anything she says over me. You know how crazy she is."

She stared into her little brother's lying eyes. After a few seconds he turned away, looking at two pretty young girls walking by the shop.

Years ago he used to call Jodie and confide in her. He even begged her to come home, but she couldn't ever live with her parents again. They'd lost a son and forgot they had any other children. Jodie and Keenan's needs were practically ignored. Now Keenan treated Jodie like a stranger. But over time she would change that. They had to stick together.

"Keenan, I understand things at home can be crazy. I grew up with her too, so I know what you're going—"

"How could you know anything about my life?" He pulled his leg back and leaned into the table before standing up. "You don't know me, Jodie. You never did." He stood up and tossed his cup into a nearby garbage can with a small opening. It went straight in.

"I'm ready to go." He walked off the patio heading for the car.

She stood and tossed her cup at the same garbage can, but missed, and the remainder of her smoothie splattered all over the ground in front of the can. The mess reminded her of her life.

She looked up at her little brother, practically a grown man now, and realized he was right. She didn't know him.

Chapter 3

William sat across from Stone's desk thinking about what his mother had told him yesterday after he told her Jodie was coming to Gator House Productions to work.

"You stay as far away from that girl and her family as you can," Geraldine warned him.

Will had finished playing a round of golf with his father and was eager to leave Clifton and drive back to Memphis. He hadn't meant to start a never-ending conversation. But, Geraldine had come from church wrung up about something and dishing out advice to anyone who would listen.

"I still can't get over the way they treated you after that accident," she went on as she turned off the stove and moved a pot of pinto beans. "His mother acted as if you shot the boy or something. I wouldn't be surprised if she wasn't to this day still campaigning to have you locked up."

Will helped his mother by pulling a country ham from the refrigerator.

"But Jodie's not like that. You remember her," Will said.

Geraldine grabbed a paper towel and wiped the sweat from her brow and damp face. She was a big woman who was well past menopause, but hadn't been able to shake the hot flashes. "Yes, I remember her. She was a cute little thing. But you get involved with that girl and you'll have to deal with her mother. And William, you don't need to keep trying to get those folks to like you. They lost their son."

His mother was the only one who called him by his full name. Her words echoed in his ear while Stone praised Jodie.

Stone reared back in his big leather chair that squeaked from the pressure and crossed his arms. "She's the best candidate for the job. She's sharp, she's worked on a sports show before, and she has the production experience we need," he said.

Will nodded and picked up Jodie's résumé for the second time that morning. "So she worked for your uncle Mack at CNN."

"That's right. She has editing experience, strong writing skills and she's willing to work our crazy hours. She's more than qualified. She's right on time, because *The Memphis Zone* is about to be picked up by a major network."

Will's curiosity was piqued, and he gave Stone a

sideways glance. "What network?" he asked. It wasn't like Stone to keep something like that from him.

Stone smiled and laced his fingers across his stomach. "I wasn't going to mention it yet, but I've been talking to my contact at Sports Central and she asked to see a tape of the show."

"When were you going to tell me?" Will asked, a little annoyed with Stone. He wondered if this contact could be the same woman Stone had been out to dinner with lately.

"Not until after she looked at the tape. I didn't want to get your hopes all up, plus I wanted the tape to be a true representation of the show."

Will laughed to himself. This might be the break he'd been waiting on since the first taping and Stone thought he would sabotage it. "So you're saying if I knew about it I'd try to beef up my show?"

Stone shrugged. "Of course *you* wouldn't, but I'm not sure about the rest of the crew. We already have a great show—we don't need to embellish on a thing. All we needed was a producer, so I hired one."

Now that a major network was interested in the show, that changed Will's perspective.

"Relax. My uncle Mack puts his production assistants to work, and it's not all grunt work. He trained me remember? So, consider yourself lucky to have someone with her experience at the price I'm paying her."

Stone's uncle Mack had been a major investor in Gator House Productions and had bailed them out of more than one jam.

Will pushed his mother's warning in the back of his mind and asked, "So, when does she start?"

Stone looked at his watch. "In about thirty minutes."

Jodie pulled into the parking lot thirty minutes early for her first day on the job. She balled up the tissue paper her egg-and-cheese croissant had been in and tossed it onto the backseat, then picked up her portfolio and climbed out of the car.

Gator House Productions was located east of downtown Memphis in an area full of old warehouses. Now on its comeback, the area boasted trendy lofts, music studios and urban clothing shops. She had no idea what awaited her behind the big red door as she pulled it open.

Her former boss Lenny Mack, known in the television industry as "The Mack Man," knew everyone in the business. He had assured her his nephew would give her every opportunity to establish herself as a first-rate television producer. So far, Lenny had never steered her wrong.

The squeak of the door caught the attention of a man in a red beret sitting behind the reception desk.

"Bonjour," he said, looking up from his desk.

The door closed behind her with a thud as she approached the desk. "Hello, I'm here to see Larry Stone."

"You must be Jodie Dickerson?" he asked, losing the French accent and extending his hand.

"I am," she replied, shaking his hand.

"Welcome to Gator House Productions. I'm Manny King. Office manager, slash receptionist, slash whatever else Mr. Stone needs. And I'll be taking care of you this morning."

"Thank you," Jodie said, taken aback by his grandiose introduction.

"Have a seat and I'll get you all settled in. Mr. Stone's in a meeting at the moment, but he will be with you shortly."

Jodie stepped back toward a chair as he came around the desk.

What the hell!

Below the black-and-white striped tank that fit snugly across his broad chest, Manny wore a pair of high-waist white linen pants with bell-bottom legs. On his feet were what resembled black bedroom slippers.

She accepted a clipboard from him, thinking at least his attire matched the accent.

"After you fill out the W-4 and this other paperwork I'll give you the full ten-cent tour."

It took Jodie all of fifteen minutes to complete everything and walk it back over to Manny's desk. He put up a Back in Ten Minutes sign, and held the interior door open, gesturing her ahead of him.

As they toured the studio, Manny introduced her to the staff, which consisted mostly of young men. Everyone gave her a friendly welcome.

"As you already know Gator House Productions is the brainchild of Larry Stone, our executive producer and CEO. We specialize in corporate and industrial videos, a few TV programs and—" he turned to Jodie with his lip curled in disgust "—infomercials."

She laughed. "I take it you don't like infomercials?"

They stopped at the beginning of a long row of offices.

"Je ne crois pas," he said, throwing up a hand, trying his best to pull off the French snob look.

Jodie stared at him, waiting for the translation. Her French sucked.

"In English," he said. "I don't think so. I prefer commercials. Has-beens do infomercials. I prefer something I wouldn't be ashamed to star in. I'm not taking acting lessons for nothing.

"And this is your new home." He gestured, Vanna-White style, for her to enter the tiny office. "I've got your desk all set up."

"Thank you." Jodie entered the closet-size office with a smile on her face. It wasn't a cubicle and it had a door. Who said she wasn't moving up in the world. She had her first ever office door.

"What happened to the last producer?" Jodie asked, as she set her purse on the desk next to a computer.

Manny flopped down on her module desk and crossed his arms. "After a month on the show, one day she walked in and just quit. She'd moved from slow-paced training videos to *The Memphis Zone*. That's our sports show, and the pace is much faster on that set. I don't believe our host thought she could cut the mustard."

"Who's the host?" Jodie asked, so she'd know who to stay clear of.

Before Manny could answer a young woman Jodie had met minutes ago, but whose name escaped her, peeked into the office. "Manny, the UPS guy's out front waiting on you."

Manny jumped up from the desk. "Oops, gotta get back to work. Jodie, I'll see if Mr. Stone is available now."

He took off down the hall leaving Jodie to sort her new supplies and test her office chair. She spun around and around in her seat and didn't care how small the office was. She'd tell Tracy it was cozy.

No more than fifteen minutes later Manny reappeared.

"*Excusez-moi.*" He peeked into her office. "Mr. Stone's ready to see you now." He gestured and Jodie followed him.

Larry Stone rose from his seat and came around the desk to greet Jodie. She walked in with a smile on her face and her arm outstretched.

Then out of the corner of her eye, she saw him.

What the hell is he doing here?

William Duncan stood across from Larry Stone's desk watching her every move. She tried not to stumble over her own feet and kept moving until she stood face to face with her new boss.

"Jodie, welcome to Gator House Productions, I'm Larry Stone."

She accepted his hand and pumped it vigorously not wanting to turn around. "Thank you. I'm excited about being here."

"Glad to hear that." He let go of her hand and turned toward Will. "This is William Duncan, host of *The Memphis Zone*, our sports show."

Oh my God, he works here! She turned to Will a little puzzled. She thought he worked for some newspaper or magazine. Wherever Tracy had read his article.

In two steps he was in her face, smiling and shaking her hand. "It's nice to meet you, Ms. Dickerson."

For a second, she was thrown for a loop. Why was he acting like he didn't know her? Her hand went limp in his, but she couldn't hide the surprised look on her face.

"I read over your résumé and I'm looking forward to working with you."

Fortunately, Larry Stone was behind Jodie.

Will let go of her hand and she turned back to Larry Stone. "I thought I was going to be working on a bridal show?"

"Here, have a seat." Stone pulled over a chair before walking back to his seat. "There's been a change in plans. We decided to scrap that show. Instead, we need your help with *The Memphis Zone*. I see you have some sports experience already."

Jodie swallowed and lowered herself into the seat. "Yes, but…" She glanced in Will's direction as he pulled his chair closer to her and Larry's desk. She tried not to look so horrified, but she had to admit it was hard. She couldn't work with him!

"The format's not that much different from the news shows you've worked on. You'll be taking over most of the day-to-day work, but I'll be around for tapings. Will here has been writing his own scripts for about the last month, isn't that right, Will?"

Will cleared his throat before nodding and Jodie caught the little smirk on his face. He appeared to get a kick out of the situation.

"Yes, I have. Ms. Dickerson, I'm not sure if you've

had much experience scripting a show, or booking guests, but—"

"Please, call me Jodie." She didn't know what kind of game he was playing, but she decided to go along with him for now.

"Okay, Jodie. What I was trying to say is around here you need to be a jack-of-all-trades. The team we've assembled for *The Memphis Zone* is the best and brightest."

"Wil—" She caught herself. "Mr. Duncan, I've had experience in everything except booking guests. But I don't see that as being a problem. I'm a fast learner."

Oh no, he's not about to make me look like a fool on my first day. Jodie didn't like his tone or his attitude, and nobody was going to run her away until she was ready to go. Whatever he could dish out, she could take.

Will's piercing ebony eyes locked on hers as one corner of his lip rose. "Then welcome to *The Memphis Zone.*"

She took a deep breath. "Thank you." When she turned her attention back to Larry Stone he gave her an unsettling look. What had she gotten herself into?

"Oh," Will said, snapping his fingers. "I just thought of something. Since you're such a quick study, I have the first five months' worth of shows on tape in my office. I can get you those to take home and watch tonight. Unless that'll be a problem?"

Five months' worth of tapes! Was he kidding? She opened her mouth to say something, but only chuckled.

Will turned to Stone who glanced from Jodie to Will

with knitted brows. "That should get her up to speed for the production meeting tomorrow morning."

Jodie finally gathered her composure. "I can't say that I'll get all five months' worth viewed tonight, but I'll certainly view a few of the tapes before tomorrow. What time is the meeting?" she asked, glancing between Will and Stone.

Stone shook his head and jumped from his seat. "Seven o'clock sharp," he said, before either of them said another word. He came from behind his desk. "Here's how I want to handle this." He paused as he gave Will a firm pat on the shoulder. "For a couple of days I want you two to work together, until Jodie gets the flow of the show."

"Excellent idea," Will chimed in.

Stone glanced down at his watch as he walked toward the door. "If you'll excuse me a moment I need to get something from Manny before I forget. I'll be right back."

The minute he left the office, Will turned to Jodie.

"What's up with you? Why all the attitude?" he asked.

"What's up with *me?*" Jodie winced. "You're the one giving me a hard time here. And what game are you playing by acting like you don't know me?"

"I can't explain that right now, but thanks for going along with me."

"Well somebody had better explain something to me because I'm a little confused. Mr. Stone must think we're crazy."

Will laughed. "He's cool."

Jodie didn't share his laughter; she just peered at him wondering what the hell she'd gotten herself into.

Will began his explanation. "Stone had already made up his mind to hire you when I looked at your résumé. I didn't really have any control over you coming onboard or not. Actually, I thought it would be cool working with you until I bumped into you at the reception."

She crossed her arms protectively in front of her. "Why didn't you mention then that you worked at Gator House Productions?" she asked.

He shrugged. "You were so short with me, it didn't come up."

"But you knew I was coming to work here, and with you?"

"Yes, I knew. But like I said, you were so short and cold toward me I didn't know what to think. We used to be friends, or so I thought."

She didn't respond. He wasn't exactly right. She'd always had a crush on him; but they were never best buds. It was more like she'd idolized him, and he'd probably enjoyed every minute of it.

"I don't like being caught off guard," she said.

"I apologize. I just didn't want Stone to think there might be some animosity between us."

Jodie focused on a glass paperweight sitting on Larry Stone's desk. A small shell floated inside, giving off the appearance of being suspended in midair. Right now that's how she felt, and she wanted to touch the ground. Her dislike for Will had manifested after years of conversations with Roz. She couldn't bring herself to literally hate the man, but she couldn't work with him either. What would Roz or anyone else in her family for that matter say?

"There isn't any animosity between us, is there?" he asked, after she didn't respond.

She slowly turned to look him in the eyes.

"I can't do this. I'm gonna have to quit."

Chapter 4

Jodie jumped up from her seat and headed for the door so fast Will had to scramble to stop her.

He held his palm against the door as she grasped the doorknob. "Hold on. Where you goin'?" he asked, as she whirled around on him.

"William, get your hand off the door and let me out of here. If I'd known you worked here I *never* would have accepted this job." She glared up at him.

Will shook his head, noticing how she used his full name. He'd been afraid of this type of reaction. "Wait a minute. I thought we were friends. What did I do to you?"

She released the doorknob and rested a hand on her hip. After a moment of silence, she ground out between clenched teeth, "You mean what did you do to my family."

Her words stung like a slap across the face. He could see her mother's cold hard eyes staring at him as she screamed, *murderer.* Will lowered his head and released the door. A tightness he hadn't felt in a long time gripped his chest.

"I'm sorry if you think I intentionally did anything to hurt anybody."

She was free to walk out of the room, out of Gator House Productions, and out of his life, but he hoped she wouldn't. He'd seen her several times since high school, and she'd never looked at him or talked to him like this before. After almost a minute, she turned around and slumped back into her seat.

"I'm sorry. I shouldn't have said that. Sometimes words just fly out of my mouth at lightning speed and I can't stop them. Seeing you again reminds me of Corey, and makes me think of the accident all over again."

Will moved away from the door and reclaimed his seat. "Nearly every day Corey comes across my mind. But I have to work past it. I hope you're not really going to quit?" he asked.

She let out a chuckle and shrugged. "Knee-jerk reaction," she said, with a roll of her eyes.

"I'm not a bad guy to work with. And I promise I don't bite." He held up his right hand and winked at her.

She smiled and turned away. He caught his first glimpse of those big sweet dimples. *Oh my God.* She had no idea how sexy she looked right now.

"I have to warn you," she prefaced, sitting up, "I haven't worked on a sports show in years."

"That's okay, it's like riding a bike. *The Memphis Zone*'s not your typical sports show anyway. Our biggest challenge is booking high-profile guests. I've been working hard on that and frankly I need some help." He reached out and placed his hand atop hers on the armrest.

"I need you. You can't quit on me."

It was nine-thirty in the evening when Jodie and Tracy finished dinner. The roommates took turns cooking, only Tracy's meals were followed by dessert, Jodie's weren't.

"So what did you say to him?" Tracy asked, as she rummaged through the pantry for something sweet to eat.

"I didn't know what to say. I just sat there looking like a deer caught on Interstate Forty. Hell, I couldn't quit if I wanted to. Do you know how hard it would be to get on at one of the local networks with no inside contacts?" Jodie scraped her leftovers in the trash and opened the dishwasher.

"In Memphis, yes," Tracy responded closing the pantry. "It's hard enough finding work with contacts." She crossed the room to the refrigerator.

"I'll have to stay and just avoid him like the plague. As soon as I figure out who does what around there I'll be able to minimize our face time."

"Jodie, you didn't buy any cookies or a pie or anything at the grocery?" Tracy asked, looking up from the refrigerator.

"Nope. Look down in the crisper though. I have some oranges," Jodie responded.

"Oranges! I've got a sweet tooth. What's an orange gonna do for me?" Tracy closed the refrigerator and crossed her arms.

"Stay off your hips," Jodie replied, eliciting a sneer from her best friend.

"Okay, Ms. Healthy." Tracy went back to the pantry for a second look. "I can't believe I don't have a candy bar stashed in the back or anything."

Jodie laughed. "Girl are you pregnant or what? You're over there craving chocolate."

"Not just chocolate, anything sweet. Got any chewing gum?"

"No," Jodie laughed. "I don't chew gum."

"Well what a perfect roommate you're turning out to be. No desserts, no gum, no—"

The doorbell rang.

"Okay, maybe that's somebody with something sweet," Tracy said.

"Expecting company?" Jodie asked.

"No, you?"

"Nope. God, I hope Roz hasn't found out I'm in town."

Tracy stopped midway across the dining room and her head snapped back in Jodie's direction. "You think it's her?"

Jodie glanced at the clock over the stove, and then shrugged. "Nine forty-five, I hope not. I'd like to think that she'd call first."

Tracy tilted her head and raised one brow at Jodie.

Jodie sighed. "You're right, it just might be her."

The doorbell rang again.

"I'm coming," Tracy called out.

Jodie put the last glass in the dishwasher and closed the door. She hesitated before turning on the noisy contraption. If Roz was at the door hopefully the noise would drive her away.

Jodie pulled the dishcloth out of the sink and wiped off the counter. The one thing she didn't want to do right now was talk to her mother. Before she was force fed on how to help Keenan she wanted to take a stab at it herself.

"Jodie, somebody's here to see you," Tracy said, peeking into the kitchen.

Jodie stopped wiping the counter and frowned. "Who is it?" she whispered.

"Go see." Tracy nodded toward the living room. She grinned and waved a stick of chewing gum before turning down the hall toward her bedroom.

It wasn't Roz, or Jodie would have heard her by now. She rinsed out the dishcloth and wiped her hands on a towel. Suddenly, a picture of Will Duncan popped into her mind. No, it couldn't be him. What the hell would he be doing at her apartment this late?

She entered the living room and found Keenan bent down by the door tying his sneakers. His presence shocked her, since they'd hardly spoken. Immediately, she thought the worst.

"Keenan, what's wrong?" she asked.

"Nothing," he responded, straightening up. "I just got out of practice and thought I'd stop by and see you." His eyes quickly turned away as he looked around the apartment.

"Come on in," she said, happy but surprised at the

same time. Maybe something she'd said had gotten through to him after all. She hoped this visit meant he was on the verge of opening up to her.

He followed her into the living room with his hands shoved into his pants pockets. "I see you and Tracy are still best friends."

"Yeah, Tracy's my girl," Jodie said, as she sat in one of the mismatched side chairs. After some awkward silence it dawned on her that she didn't know how to act around Keenan. She wasn't sure how to be a big sister.

He sat on the couch and picked the remote up from the coffee table. "Mind if I turn the channel?"

"Help yourself."

He turned to ESPN and Jodie was reminded of her day with Will.

"Did you just come by to hang out?" she asked, after a few minutes.

He shrugged and pointed at the television with the remote. "It's okay isn't it?"

She glanced at her watch. "Sure it's cool. Stop by anytime, but it's kind of late and I'll be going to bed soon. Don't you have school tomorrow?"

"Yeah, but I like to unwind after practice."

It sounded good, but Jodie wasn't buying it. "What did she do now?" she asked, referring to Roz.

"Who?"

"Your mother."

He shrugged. "Nuttin'. Everything's cool. She's about to go to Jamaica with her husband."

"You mean Marion?"

"Yeah, that dude."

And therein lay part of the problem, Jodie thought. Keenan had never gotten along with Marion. Jodie didn't care for the cigar-smoking councilman herself, but then she didn't have to live with him.

She contemplated broaching that subject, but didn't want to run Keenan away. When he was ready to talk she'd be there to listen. She let him watch television while she prepared for work.

Some time later, he was standing in the doorway to her bedroom.

"Jodie, I need to ask you something."

She turned around to see Keenan shifting from one foot to the other. "What's up?"

He stepped into the room with his hands in his pockets. "You got fifty dollars?"

Jodie blinked. She hadn't seen him in a couple of years and here he was asking for money. "What do you need fifty dollars for?"

"I want a pair of Air Max and I'm fifty dollars short."

"What are Air Max?" she asked.

"Sneakers. I'm gonna wear them in the All-Star Game. I guess you'll get to come to my games this year, huh?" A little smile touched his lips giving him an almost cocky appearance as he looked around her room.

"I hope to make them all," she said, before looking down at her watch. "Keenan, it's ten o'clock and you're just now realizing you want those shoes?"

"Yeah, well, not actually. I just wasn't sure how to

ask you for the money. See I've been saving up, but I don't have enough money to buy them retail. The guys are going to the outlet mall tomorrow after school where they can get them cheaper. Me too, that is if I get fifty more dollars."

Jodie walked over and sat down on the bed where her purse was in reach. "How come you didn't ask Roz or your stepfather?"

"What? Me ask Marion for money. You don't know him do you? Before I get the money, *if* he decides to *loan* it to me, I have to answer fifty questions. One for every stinking dollar that comes out of his pocket."

"And I'm not going to ask any questions?"

He exhaled. "Come on, Jodie, you gonna give me the money or not?"

"Is this a loan?"

His eyes bucked. "I have to pay it back?"

"Of course. What makes you think I don't need my money back? My money doesn't come as easy as Marion's."

"Yeah, well you don't do favors for money."

"Is that what he does?"

"*Pst,* he's a sleazeball. Daddy might drink, but he's not sleazy."

Jodie produced the only fifty-dollar bill she had and handed it to him. She pulled back when he reached for it.

"I want to see these sneakers when you get them."

"Yeah, okay," he said, taking the bill.

She tucked her wallet back in her purse and walked

over to hang the purse on the closet doorknob. When she turned around—Keenan was gone.

A beat-up black Toyota Corolla slowed as it pulled to the corner. The passenger side door opened, and Keenan jumped in before the car sped off.

"Man, what took you so long? I been driving around the block for 'bout fifteen minutes." The driver, a teenager half slumped in his seat with a black do-rag tied tight around his head frowned at Keenan as he passed a joint behind his back to another passenger.

"I couldn't just come right out and ask for the money and leave," Keenan said.

"Why not? She yo' big sister ain't she? That's what they do—give you money."

"We ain't exactly that close."

"Yeah, I hear ya. You had to play up that little brother role. Cool man. How much you get?" he asked, as he stopped for a traffic light.

Keenan pulled the bill from his pocket. "Fifty," he said, with a big grin.

"Man! We can get half a ounce with that," the scratchy voice in the backseat said jubilantly.

"*I* can get half a ounce," Keenan corrected him. "You might get a joint."

"Be like that then." The young man tapped Keenan on the shoulder and passed the joint. Keenan took it and pressed it between his lips and inhaled.

"I got a few more weeks before the all-star game, so let's get wasted," Keenan suggested.

"We're with ya dog." The driver reached over and tapped fists with Keenan.

The smoke-filled car rolled away from downtown, and headed toward their neighborhood drug dealer.

Chapter 5

The alarm blasted off at 5:00 a.m. Jodie rolled over and slapped her palm across the top of the clock to cease the annoying sound. She threw the covers back, stepped out into her house shoes, and shuffled into the bathroom.

In forty-five minutes, she'd showered, fixed her hair, made her face, and bounded out of the bedroom eager to get to the studio. She grabbed her multicolored tote bag, a Target special full of books on sports, and left the apartment.

On the floor in the backseat of her car were the wedding magazines she planned to dispose of as soon as she passed a recycling Dumpster.

Producing was hard work with long tedious hours, but Jodie loved every minute of it. What she actually loved was the aftereffects of the show. Once she settled all the offscreen near-disasters, she sat back happy and proud. The final product was always worth all the stress.

By 6:45 a.m. she was at her desk with her door closed. She didn't want to appear antisocial, but until she figured out Will's schedule she didn't want to take a chance on him popping in.

However, her stomach had been doing a little flip flop in anticipation of seeing him again. On one hand, the sight of him brought back her teenage crush. But on the other hand, he reminded her of angry family fights.

She buried herself in paperwork, reading up about the show and Gator House in general, when she was startled by a brisk knock at the door. She jumped in her seat, then stood up and made her way around the desk. *Please don't let this be Will.* She opened the door.

"Hey! You're in. Good. I wanted to run a few things by you before the meeting." He paused and glanced at his watch. "In the next five minutes."

Dressed in a navy jogging suit and a white nylon T-shirt that fit snug across his chest, he looked like the co-captain of Clifton High School's Mighty Cobras that she used to idolize. She smiled outwardly, but cursed inwardly.

"Sure," her body responded instead of her head.

"Great," he responded, and walked past her into the office.

As if her feet were glued to the floor, all she could do was turn and watch his backside. Her eyes lingered down his strong back to his tight little butt. No, no, she chastised herself and tore her eyes away.

"Have you had a chance to look over my script yet?" he asked, turning around to face her.

She shook her head.

"You know you don't have to keep the door closed. We're a pretty tight-knit group around here," he said, pointing to the door she was closing.

She released the doorknob and tried to regain her composure. It was happening again. Will walking into a room and her turning into a fifteen-year-old. She cleared her throat and walked past him back to her chair, all the while trying her best not to touch or brush against him in any way.

"I'm sorry, I didn't get a chance to read over the script yet." She picked up her pages and leafed through them. "Is this the proposed show, or is this final?" she asked, glancing up at him.

"Proposed," he replied, and then licked his lips.

His tongue darted out to stroke his top, and then his bottom lip, leaving behind a moist, full mouth that drove her to distraction. She remembered with fondness that wicked habit of his from high school.

He continued. "The final won't be ready until right before the show. Literally, thirty minutes before if I'm lucky."

"I see."

She started to apologize for not having read the script that was on her desk when she arrived, but then he relaxed his arms and sat on the corner of her desk making himself at home.

"Jodie…I'm really glad you're here," he said with a cheerful smile.

"Thank you," she said. *I wish I could say the same.*

"It's going to be interesting to see if the stubborn

little Jodie I remember is still in there." He pointed at her and his smile transformed from cheerful to wicked.

She reminded herself of what he was responsible for, and wiped the smile from her face. "Let me warn you. I'm not the same little Jodie as you put it. I'm an ambitious woman who takes her job seriously." She stood up and picked up the script.

"Well, I guess we'd better go on to the meeting since I haven't read this," she said, holding up the script.

"We've got time," he said, not moving from his spot.

He shifted to a more comfortable position and crossed his wrists.

"Relax, we haven't had a chance to have a good talk. How do you like being back in Tennessee?" he asked.

She shrugged. "It's okay. It's grown."

"Have you been to Clifton yet?"

She shook her head. "No."

"Your father's still there, isn't he?"

Conversations about her family were off limits—way off limits. She turned away and picked up a tablet and ink pen. "Nothing's changed," she said in a harsh tone, hoping to squash any other questions he felt compelled to ask.

He seemed to catch the hint and gave her a knowing smile. "I understand. My family's still there, too. The town is dying around them, but they refuse to leave."

He didn't understand her situation. How could he? His family hadn't fallen apart like hers. "You brought your parents a house a couple of years ago, didn't you?" She remembered Tracy reading her the newspaper article over the phone.

"Yeah. I had a nice little ranch house built. That's one of the best things I ever did with my money from the NFL."

"They must be very proud of you." An apprehensive look crossed his face as he nodded. "My dad lives in the same house we grew up in on Fountain Street. He still drinks himself into a stupor, and I doubt that he's ever thought of leaving Clifton."

Will absently brushed the side of his nose with his finger and nodded again. Jodie wanted him to understand that being from Clifton was the only thing they had in common anymore.

"Does he still work for the power company?"

"No. He retired early. I think working got in the way of his drinking."

Regret shot across Will's face and his jaw clenched as they stared into each other's eyes.

"I'm really sorry," he finally said in a low whisper.

Jodie twirled her ink pen between her fingers and shrugged. She didn't feel compelled to accept his apology or say anything else. What she wanted was for him to leave her alone, but she knew that wouldn't happen.

"Well," he said, after several seconds of dead silence. "I'll show you where the meeting is if you're ready." He rose and glanced down at his watch.

"Now we're probably late," she said, coming from behind her desk. She hadn't seen anyone pass her office, but it was now well after seven-thirty.

"We don't actually get started until about eight. We're right on time."

As they walked out of her office he guided her in the

right direction by placing his hand on the small of her back. The touch jolted her awake more than the cup of caffe latte she'd gotten from Starbucks on her way in. She followed his lead into a large conference room at the end of the hall.

The small staff of Gator House Productions had already assembled, and a box of doughnuts was being pushed around the table. Larry Stone stood at the credenza pouring hot water from a carafe and then dunked his tea bag in and out of his cup. Jodie would never have pegged him as a tea drinker.

Three seats remained at the table. Jodie carefully avoided the one next to Will.

Stone kicked the meeting off and then Will took over. He handled his business more like a corporate executive than an ex-jock. Jodie was impressed, but not surprised by Will's knowledge of sports and his ability to articulate his ideas for the show into concepts that everyone understood. In high school, he never was the dumb one. That was Corey.

The crew's excitement bubbled over and everyone seemed eager to get started. Will had even managed to motivate her, and for a moment she, too, was excited about working on the show.

"Before we move on I'd like to suggest something that would attract more females to the show." Leta, the only other full-time female on staff introduced the new topic and turned to Stone. "Last week you discussed broadening the audience base. Will's 'guy talk' format is working great for the guys, but we're alienating women fans."

"Women are watching to see Will, not to hear about sports anyway," someone offered.

Stone tilted his head toward Jodie. "Leta played for the University of Memphis Lady Tigers, which is why she pushes women's sports so hard."

"But Larry, you know we don't cover women's sports like we should. Will gives it what?" She shrugged. "All of five minutes if that long to run down some scores?"

"When there's something to cover, I cover it," Will retorted.

"How about an interview with Coach Savage?" Leta continued. "I could get her to come down. The Lady Tigers could use our support," she added with a big grin.

"Leta's our very own Billy Jean King," Jeffrey, another staffer, said in a low voice meant for Jodie, but heard around the table.

"Watch it, Jeffrey, or I'll tell everyone you prefer men's gymnastics over basketball," Leta threatened.

Everyone around the table laughed.

"Oops, did I say that out loud?" Leta teased with a hand over her mouth.

Jeffrey balled up a piece of paper and threw it across the table at her.

"Talk to Jodie about that," Stone responded to Leta.

All eyes were on Jodie now, including Will's. Her second day on the job and she was being thrust into making decisions.

"I'm sure we can make that happen," she said to Leta, and then turned to Will. "Coach Savage will fit into your 'guy talk' format, won't she?" She tried not to sound so condescending, but she didn't think she'd been successful.

Several heads at the table lowered, and someone snickered.

"As long as she talks sports she will. I asked her last year, but the timing wasn't right. By no means do we discriminate on this show."

Leta cleared her throat.

Jodie had a feeling it was going to be the girls against the guys, like in a game of kickball.

After the meeting, Jodie spent over an hour in her office listening to Leta talk women's sports.

By midday Jodie sat across the desk from Stone who informed her he was putting her in charge of the interns and the company's two P.A.'s, along with her producer responsibilities. For a brief second, she considered protesting, taking into account the small amount of money he was paying her. But Mack told her she'd be given all the responsibilities of a full-fledged producer. Plus, the experience would look great on her résumé, so she sucked it up.

"Until you've collected a sufficient amount of local sports contacts feel free to tag along with Will on some of his interviews. He also writes articles for *The Commercial Appeal* every now and then, so he has more sports contacts than anyone else on staff."

Jodie wanted to plead with him not to have her shadow Will. Anybody but Will. "Doesn't Leta do interviews as well?"

"She does, but with Will's previous NFL background

he has better contacts. He can get you into places Leta can't. She basically researches women's sports or issues in sports pertaining to women. You'll need a good understanding of local men's and women's sports."

Jodie nodded her understanding, but hoped to be able to get out of it somehow.

"Will and I were talking, and I want you to handle the day-to-day operations of *The Memphis Zone*. Stick with Will, and he'll have you up to speed in no time. I think you two have great chemistry. You'll work well together."

She mustered up a pitiful smile. *That's what I'm afraid of.*

Will sat at his desk staring into the computer screen. He needed to make adjustments to this week's script, but he couldn't get Jodie off his mind. His morning greeting hadn't gone quite as planned. The mature, all grown up Jodie aroused him in a way he hadn't expected.

The first thing he'd noticed when she opened the door was she hadn't pulled her hair back today. Soft black curls framed her beautiful brown face, and that pouty mouth caused his throat to go dry. The urge to kiss her had been so strong, he kept telling himself she was Corey's kid sister. Only, she most certainly wasn't a kid anymore.

"Hey, got a second?" Jeffrey stood in the entrance to Will's office.

"Sure, come on in." Will closed his laptop and spun his chair around.

"I just heard that Keenan Dickerson is Jodie's little brother. Is that true?"

"Yeah," Will replied, nodding.

"That's cool man. You think we can get him on the show?"

Will shook his head. "Too close to the all-star game, I doubt it."

"What if we came at it from another angle? You know, like one of those human-interest pieces you do for the paper. This kid just happens to play basketball. He doesn't have to be the whole show, and still all the kids would tune in. We can do a quick interview during practice."

Will thought for a moment. Jeffrey's idea wouldn't work; but he had just given Will the idea for another show. "You know, you might have something there. I don't know about Keenan, but I've got some other high school athletes in mind."

"You mean the kids from your foundation?"

Will leaned forward resting his elbows on the desk. "Yes. We've got a good program and I've thought about writing it into one of my shows, but you've given me a better idea. Grab a pen and paper and let's map something out."

"Great, I'll be right back." Jeffrey turned to leave.

"Hey, Jeff." Will stopped him.

Jeffrey looked back over his shoulder with raised brows.

"Until I talk to Avery, my business partner, don't mention it to anyone yet. Let's just keep this to ourselves for now."

Jeffrey nodded. "Sure, that'll be easy. Even I don't know what *it* is yet."

Will chuckled and opened his laptop again to start a new file. He labeled it, *A tribute to Corey Dickerson.*

Chapter 6

Lately, Will had been spending so much time at the studio he hadn't seen Avery Douglas, his partner with the Forward Motion Foundation, or their secretary Belinda in a couple of weeks. So, he spent time on the phone with Avery this morning discussing their newest kid.

"Have Belinda start a new file and let's see what counselor's next on the list," Will said, with his phone on speaker and turning around to his computer.

"Belinda already has the folder ready. I thought I'd take this kid, and I was thinking about Ron Griffin for his counselor," Avery said. "The police stopped our boy because the license plate light was out. They found a couple of joints and somebody had an open can of beer. Our boy wasn't in possession of either, but he was high."

Will shook his head. "These kids will never understand the dangers of drinking and driving. Ron's a good choice," Will replied, as he scanned the list of counselors. He sat back in his seat. "Sounds like you've got it all worked out."

"I thought it out before I called, but I wanted to clear it with you."

"Let's run with it. That gives us how many kids now?" Will asked, turning away from his computer.

"A total of six. Let's hope we don't get any more for a while," Avery replied.

"If we do we'll have to refer them out," Will said.

"Oh, yeah, one more thing," Avery said. "You had a visitor stop by the office today."

"Who?" Will asked surprised.

"Allyson Pendleton. Said she just stopped by to see if you were available for lunch."

Will snorted at the teasing tone in Avery's voice. "I don't know why she came by there. She has my number here if she wants to reach me."

"Are you two still hanging out?" Avery asked.

"Man, that's history."

"I didn't think so, but when she popped up I thought maybe, you know, you were revisiting the past."

"No way. I saw her at Walter Oats's wedding Saturday and she tried to get me to hang out with her and some of her friends. I took a pass and haven't heard from her."

"I hear you. What do you want me to tell her if she pops in again, or calls?"

"Tell her I'm unavailable," Will said, in a flat disinterested voice.

The second line on his phone buzzed.

"Hey, man let me get that. I'll holler back at ya."

Will clicked over to his second line, hoping it was retired NBA player Charles Ealy's secretary. Will had been trying to reach him for the last couple of days.

"Hello, Will Duncan."

"Hey, Will, it's Nina."

"What's up, baby girl?" He was always glad to hear from his little sister.

"My car finally died on me and Kristen has a doctor's appointment this afternoon. Think you can help me out?"

"Sure. That's what big brothers are for. What's wrong with Kristen?" he asked. He adored his one and only niece, and stepped in whenever he could since her father was nowhere to be seen.

"She's got a bad cold. Or some type of virus, I'm not sure. I just want to get her something before it gets worse."

"Okay, give me a few minutes to get out of here and I'll be right over." He hung up.

He shut his computer off and decided he'd finish up at home later instead of coming back to the studio.

As he walked down the hall nearing Jodie's office, he thought about how much Nina depended on him, and wondered who took care of Jodie. Corey would have if he'd been there. Just thinking about how Corey used to protect his little sister got under Will's skin. He remembered one day after school commenting on how Jodie was developing and looking good. Corey punched him in the arm harder than he had when they'd been playing around. The look in his eye said, "go near my sister and I'll hurt you."

Old feelings of guilt returned. Will tried to shake them as he stopped outside Jodie's open door. Inside was a beautiful woman who'd been robbed of the pleasure of growing up with an older brother. Will felt like a thief.

She sat with her hands on the keyboard typing her little heart out. She looked as sweet and innocent as she had in high school. Her long black hair was tucked behind an ear making her profile extremely enticing. One hand left the keyboard and slid up and under her hair. Her fingers pulled through to the end in a slow sub-conscious gesture. She twisted the ends around her finger and seemed to find the answer she'd been pondering over, because her hand returned to the keyboard.

He tried to make himself move on down the hall, but she straightened her back and rolled her shoulders. The graceful movement called attention to her breasts, which made his stomach tighten and a long ignored ache move down into his groin.

Jodie almost jumped out of her seat when she turned and noticed him. A hand quickly covered her chest.

"God, Will! You scared me to death." She spun around from her computer facing him.

"Sorry," he said, as he walked into her office. "I didn't mean to. I'm about to leave, but I stopped to see what you're doing after work. Thought maybe I could talk you into dinner. We could discuss next week's show," he added as an afterthought.

She shook her head swiftly. "Sorry, but I can't tonight. I'm busy." She pointed at the computer.

He nodded. "Maybe another time then?"

"Yeah, maybe." She nodded and slowly turned back to her computer. "I really need to finish up these notes."

"Sure," he said, backing out of the office. "I'll let you get back to work. We'll talk tomorrow."

Jodie spent the next two days following Stone around from sunup to sundown, gaining a full under-standing of her job. He issued her a cell phone and called her with work the same night. Time spent with Will was brief and in the company of others. She sat in on the script consultation where Stone informed her he would be turning this job over to her beginning next week.

By the time Friday rolled around, and they started taping *The Memphis Zone,* she felt like a member of the team. Everyone had been so nice to her, and Stone had given her more control than she ever could have imagined.

From the side of the stage she watched Will inter-view his guests, two local sports writers, and witnessed the relaxed "guy talk" format in action.

Like three buddies casually sitting around talking about local sports Will asked, What were the Grizzlies doing? Who's going to the Riverbend Classic this year? And, was there any truth to the allegations that coaches were being paid to steer players to specific colleges?

The format even put Jodie at ease. Will's casual con-versational style was meant for television. He had complete control and was definitely in his element. He laughed heartedly and played around with the guys being interviewed as if they were all old friends, erasing whatever discomfort either of them may have had about being on television.

After the show wrapped, Manny and Leta talked Jodie into joining the crew for drinks and dinner at Clicks.

Televisions lined the walls of Clicks Billiard's and Sports Café where a different sporting event was displayed on every set. A sign in the entrance boasted, Best Wings in Town.

The crew from Gator House Productions had pulled a few tables together in the back of the room. Platters of wings were already on the tables when Jodie arrived. So she ordered a Coke.

Manny pulled out the seat on her left. *"Comment allez-vous?"*

"Très bien, merci." Jodie shot back with a cunning smile.

Manny snapped his fingers and smiled. "I'll be damned. You speak French?"

She laughed at how fast he switched from French to Memphis Southern twang. "No. But, 'very well, thanks' is one of about three phrases I remember from high-school French."

"Man, I thought I was going to have somebody to practice with." He picked up his pretty blue drink, a far cry from all the bottles of beer on the table, and took a sip. "So, how are you and Will getting along? I hope you're doing better than our last producer."

"Oh, he won't be running me away," she said, with conviction.

"Who's that?" Leta asked, as she sat down across from them.

"Will," Manny volunteered. "I told her about Cindy."

Leta frowned and poured her beer from the bottle into a frosted glass. "Cindy, huh. That woman had problems. I think she was kinda diggin' Will until she found out he had a woman. That's when she started wiggin' out on us. I thought I was gonna have to slap her one day."

Manny choked on his drink, and Jodie quickly reached over to pat him on the back. "You okay?" she asked, concerned and trying not to laugh.

He alternated between laughing and choking until tears filled his eyes and he leaned back and fanned himself. "Whew, let me tell you. I was just getting a mental picture of you bitch-slapping Cindy." He pointed to Leta. "And honey it was funny as hell."

Leta rolled her eyes at him. "Screw you, Manny." She turned to Jodie. "Anyway, Will's great to work with. He's a tad bit chauvinistic, but it's all that testosterone. We'll break him of that."

A cheer broke out from the crowd and all heads turned toward a television to see who scored.

Jodie looked up at the screen, but she wasn't interested in the game. Leta had said Will had a woman. Did he have one now, she wondered.

"You know she's partly right," Manny said from her left. "Will's a doll. Everybody at the studio loves him. I mean what's not to like. He's intelligent, hardworking, and not at all bad on the eyes. Plus, he's not just another rich jock, you know what I mean?"

With a mouth full of food, Jodie swallowed and shook her head. "No, I don't know what you mean. What makes him not just another jock?"

Manny stopped eating and gawked at Jodie.

"Honey, the minute William Duncan retired from football his phone started blowing up. Everybody wanted a piece of him."

"Really?" Jodie asked, somewhat surprised. She glanced at Leta, who remained glued to the television as she fussed at the referee about a bad call.

Manny nodded, and sipped his drink. "In college, Will was the Tigers' designated interviewee. Whenever a television or radio crew wanted comments after a game, the coach sent Will out there because he was articulate and they didn't have to worry about him sounding stupid. The guy has a great voice, you have to admit that."

Jodie nodded in agreement. "Yeah, he does have good on-camera presence. So why isn't he working at ESPN or some other major studio?"

"Honey, he loves Memphis. I don't think you could pry that man away from here. Besides, a major network wouldn't give him control of his own show. Here, he can get that."

"Anybody want something else to drink?" Leta asked, as she motioned for the waiter.

"I could use a refill." Jodie sucked the remains of her Coke from the glass and looked over her shoulder for their waiter.

"Speak of the devil," Manny said.

Jodie turned around and looked up right into Will's beautiful ebony eyes, and choked on her Coke. Manny reached over and patted her on the back.

"You okay?" he asked, laughing.

She cleared her throat and shook her head. "Yeah, I'm fine. It just went down the wrong way." She hadn't expected to see Will. Especially after she told him she had something to do tonight. He'd changed into a casual shirt and a nice-fitting pair of jeans.

"Was anybody sitting here?" he asked, as he sat down.

"Naw, cop a squat," Leta said, shoving the plate of wings in his direction.

Then the crowd erupted into another round of cheers after a touchdown, three-pointer or something. Jodie didn't turn this time to see, she wasn't interested.

Neither did Will. Instead, he asked her something but she only heard the tail end of the question.

Jodie leaned into the table. "What did you say?"

He stood up and came around the table, pulling out the vacant chair next to her, and sat down.

"I didn't get to talk to you after the show," he said, with his face inches from hers so he could be heard over the loud noise. "I wanted to get your opinion of the show."

His knee pressed against her thigh as he talked. The contact sent a shiver through her body. She crossed her legs at the ankle, which pulled her thigh away from his knee, and she took a deep breath.

"It was good," she said, giving him a quick glance.

He pulled his arm away. "Just good?" he asked impatiently.

She could almost see his ego shatter and fall all over the floor in a million pieces. "It's a different kind of sports show than I'm used to," she clarified. "I mean I don't watch a lot of sports. Or, I didn't anyway until recently." Stop babbling, she scolded herself.

He nodded, and stared down at her. "Just good, huh?" he repeated.

She relented. "Actually, a little better than good, but I did see room for improvement."

He looked about ready to burst until the waiter set a platter of wings and a bottle of beer in front of him.

"Well, we'll have to get together to discuss those improvements." He turned around to his food, but not before giving her a sweeping, admiring glance.

She nodded and shrugged cheerfully. "That's part of my job." What had he expected from her? He probably only wanted her praise for the show and his skills as a host. In other words, a yes woman.

Jodie could feel him stewing over her lack of enthusiasm. Then his attention shifted to a television and one of the games as he ate.

Two separate conversations had started about today's show, one at each end of the table. Jodie realized she was sitting dead center and didn't know which group to listen in on, so she listened to bits of each one. Then Will said something that caught her attention.

"Thanks, Jeffrey, but our new producer thinks the show could have been better."

Jodie's eyes popped when the crew looked at her. "I didn't say that," she protested.

Will turned to her and smiled. "You didn't?"

"I thought that was one of the best shows in months," Leta said.

"Yeah, everything went off without a hitch," Jeffrey added.

Jodie turned in her seat until she faced Will. "Your

timing was a little off, and some things could have gone smoother, but other than that everything was fine."

"My timing?" he shot back.

"Yes. I think it needs work."

He leaned over and scratched the side of his head and smiled. "So, it's not the show you have a problem with, it's me?" he asked.

Manny elbowed her and whispered, "Give him hell, girlfriend."

Before Jodie could respond, Will's cell phone rang. Without taking his eyes off Jodie, he unclipped it from his belt and flipped it open.

"Yeah," he said into the phone.

Conversations at the table resumed until Will stood up.

In a rushed voice he asked, "Is he okay?" Then nodded. "I'll be there in fifteen minutes." He closed the phone and clipped it back to his belt.

"Everything okay, Will?" Leta asked.

He shook his head and wearily said, "No, I've gotta run."

He leaned down and whispered in Jodie's ear. "We'll talk about my timing later."

She nodded and held a straight face. His lips were so close to her ear she could feel the warmth from his mouth.

"Is it one of the kids?" Leta asked.

Will nodded. "Yeah. I'm headed down to the hospital." He waved goodbye and was gone.

Kids! Jodie thought. *He has kids!*

The minute Will left Jodie turned to Manny and asked, "Is he married?"

Manny shook his head. "No, but half of the women

in Memphis are fighting for the pleasure. Why, you interested?"

Jodie shook her pinched face, and in a voice a few octaves from her norm, she said, "No way."

Manny nodded as he peered out of the corner of one eye at Jodie. "Uh-huh. If you say so, missy."

Chapter 7

Saturday morning Jodie woke from her first night out with Tracy and her friends. They closed down Beale Street one drink at a time. For a preacher's kid, Tracy knew how to party. If Jodie hadn't been the designated driver she knew she wouldn't even be conscious right about now.

She pulled herself out of bed, and across the hall into the bathroom. Late nights were not for her. If she wasn't in bed by ten she was no good the next day.

She turned on the shower to the sound of singing and dishes clinking in the kitchen. Tracy was already up being her cheerful self this morning.

Minutes later, dressed in jeans and a T-shirt, Jodie walked out of her bedroom and started down the hall. She froze when she heard a familiar loud voice that caused her body to stiffen.

"Oh God, no!" she said, under her breath and then quickly spun around.

"There's sleepyhead now," Tracy called out from the other end of the hall. "Jodie, you have company."

Jodie gritted her teeth and stopped. She turned around as the Wicked Witch of the West appeared behind Tracy.

Rosalyn Roberts sashayed around Tracy down the hall with her arms extended. "Well, if it isn't my middle child. I keep telling everybody I have a daughter, but these folks around here don't believe me."

Jodie improvised a lackluster smile.

In high heels, a lime-green suit that fit like a glove, and a face that cost a fortune, Roz pulled Jodie into a hug. Jodie's shoulders shrank like a child's as she let Roz embrace her. Her nostrils filled with a flowery perfume she hadn't smelled on Roz before. Then she was thrust back at arms' length, and scrutinized from head to toe.

"Now. What I'd like to know is how could you move to Memphis and not have the decency to call your own mother to let her know you were here?"

Jodie glanced past Roz down the hall. Tracy had deserted her.

"How did you know I was here?" Jodie asked.

Roz lowered her arms and turned to walk back into the living room.

"Keenan told me."

"I was going to call once I finished settling in." Jodie wanted to kick Keenan's narrow behind.

"Sure you were." Roz walked over to the couch and

picked up her clutch purse with a big Prada emblem on the front, and pulled out a pack of cigarettes. She glanced over her shoulder at Jodie and waved her hand in a show of disgust. "What's wrong with your hair? When's the last time you visited a salon?"

Tracy poked her head out from the kitchen. "If anybody's hungry breakfast is ready."

Jodie ignored the snide remark about her hair, but didn't take her eyes off Roz. "Please don't smoke that in here. You know how much it bothers me."

Roz raised her chin and headed for the patio. "Oh, I'll just step out here."

Jodie crossed her arms in silent protest as Roz lit her cigarette, and then opened the sliding glass door to step out. She gently closed the door behind her.

The smell of smoke quickly filled the room as Jodie walked into the kitchen.

"I told you, you should have called her," Tracy whispered.

"That woman is going to get on my last nerve. She knows cigarette smoke stops me up, yet she lit that cigarette in here anyway." Jodie jerked the refrigerator door open.

"So Keenan ratted you out?" Tracy asked.

The silk plant on top of the refrigerator shook as Jodie closed the door. "Can you believe it? I asked him not to say anything, and he runs home and tells her."

"Girl, like I said, sooner or later you have to face the music. And your orchestra is out on that patio," Tracy said, as she passed Jodie with her plate and sat at the dinette table.

The patio doors slid open and Roz walked back in. "Ladies, I'm hungry enough to eat a horse. Jodie, why don't you fix me some of your famous blueberry pancakes?"

"Sorry, we're all out of fresh blueberries," Jodie proclaimed proudly, about to help herself to some eggs Tracy had cooked.

"No we're not," Tracy announced. "I bought some yesterday." She turned around to Jodie with an innocent look on her face and pointed at the refrigerator. "Look down in the…crisper," she trailed off at the sight of Jodie's narrow eyes, and turned back around to eat her bacon.

"Wonderful," Roz said. She walked into the dining area to sit at the table with Tracy.

"Are you sure you can't eat bacon and eggs like the rest of us?" Jodie asked.

"Oh honey no, I don't eat pork. And I only eat egg whites, but I wouldn't put you through the trouble of separating any for me. I'm on a special diet. Marion and I are about to go to Jamaica, and I need to be ready for the beach."

"Mrs. Roberts, you don't need to lose any weight, you look great," Tracy said, between bites.

"Well, thank you, honey. It does look like you've put on a few extra pounds since the last time I saw you."

Tracy stopped eating and shook her head. "I don't think so," she said, looking down at herself.

"Well, maybe it's just the way those sweatpants fit you."

Jodie banged the griddle against the stove as she pulled it out.

"How are we coming with those pancakes? Do you need some help?" Roz asked.

Sixteen-year-old Jodie had reluctantly returned. Roz reduced her to childlike status every time they were together, which is why Jodie didn't like coming home.

"No, I've got it. How many would you like?" Jodie asked between clenched teeth. *Would you like a little arsenic with that?*

"Two will be fine. And don't make them too big. I hate big fat pancakes. Oh, I hope you have some two percent milk? Whole milk doesn't set well with me these days," she confided to Tracy.

"It's whole milk or no milk." Jodie's attempt to mask the frustration in her voice failed.

"I guess I can stomach it. It's not every day that my Jodie fixes me breakfast."

Jodie prepared the pancakes while Roz and Tracy chatted about the latest Memphis happenings. Roz had turned into a social butterfly. She knew a little something about everybody and everything.

In the kitchen, away from their conversation, Jodie remembered the last time she cooked Roz breakfast— the weekend before she left for college. Roz complained that the pancakes were cold, the juice was warm, and she'd forgotten her side of turkey bacon.

With two perfect blueberry pancakes topped with a dot of butter, Jodie walked into the dining room and set the plate in front of Roz. She returned to the kitchen for a glass of chilled orange juice. Just how Roz used to like it.

"Aren't you going to join me?" Roz asked, as she poured fat-free syrup over her pancakes.

"I lost my appetite," Jodie responded.

"Then grab something to drink and sit down. We need to talk." Roz ate her first forkful of pancakes and closed her eyes.

"These are wonderful, Jodie," she praised.

Tracy scrambled up from the table and set her dishes in the sink. "Well ladies, I'm going to hit the shower."

"Honey, you don't have to run off on my account. Sit back down and talk with us. I haven't seen you since you used to come around to the house."

"It's good seeing you, too, Mrs. Roberts, but I'll let you two have some privacy."

"Nonsense, sit down. You're like family. You know all of our business anyway. How are your parents? Are they still in Clifton preaching to the neighborhood?"

Jodie pulled back the chair Tracy had just gotten up from and gave her roommate a helpless smile. "Have a seat, we might as well get this over with."

Roz continued to eat, oblivious to the girls' reactions to her.

Reluctantly, Tracy sat down. "Yes, ma'am, they're still in the ministry if that's what you mean. Right now they're in Belize on a missionary trip."

"That's wonderful. You always were an honest child." Roz pointed at Tracy with her fork. "Maybe you can tell me why my daughter moved to Memphis without letting me know, and instead of doing anything to help her little brother, she gave him money to buy drugs."

Jodie wanted to scream. "He did what?"

"He came home two nights in a row high as a kite.

Marion is fed up with it and threatened to put him out if he didn't tell us where he got the money. Imagine my surprise when he said his big sister gave it to him."

Jodie shook her head. She'd had a feeling Keenan wasn't being straight with her about why he needed the money. But she didn't think he'd use her like that.

"You know I didn't intentionally do that. I thought he needed it to buy basketball shoes."

"I told you the boy's on drugs. He's not going to come out and say he wants money to buy drugs." Roz turned to Tracy. "You don't have any brothers do you, honey?"

"No, ma'am. I'm still an only child."

"And you come from a good Christian family. I wish some of your Christian ways would rub off on my daughter here."

Jodie and Tracy shared a knowing smile.

There had been no walking away from Roz this morning. She was as abrasive now as she'd ever been. How Marion put up with her behavior Jodie didn't know. Roz was too much for her father, Lou, who searched for an out in liquor bottles.

With Tracy backing her up Jodie detailed how Keenan conned her. She apologized again for not calling Roz the minute she arrived in town.

Satisfied with the explanations, Roz and Jodie walked into the living room. Jodie caught Tracy sneaking off down the hall.

"You girls really could use some help decorating this place," Roz said, as she looked around the room.

"It's coming together. We've only been here a little over a week."

"I've got some old furniture in the garage you can have. It's far better than this snap-together, slip-covered stuff you have here."

"What we have is fine for now."

"Are you working yet?"

Jodie scrambled for an answer. "I'm still in television," she said, walking over to the fireplace.

"Exactly what do you do?" Roz persisted.

"I was hired to produce a bridal show, but—"

"For what station?"

Jodie didn't really want to lie, but Roz wouldn't let it go. Desperate times called for desperate measures.

"It's an independent studio that's affiliated with CBS, I doubt that you've heard of it." Considering how Marion's lifestyle had pushed Roz into the Memphis social scene, Jodie didn't want to risk mentioning Gator House Productions.

"You should have let me know when you were coming, Marion has connections all over town. He could have gotten you on at one of the major networks."

"Thanks but with everything you guys are dealing with I didn't want to inconvenience you." Jodie walked back over to the couch and sat down.

Roz sighed and uncrossed her legs. "Jodie, about Keenan, you should have known better. He's different when he's on those drugs. I don't know him anymore. I don't know any of his friends. He never brings them by the house." She paused to pull the pack of cigarettes from her purse again. "When he's not playing basketball he's asleep. I don't understand him. He's not at all like Corey."

Jodie blinked in surprise at seeing this gentler side of Roz.

"Everybody loved Corey. He had lots of friends," Roz said, with a hitch in her voice. "I understood Corey."

"He was like Daddy," Jodie thought aloud. When Roz turned and looked at her, Jodie corrected herself. "I mean Lou." Her parents had never liked being called Mom and Dad, and it wasn't a term she usually used.

"What I'm trying to say is Keenan's a loner."

"God help him if he's anything like Lou," Roz said, with her lighter in hand, and stood up. "He still lives in that dive in Clifton with that dime-store woman. She looks like a slut. I bet you she's a retired stripper."

Listening to Roz rant and rave, Jodie realized, *Keenan's cursed either way.*

"But," Roz continued, as she walked over to the patio door. "Unless we find him help, Keenan will squander his life away just like Lou. Living hand to mouth."

"Like father, like son," Jodie said absently.

Roz jerked her head around from the patio door. "That's not true. Corey was nothing like Lou." Then she opened the door and stepped out.

"And thank God I'm nothing like you," Jodie said, this time under her breath.

The long stretch of highway that lay between Memphis and Clifton was just what Jodie needed at the moment. After attending morning service at Greater Bethel with Tracy, she dropped her roommate off and kept going. She had a lot of thinking to do.

She'd given up a promising job, a fun single life in Atlanta, and an hour-long commute to work, the latter of which she wouldn't miss, all to try and save her little brother's life. And what's the first thing she does? Give him money for drugs. She wanted to beat her head against the steering wheel for being so dumb.

And although she was beginning to like her job at Gator House Productions, the minute Roz found out Will worked there, she would make Jodie's life a living hell. And this time, Jodie couldn't run away from her.

All of these thoughts ran through her head as she admired the picturesque landscape and beautiful mountains of Tennessee.

When she turned off Interstate 78, beads of sweat formed on her upper lip. She lowered the window to let a little air in. Clifton. She hadn't set foot in the little town of six hundred and twenty in over five years. Since her mother's move to Memphis she'd been back only twice.

She drove through the quaint little town noticing several new buildings and spruced up landscaping all around. She wondered if any of her relatives still lived in town?

In no time at all she found herself at the corner of Fountain and Sundial. She sat there gripping the wheel until a car horn behind her startled her into moving. With her left signal on she turned down the street full of small run-down clapboard houses. This used to be her stomping ground, she thought as she cruised down the street.

Two blocks ahead was the house she was born in, and her father's home. Her palms grew sweatier the closer she got. She turned the air conditioner off and let the window down. She wanted to smell Clifton, to see if it smelled like home to her.

Suddenly, she hit the brakes. She was within her block and a Ford Focus had just pulled into their driveway. The passenger side door opened first and Lou slowly stepped out of the car closing the door behind him. For once, he looked sober.

Jodie's foot slowly rose from the brake and her car began a slow roll toward the house. A few houses away now, she noticed Lou had more gray hair than the last time she'd seen him. There was a little hesitation in his step, as if he needed a few minutes to get his legs working.

Then the driver side door opened and a woman got out of the car with a cigarette dangling from her mouth. She had on a black skirt, white shirt, and a pair of sneakers. More than likely a waitress uniform, Jodie assumed. She walked around the car to the front door and opened it as Lou reached the small porch. Together they went inside and closed the door.

Actually seeing them together for the first time gave Jodie such an uncomfortable funny feeling she couldn't bring herself to stop the car in front of the house. She kept going until she reached the stop sign at the corner. In the rearview mirror she looked back at the house as her eyes filled with tears. What had at one point in her life been a home filled with love, was now a dilapidated home, possibly beyond repair.

Chapter 8

A̲ll Monday morning Jodie kept expecting Will to pop into her office wanting to discuss his timing, but he never did. She saw him once that morning, and then he left for the day. According to Leta, he'd gone out researching a story involving the Grizzlies.

Come Tuesday, her luck wasn't as good. She found herself at George Washington Carver High School with Will and Jeffrey doing an interview and shooting some footage for a later show.

Afterwards, Will thanked the coaching staff for their time and stood around shooting the breeze for a few minutes while Jodie helped Jeffrey load the camera equipment into the studio's Astro Van.

She didn't think a producer normally went out on an interview, but Stone wanted her to experience every aspect of the show, and she appreciated that. More than that, she appreciated Jeffrey letting her ride along with him instead of her having to ride with Will.

"That went pretty well," Jeffrey commented, about the interview.

"Yeah, I thought so, too," Jodie agreed. "We got some great sound bites to choose from. After he interviews Coach Harris tomorrow I want to get some shots of both schools."

"Got it." Jeffrey closed the van door. "Sorry, but I gotta run. I need to pick my son up on time today. My ex-wife gets all bent out of shape when I'm late. Will said you could ride back with him if that's okay?"

Jodie went brain dead. "Do what?" she asked, momentarily confused.

"I'm not going back to the studio." Jeffrey held up his watch. "This took so long I'm gonna be late picking up my kid."

"Oh, sure, sure. You do what you gotta do. I'll ride back with Will. No problem."

"Thanks, Jodie." He opened the van door and climbed in. Before shutting the door he said, "Tell Will I'll drop the footage off tonight."

"Okay." Jodie nodded and waved goodbye as Jeffrey pulled off in the van with the red-and-black Gator House Productions logo on the side. Her eyes followed the van until it pulled out of the school lot and disappeared around the corner.

Parked next to the van's empty spot was Will's silver Range Rover. She'd never ridden in a Range Rover before, and she didn't care to now. When she turned around toward the school, Will stood in the bright sunlight staring at her.

He pulled a pair of shades from his jacket pocket and crossed the lot. She couldn't get over how good he looked in a suit and tie. He literally took her breath away. Everything about William Duncan said class, charm and sophistication. He drove a classy SUV, wore classy suits and could charm the pants off any woman. Or so she'd heard. But she wasn't game to find out. At least she didn't think she was.

"Sorry if I kept you waiting," he said, as he opened her door.

She shook her head. "You didn't. Jeffrey pulled away a few seconds before you walked out." She reached for the handle to pull herself up into the SUV, but Will took her hand in his and helped her up instead. Once her butt hit the seat she pulled her hand from his, and he smiled.

He closed her door and walked around the back toward the passenger's side of the SUV to hang his jacket inside the door.

"What did Jeffrey say about the footage?" Will asked, before closing the door.

"He said he'd drop it off tonight." Jodie glanced over her shoulder, but Will had closed the door and was opening the driver's side door.

"He has to pick up his son," she continued as Will buckled himself in and started the engine.

"Okay, great, I'll get to check out the tape before tomorrow's interview." He pulled out of the school lot and shot Jodie a quick glance. "Want to watch the playback with me tonight?"

"You're working tonight?" she asked.

He laughed. "No. Jeffrey always brings the tape by my house and we check it out. You're welcome to join us."

She shook her head and turned away, watching the passing houses. "Afraid I can't. I'm busy tonight."

Will nodded and turned the radio on. "Could somebody have a date already?"

"Because I'm busy doesn't mean I have a date," she said with a roll of her head.

"No, it doesn't." He reached up and worked his tie off with one hand and tossed it into the backseat. As he turned Jodie sensed his eyes moving up and down her body. Instead of being revolted or upset, she felt desired, excited, and better than she had in a long time. When he turned his attention back to the stop-and-go traffic, she slid a hand down and pinched her thigh. She had to make sure this wasn't a dream. She was riding in Will's SUV, and he was checking her out like he used to check out the older girls in school.

"You know, Corey told me to keep an eye on you."

She gave him an incredulous, gape-mouthed, "Huh?"

"Yeah." Between watching out for the traffic, he glanced at her. "I'm not supposed to let anything happen to you. So maybe I'd better check out your dates."

"You must have fallen and bumped your head back there somewhere," she teased.

"No really, he did ask me to keep an eye on you."

"Then where have you been for the last fifteen years?"

"Sorry, I got sidetracked, but I'm here now. So who's this guy you're going out with?"

"My, my, aren't you the mother hen. What makes you think I don't already have a man?"

"Do you?"

She hesitated for effect more than anything. She didn't want to make up some man she'd never be able to produce later. "Presently, no I'm not seeing anyone," she admitted.

"So you're single?" he asked.

"And you?" she retorted.

Will slowed in the heavy traffic ahead of him merging onto the interstate. He turned to face Jodie. "Yes, ma'am, single as a dollar bill."

"Any children?" she asked.

He shook his head. "None, you?"

"Then who did you run to the hospital to see the other night? I thought Leta said it was one of the kids."

Will grinned. "It was one of the kids from my Forward Motion Foundation. He was in a car accident. I'm his mentor."

"Oh, I hope he wasn't hurt."

"Naw, just a little shook up."

The Range Rover finally inched onto the interstate only to be stuck in thicker traffic. Will turned the air conditioner on and dropped in a CD. A jazz artist Jodie wasn't familiar with blew beautiful saxophone music that filled the car. They listened to the number in silence for a few minutes.

"What about you?" Will asked. "Any children?"

She shook her head. "No."

"You know, I thought you'd be married with at least one child by now. I'm surprised to hear that somebody in Atlanta didn't snatch you up."

Jodie arched a brow. "What makes you say that?"

"Because, you're the marrying type. You're ambitious, smart, still beautiful as ever and I know you'd make a great mother."

She laughed.

"I'm serious," he said. "Your biological clock hasn't started ticking?"

"Will, you don't know me. You haven't seen me since high school."

"Hold on. I've seen you a couple of times since then."

"We've bumped into each other in the street a couple of times during one of my brief visits. That's it. How do you know what type of mother I'd make?"

He licked his lips and flashed a cocky grin. "I know women."

"Something Mrs. Geraldine taught you?" she asked, remembering how nice his mother was.

"No, something I learned from my ex-wife."

Jodie's eyebrows shot up in surprise. "I didn't know you'd gotten married." Tracy hadn't told her that little bit of news.

"Briefly. When she told me, 'I ain't the type of woman to be raising no kids,'" he mimicked her high-pitched voice, "I thought she was joking, but the joke was on me. About a year later I found out she meant it."

"Is that why your marriage broke up?" she asked.

He frowned and shook his head. "I'm not in the NFL

anymore, that's why she's my ex-wife. She found somebody who had better knees, so I guess you could say she traded up."

Although he tried to look nonchalant, Jodie could detect the pain in his expression. "You blew out your left knee, right? Is that when you retired?"

"Retired, got a divorce and moved back to Memphis. All in about three months' time."

"Wow, talk about life changing."

"Yeah, but I don't have one single regret. I love my life right now."

"How long were you married?"

"Two years and four months."

"Bitter?"

He glanced at Jodie. "Me?" And shook his head. "Naw, it just wasn't meant to be. She's better off anyway. Her new boyfriend's salary made mine look like chump change. She has the life she wanted, and I learned a valuable life lesson."

"And that is?"

"People really do show you who they are, if you're paying attention."

Traffic let up a bit and Will changed lanes. They were almost at the studio when he finally mentioned the show again.

"Instead of riding out to Hillcrest High School tomorrow with Jeffrey, you can ride with me. I'll be in early."

Surprisingly, she had enjoyed the conversation, and the Range Rover ride beat getting tossed around in the

Astro Van the way Jeffrey drove. But, getting closer to Will wasn't what she'd wanted to do.

"I might have to meet you there. I'm trying to set up a meeting with Keenan's school counselor for tomorrow."

"How's he doing, by the way?"

"He's doing good," she lied.

Will pulled the Range Rover into the studio parking lot. "I caught most of his games last year. He's got a lot of natural talent. He just needs to learn a little more control and he'll be ready for college ball. Have the scouts been hounding him yet?"

She shrugged. "Not that I know of, but it's his last year, so I'm sure they'll be coming around."

Will chuckled. "You can bet they've been around for years." He parked next to Jodie's Cavalier and turned off the engine.

"Thanks for the ride." She unbuckled her seat belt and opened the door to get out, but stopped and looked back when she felt his hand on her arm.

"I'm not going inside—I've got a few things to do, but thanks for coming along today."

"No, I should be thanking you. I'm the one learning in this process."

"Yeah, but I know this isn't what you had in mind when you took the job. Trust me, it'll work out, though."

She nodded. "I'm sure it will." Then she climbed out and closed the door.

Jodie entered the building before Will pulled out of the parking lot. The whole ride, she sat stiff as a board afraid to move or touch anything. He didn't like that. He wanted her at ease and relaxed around him. It was bad enough she managed to avoid him all the damned time. But that would have to change if she continued to work there, and he'd make sure it changed sooner rather than later.

After a quick stop by his Forward Motion office to catch up with their part-time secretary Belinda, he left for home.

Before the guys came by, Will spent a couple of hours working on what he'd dubbed his Special Project.

When the doorbell chimed at nine-thirty that night, he answered the door fully expecting Jeffrey.

"Hey man, sorry I'm a little late. You'll never guess what kind of bull I had to go through this afternoon."

Will stood back and let Jeffrey and his oversized Gator House bag full of tapes inside.

"What happened?"

"I picked up my son because my wife had some important meeting, so she claimed. Man, when I dropped him off a little while ago, she was getting out of some dude's car. Can you believe that shit?"

"He was her important meeting?" Will asked.

"Yeah man. She had a freaking date. She had me babysit while she went on a freaking dinner date."

Will shook his head as he led the way through the house into the family room. "Why didn't she just tell you she had a date?"

"Dude, I don't know. But she made me look like a chump, sitting there waiting on her to come in from her date."

The sixty-two-inch screen was turned to Sports Central, while the picture in picture was on ESPN.

Jeffrey dropped his bag on the floor next to the couch and took a deep breath. "Mmm, mmm, what's that I smell cooking?"

"Rita whipped up a little something before she left today. I warmed it up in case you guys got hungry. Beer's in the fridge, help yourself."

"Don't mind if I do," Jeffrey said, rubbing his palms together. He left Will sitting on the couch and walked into the open kitchen.

"Dude, you must be the luckiest man on the planet. You've got a housekeeper who doubles as a cook. And a damned good one if I might add. Whatever that was I ate last week was da bomb."

"Chicken cacciatore, it's her specialty."

"Well, it was slammin'. I need to find a woman that can cook like that. Jessica's idea of a good meal is some KFC."

"Is the tape in your bag?" Will asked, eager to get started.

"Yeah, go ahead take a look. Where's Avery?"

"He's on his way. Both of you slackers are running late tonight." Will found the tape that Jeffrey had managed to round up for him and popped it into the recorder.

"What did Jodie say about the interview?" Will asked, as the Clifton High Wildcat mascot displayed on the television.

Jeffrey walked out of the kitchen with a plate of food and a bottle of beer. "She said she thought it went well." He set his food and beer on the coffee table and clasped his hands together. "Dude, I love hanging over here. You live like that cat, Felix Unger from *The Odd*

Couple. Everything's all neat and clean." He sat on the couch and reached for his beer. "I'm not sure if I should eat in here or in the kitchen," he teased.

"Man, sit your ass down and eat."

Jeffrey took a couple of swigs of beer before saying, "Oh, yeah, at one point Jodie even whispered in my ear, he's pretty good at this isn't he. I said he's all right I guess." He snickered and started in on his dinner.

"You guess my behind, you know I'm good. So are you. Thanks for coming up with that bit about having to pick up your son."

With a mouth full of food Jeffrey gestured, "Yeah man," then swallowed and wiped his mouth with a paper towel. "It was kinda true, I just didn't have to leave that early." Then Jeffrey lowered his voice. "Dude, you gonna tell me what that's all about, right?"

Will's lips turned up as he smiled at the television screen. "In time."

"Cool that, cool that, keeping it on the down-low, I got ya." He took another swig of beer and watched the screen.

The footage was old, but in good shape. The bottom corner of the screen displayed the date, November 1990.

"That you, man?" Jeffrey asked, pointing to the screen.

Will shook his head. "Yeah, my senior year."

A young man ran for a touchdown and the crowd cheered wildly. Will fast-forwarded to a close-up shot of his best friend.

"Corey Dickerson," Jeffrey read off when the screen displayed his stats. "Any relation to Jodie," he asked, in a rather nonchalant way and continued eating.

"Yeah, he was her older brother."

Jeffrey's fork stopped in midair. "Was?"

The doorbell rang and Will stopped the tape and stood up. "Yeah, he died in a car accident."

"Bummer."

The minute Will left the room Jeffrey grabbed the remote and hit Play. He'd intended to laugh at Will during his high school years, but the game was over. A reporter was talking with the captain and co-captain of the team. Jeffrey set his beer down when a much younger Will and Corey appeared side-by-side smiling into the camera. Puzzled, he rewound the tape. *If Will knew Corey, he had to have already known Jodie,* he thought. But for some reason Will wasn't ready to tell him about it yet.

At three hundred and twenty pounds, when Avery Douglas entered a room he caught everybody's attention, and Jeffrey was no exception.

"What's up, Jeff?" Avery said, as he crossed the room to grab Jeffrey's hand.

The greeting always pained Will. He could imagine Jeffrey's arm being ripped out of its socket every time Avery affectionately greeted him by gripping his hand and slamming his featherweight body in for a firm pat on the back.

However, Jeffrey never seemed to mind and greeted Avery with a smile.

"You, dude."

"Man, what you grubbing on?" Avery asked, looking down at his plate.

"Chicken something another." Jeffrey turned to Will. "What's this again?"

Will slapped Avery on the back. "One of Rita's specialties. It's on the stove. Grab yourself a plate and a beer and let's get started."

"Don't mind if I do. You'all go ahead, I'll be right with ya," Avery said, taking off his jacket and tossing it on the couch.

He walked into the kitchen while Will returned to his spot on the couch and flipped open his laptop. The file titled, *A tribute to Corey Dickerson,* was already on the screen.

Chapter 9

Two nights later, Jodie pulled up to Fairley High School before basketball practice ended. She'd worked so late every night she kept missing Keenan. But tonight she'd finally catch up with him.

The school doors finally opened and young men began pouring out. All of them were tall with gym bags across their chests, or over their shoulders, and African American. Jodie sat up in her seat waiting for Keenan to walk out before she started the car. Several young girls dressed too provocatively for her taste stood by the door waiting for what must have been their boyfriends, from the way they were greeted. Keenan was the last player to exit the building, followed by what looked like a couple of assistant coaches.

Jodie started the car and pulled over to the curb next

to him. A car of young men had been waiting for him, but she cut him off.

When he stepped back and noticed her his shoulders slumped.

She stopped the car and got out as the coach looked back and called out Keenan's name.

"Yes, sir," Keenan responded.

"Make sure you're here on time tomorrow. Practice starts at six o'clock, not six-thirty or seven."

"Yes, sir," he said, before tilting his head in Jodie's direction.

"I don't need a ride home."

"I know you don't, I can see that. But you owe me an apology."

He took a deep breath, and bent over holding his knees. "Jodie, what did you move to Memphis for? To follow me around town being a pain in the ass?"

"No. I'm here because of my job, but while I'm here you and I are going to get better acquainted. Like it or not."

"Hey, Keenan, you coming or what?" A young man from the beat-up Mustang called out.

Keenan straightened up and shook his head. "Man, I don't believe this," he said, under his breath. "Go ahead, I'll see you tomorrow," he finally called out to his friends.

After the car pulled off he turned to Jodie, leaning against her car door. "Look, I'm sorry about the money. If you need fifty bucks that bad I'll give it back to you."

"It's not about the money, and you know that. You

took my money and bought drugs with it. That pisses me the hell off."

"Aw, here we go," he whined and ran a hand down his face.

"That's right, here we go. How do you think I felt when Roz knocked on my door accusing me of supplying you with drug money?"

He took a deep breath and walked around to the passenger's side of the car. "Hey, why should I have all the fun. She accuses me of something every day."

He opened the back door and threw his gym bag on the backseat where it fell off of a stock of tote bags onto the floor. "I see you cleaned out your backseat."

Jodie yanked her door open. "Just get in the car."

They rode in silence for a few minutes, while Jodie tried to cool off. Keenan never opened his mouth. He just looked out the window.

"Does your coach know you're doing drugs?" she finally asked.

"I don't do drugs. I just smoked a joint that's all."

"Boy, what do you think a joint is? It's marijuana. A mind-altering drug."

"And you never smoked a joint?" he challenged her.

Jodie turned to look at him. "No. Never."

He turned from her and continued to look out the window.

"Keenan, I can't believe you'd do that to yourself. Especially with the way Lou drinks and after what happened to Corey."

"I don't drink," he said without hesitation.

"No, you do something just as bad. Don't you want

to play college basketball and then get drafted by the pros?"

"And I will. Smoking a joint isn't going to stop that."

She shook her head. How could she get through to this little know-it-all? "Keenan, the minute you don't pass a drug test, your career is over."

"I know what I'm doing, and I'll never fail a drug test."

"Keenan, promise me you'll stop smoking marijuana and doing whatever else you've been doing to get into so much trouble."

He leaned his head back into the headrest. "Man, I can't wait until I can get out of here. Roz is all over my butt, and now you. Why don't you guys just leave me alone?"

"Because we love you, fool."

The fearful emotions she'd been holding in for so many days teetered on the edge, about to spill over as tears blurred her vision.

She'd left her job in Atlanta, and given up her quest of keeping as much distance between her and Roz as possible, all to try and save her little brother's life.

Her hands gripped the steering wheel as her bottom lip began to quiver.

Keenan finally reached out to turn the radio on and glanced at her before turning away. "Why don't you come to the game this weekend?" he asked. "I'll put your name on the list and you can get in free, unless you have to work."

Jodie nodded. "Do Roz and Mack come to the games?"

"Sometimes, but they leave for Jamaica this week. They won't be in town."

She sniffled. "I'll be there."

* * *

The only time Keenan's counselor had available was Friday morning, the busiest day of Jodie's week. But, she made the appointment.

"From everything you're telling me it sounds like he's just seeking attention. Keenan's a very bright young man, when he applies himself. He does just enough work to stay on the team and out of academic trouble, but he has the potential for so much more. I shared all this with your mother a few months ago."

Jodie sat across the desk from Mrs. Carey, Keenan's school counselor, hoping to get some help. She filled the counselor in on Corey's death and her mother's divorce, all of which Jodie believed contributed to Keenan's behavior even though he was a small child at the time.

"Yes, my mother—" the words sounded awkward coming out of Jodie's mouth "—she told me everything you said. I wanted to know if I could do anything to help." Jodie didn't dare tell Mrs. Carey about the drugs.

"Keenan lacks focus and concentration. Half of the time he comes to school to go to sleep. And if I didn't know better…" She hesitated. "I'd swear he's high some of the time. But Keenan's a real quiet type—he doesn't run with that crowd. He's a ballplayer, and they pretty much run together. We have problems with them drinking from time to time, but not much drug use. I do think he could benefit from counseling though."

Mrs. Carey pulled her desk drawer open and rifled through for something. "I'm surprised the coach hasn't had a talk with your parents yet." She handed Jodie a business card and closed Keenan's file. "If you'd like for me to set something up for him I can, or you can give them a call?"

Jödie read the card before putting it into her purse. "I'll have to talk to him first," she said.

"I won't lie to you, the hardest part will be talking him into going," Mrs. Carey continued. "Teenagers tend to think counselors are for crazy people. But with all the changes in your family dynamics he needs to express his feelings about that."

"Thank you, I'll see what I can do."

Jodie left Fairley High School and drove back to work wondering how in the hell she was going to talk Keenan into going to see a counselor. Maybe if she told him she was seeing the same person, he'd go. She gripped the steering wheel and shook her head. That was lame and she knew it. He was a better con artist than her and he'd proved it. She'd have to come up with something better than that.

Jodie almost didn't recognize the studio when she walked in. The dingy reception area looked as if someone had thrown the sun inside. Bright light from new lamps illuminated the new furniture that replaced that beat-down junk she'd always been afraid to sit on. Even Manny's desk looked like a prop out of a magazine spread. For once, everything was in its proper place. Had she wandered into the wrong studio?

Manny came fluttering into the room like a storm, carrying a large box of Dunkin Donuts.

"What's going on?" Jodie asked, pointing around the office.

"Enterprise Rental. A new contract Stone negotiated. We'll be doing Enterprise commercials from now until doomsday. Take a test ride and tell me what you think." He walked around the desk over to the couch. "I picked this one out."

Jodie had to do a double take on Manny. He had on a pair of blue jeans, loafers, and a button-up blue-and-white striped shirt. On him, the outfit looked like a costume.

He noticed her stare and glanced down at himself. "Anything for Mr. Stone, honey. He's all jazzed about the show today."

She nodded and sat on the couch. "Nice," she said, giving it a little bounce.

"Better than the filth that was in here." He motioned around the lobby. "Everything compliments of Enterprise. I just love their stuff, although I wouldn't have any of this cheap crap in my house for free."

Jodie had seen the Enterprise commercials on television, but couldn't say if their product was cheap or not. Regardless, she liked it. She stood up and followed Manny through the door into the studio.

"Are we having a late meeting this morning?" she asked, pointing at the box of doughnuts. After leaving Keenan's school, she stopped at Starbucks for her usual caffe latte, which would go great with a doughnut.

He held the box up. "No, these are for the kids. I told Will he'd have them bouncing off the walls if he fed them this stuff, but it's what he said to get."

"What kids?" she asked.

"Those." Manny pointed toward the set.

On the set Jodie spotted Will surrounded by a group of what looked like high school students sitting and standing all around him.

"Who are they?" she asked.

"Part of his Forward Motion Foundation. They come from local area schools. He brings them in once a month and gives them a tour around the studio."

So those were the kids, Jodie said to herself and smiled.

Manny strutted over to them calling out, "Donuts, fresh donuts."

All heads turned and hands reached out for the box.

Jodie continued down the hall glancing back over her shoulder at Will. He had a few students taking turns sitting in his seat.

The minute she reached her office, Stone's head popped out of the conference room at the end of the hall.

"Jodie, we need you down here," he called out.

"On my way," she replied. She dropped her purse on her desk and found Stone and the rest of the crew in the conference room huddled around the table.

"What's up?" Jodie asked.

"Have a seat." Stone pulled out the chair next to him while holding his cell phone to his ear.

Leta slid some papers across the table. "Your copy."

Jodie caught the papers as they slid in front of her, and picked them up. It was today's script. And the name of the guests surprised her.

"Charles Ealy?" Jodie said aloud, unable to believe her eyes. He used to be one of the biggest celebrities in the NBA.

"Surprise, he's in town today so we tape in two hours, or not at all," Leta said.

Two hours! Jodie looked around the table in shock. You couldn't prepare for an interview with somebody of Ealy's caliber in two hours.

Leta must have noticed the lost expression on her face and volunteered, "He called Will at home last night and said he'd be in town. He flew in this morning, and he's flying out this evening. Will pulled the script together last night. Everybody's scrambling."

"He called Will at home?" Jodie asked.

"It's those NFL contacts I told you about," Stone chimed in, snapping his cell phone closed. "Okay, people let's get ready to make this happen."

Gavin, another staffer, walked in and grabbed a seat. Manny walked in behind him. The whole room looked at Manny as if he'd dyed his hair blond. He'd dressed better than anyone in the room other than Stone.

"Okay, the caterer is on the way, the limo will pick him up at ten o'clock sharp, and our little makeshift audience is all set up," Manny announced.

Jodie frowned. "Makeshift audience?"

"Will's kids," Stone said. "They're going to sit in on the interview and we'll do a round of questions and answers at the end."

Jodie looked up at Stone. "Quick thinking."

Stone shook his head. "Luck. Thank goodness today was their scheduled visit. Will's the luckiest SOB I know."

After the brief meeting to make sure everyone knew their assigned jobs Stone let them go. Everyone that is, except for Jodie.

Chapter 10

Once the crew returned to work, Stone strummed his plump fingers against the desk and looked at Jodie as if he were trying to figure out what to do with her.

"Is everything all right?" he asked.

Dumbfounded, she glanced around the room wondering what he was alluding to. "As far as I know," she responded, in puzzlement.

"I mean at your brother's school. Isn't that where you went this morning?"

Eyes wide now, she'd forgotten she told Stone she was going to talk to Keenan's counselor. "Yes, everything's fine. And thank you for asking."

He nodded. "Good, I'm glad to hear that." He leaned back in his seat. "Well, this is probably the only quiet moment we'll have today. Once we open that door and step onto the set the day is going to fly by. I want you to know I have complete confidence in your abilities to make whatever decisions you feel you have to today. I'll be with Charles's people most of the day, but I'll be available if you need me. Do you think you're ready for it?"

"I think I am. But, we'll know for sure after today."

He nodded his understanding. "Great," he said, picking up the script. "Will worked this out last night. Read over it, discuss it with him, and let me know what you think. It works for me. So tell him not to make any major changes."

"I'll do just that," she said, picking up her script. A tingle of excitement that reminded her of her first day at CNN flowed through her body. She was ready to work.

After she finished making minor adjustments to the script, she found Will in his office pacing back and forth behind his desk. While he held the telephone to his ear, she tiptoed in and placed the script on his desk. Before she could turn around, he reached out and wrapped his big hand around her wrist.

His movement startled her so she jumped and cursed under her breath. He let go and she took a step back away from the desk.

He held up a finger and motioned her closer. "That's right, tonight at seven-thirty," he said into the phone. "Got it?"

She didn't actually move any closer to him, but she stopped backing up. She caught a whiff of his cologne as he turned and ended his conversation while keeping his eyes on her.

"Okay, thanks." He reached over and hung up the

phone, then took a deep breath and smiled. "Are you ready for today?" he asked.

"Ready as I'll ever be," she said, for hopefully the last time. "I've just never worked a show where the guest wasn't known until a few hours before taping. It's a good thing we're not live."

He spread his arms wide. "Welcome to the world of independent television. Here we're free to do whatever we want and we've been known to pull a rabbit or two out of our hats."

"I'm impressed," she said, folding her arms.

"Hold that until the end of the day. We've got to pull this off first."

She pointed to the script on his desk and said, "Well, you've got a good script to start with. I made a few corrections, and had a few questions, but all in all, it really doesn't look like something you whipped together last night."

He picked up the script and flipped through the pages. "You know, I might be wrong, but I think you just paid me a compliment. Was that a compliment?" he asked jokingly.

She blushed and lowered her gaze to the few pieces of paper on his clean desk. "I suppose it was," she said, sweating under the intensity of his gaze.

Will laughed and sat down. "You know we never did get around to discussing my timing, so I'm glad to see you think I do something well."

"You're a writer too so I would expect your script to be well written. Like your articles."

His eyes widened and he nodded with a pleased smile on his face.

"Plus, it's better to discuss your timing while watching the tape. When you get a minute this week I can have Jeffrey cue it up."

She unfolded her arms and then dropped them to her sides. *What to do with her arms?* she asked herself, and settled for tucking her thumbs into her pants pockets. She didn't like the effect Will had on her. She had to get away from him.

He turned around to his computer. "Let's take a look at this script now."

Jodie stepped back up to his desk and propped her hands against the edge. She peered over at the computer screen. He opened the document while looking down at the paper copy.

"Grab a chair and come on around," he said, without looking up. "We can make these changes in no time."

"We!" she said. "Do you need me for that?" She wanted to have something more important to do, but at the moment, the corrected script was her number one priority.

"It won't take long. That way I won't have to look for you if I have any questions."

She gripped the back of one of the black chairs across from his desk, and slowly pushed it around the desk. He slid his chair to the left, providing room for her next to him.

With her chair several inches away from his, she stopped and sat down. She could see the screen well enough from where she was. His desk drawer was in her left side, and his cologne was flirting playfully up her nostrils. He smelled good enough to eat, which prompted her to give one more scoot to her chair. When she did, her chair bumped his.

Will reacted by sliding over a little more. "Come on up here," he said, patting the armrest of his chair.

"This is fine. I can see from here," she responded, not wanting to get any closer.

Will looked over his right shoulder at her, and grinned. "I think we've already established that I don't bite." He reached down and pulled her chair closer until it was almost directly next to his.

"I'm not trying to get in your lap," she replied, bracing her hand against the edge of his desk. "I can see from here."

He adjusted his fingers over the keyboard, but then relaxed them before turning to her again. "You know, that might not be a bad idea." He pushed back slightly. "You could sit here—" he rested a hand on his thigh "—and type, while I read the changes to you. What do you think?" he asked, with a crafty smile on his face.

"I'm thinking sexual harassment," she said bluntly to his dancing eyes.

"Then again, I wouldn't be able to concentrate anyway," he retorted, turning back to the computer screen.

He's flirting with me. Maybe it was all harmless play to him, but he was still flirting and she enjoyed it. But, she quickly reminded herself that she wasn't supposed to like this. She was supposed to be avoiding him. *Just get this script changed and get out of here.*

Will began making the corrections and Jodie gave justification for each one. They worked together on the script for the next thirty minutes. Then, Jeffrey poked his head into Will's office.

"Will, I need you for a quick—" he stopped.

Before Will could respond, Jodie blurted out, "We're making script changes."

Jeffrey arched one brow, and nodded. "Okay," he said, with a slow drawl. "Will, I need you on set for a quick second. If you can spare it?"

"Come on in," Will said. "I'm just about finished."

Jodie straightened up from being hunched over the paper, and turned to catch the goofy smile on Jeffrey's face as he walked in. She hoped he hadn't gotten the wrong impression as to what they were doing. She pushed her chair back and stood up, giving Will the room he needed to stand.

After saving and printing the changes, Will followed her around his desk.

"Jodie, today you get to show what you're made of," Jeffrey said. "And you'll discover that we kind of make this stuff up as we go."

Jodie laughed. "I hope that's not true."

Jeffrey looked at Will. "Tell her, man. We don't know what's going to happen today." Then he glanced back at Jodie. "Say a prayer that Stone doesn't pass out before the day's over with."

Will and Jeffrey laughed a little too hard at that.

Jodie figured it was an inside joke, but laughed anyway.

They followed Jeffrey out to the set.

The next two hours went by in a whirlwind. Jodie was ripped from one end of the studio to the other. To say things were hectic would be an understatement.

However, in all the chaos she was able to witness how much of a team the crew was, and why Stone never doubted they could pull this off.

Jodie was going over the format of the show with Leta when Manny pranced through the door with Charles Ealy and his entourage. A young white woman who was probably his publicist, and another black man a few inches shorter than Charles walked alongside him. Behind him three other young folks followed with wide eyes.

The sports coat and loafers only dressed up the fact that Manny was sweeter than a bag of cotton candy. He practically glowed as he strutted onto the studio floor with all that testosterone behind him. But today, he'd shown why he was so valuable. He'd handled refreshments for everyone, took care of Will's students making sure each one ate before they left the set, and saw to Charles's entourage.

Stone however had turned into a madman. He ran around barking orders at everyone in his way. Every time he turned around to yell Manny's name, Manny was right there in his face—sometimes to Stone's obvious annoyance. Jodie realized today that Manny was much more than an office manager. He was also Stone's assistant.

Interns and production assistants were scurrying around the building being sent on errand after errand. When Jodie's favorite production assistant, Anastasia, walked into the control room almost in tears looking for Stone's favorite pen, Jodie stepped in to help her. The teenager reminded her so much of herself she couldn't let her shed tears in front of the predominantly male crew. She ushered Anastasia into her office.

"Okay, just take a deep breath and relax. I've got a pen just like the one he uses." Jodie reached into her desk drawer and pulled out a Gator House Production ink pen that Manny had given her on her first day. The special pens were Stone's favorite.

"Here." She handed Anastasia the pen. "Tell him you found it in the conference room. He'll never know the difference."

Anastasia pulled her braids back out of her face and looked up at Jodie with grateful eyes. "Thank you so much Jodie. I couldn't find his stupid pen and I don't know why he's so bent out of shape over it."

Jodie knew it wasn't the pen, but the resourcefulness of producing a pen that Stone was interested in. What better time to test a P.A. than when under pressure. Jodie had been tested several times by Stone's uncle Mack. The objective was to break the P.A. down, and then make them stronger. Jodie hoped Anastasia passed the test.

At six o'clock that evening Jodie's stomach began to growl. She'd been too busy to break for lunch. Then Manny, like Johnny on the spot, informed everyone that food was served in the conference room.

An hour after taping, the excitement of the day had dwindled and the staff began drifting out for home. Jodie joined Gavin in the control room where they continued to work. She was exhausted, but running on adrenaline from the rush of the day.

"Jodie, I hate to do this to you, but I'm gonna have to run," Gavin said, after about an hour.

"Don't worry about it. I've got it from here. You've shown me enough."

"Stone will probably be in to look at the tape, if he didn't get on the plane with Charles's people. The man was in heaven today." Gavin stood up and stretched his long arms over his head.

Jodie laughed. "I noticed. I gather you don't do many celebrity interviews?"

"Not of Charles's caliber. Local coaches don't excite Stone, but somebody as famous as Michael Jordan gives Stone an orgasm."

She bit her lip trying not to laugh. But, she had to admit she'd never seen that side of Stone before. The minute he walked out of that conference room earlier, he had turned into a different man.

"Well, the taping went well, so he should be happy," she replied.

"Yeah." Gavin hesitated and looked down at Jodie. "He should be."

Gavin gathered his things and pulled his laptop bag up onto his shoulder. "Don't you sit in here all night now," he said, pulling his car keys from his pants pocket.

She leaned back in the swivel chair and shook her head. "Not a chance. I've got a date with Fire and Ice tonight."

Gavin tilted his head and jingled his keys. "Fire and Ice?" he asked. "Don't believe I know him."

She laughed. "It's a night club. I'm meeting my roommate and a few of her friends there. She doesn't think I know it, but this is her attempt to introduce me to some unsuspecting guy. I detest hook-ups."

Gavin shook his head. "Young folks. How you work as hard as you did today and still have the energy to party tonight, I'll never know."

"Oh, trust me, I'm tired. I wouldn't be surprised if I fell asleep right here watching the playback. Especially with this nice mood music you've got going on here." She referred to the jazz music piped into the room.

"Yeah, it's nice. If you get tired of it, just hit the green button on the end there, and shut it off."

"No, it's nice. I like it."

He laughed and headed for the door. "Yeah, well just don't fall asleep and wind up spending the night. I'll be in tomorrow for a few minutes. If you need to, leave me a note."

"Will do." She saluted him as he walked out the door.

Jodie glanced at her watch and told herself she'd stay thirty minutes tops. That way she'd have time to get home, shower, dress, and meet Tracy at the club by ten-thirty. With her luck, she'd be asleep at her table by eleven.

While viewing the footage Jodie pulled out a tablet and jotted down a few quick notes. If she had to say so herself, she and Gavin had done a good editing job.

She looked at Will smiling at her through the camera lens and she realized no matter what he'd done, she could never hate him. The past was the past. Her family may have held grudges, and she'd tried her best to do the same, but she couldn't.

Every minute of attention Will showered her with in school was as vivid as the day it happened. Even when he wrapped his arm around her in the hallway and called her kid, she couldn't have been happier. Maybe he'd treated her like a little sister, but he had liked her.

But then it was her erotic dreams that she remembered most. In her dreams she wasn't a freshman and he wasn't a senior, but they were equals. He'd wanted her more than any of the pretty girls that used to chase him around school. In the halls their open displays of affection always left her flaming and gasping for breath.

On the tape, Will did that little thing with his tongue again, and she had to hit freeze frame. My God, what that man did to her. She gripped the arms of her chair and slowly pulled her almost-asleep foot from underneath her and crossed her legs. Was it possible that he turned her on even more now than back then?

She heard a faint click and turned to see light shining in when the control room door opened.

And then, Will walked in.

Chapter 11

"Ah, here you are," Will said, as he walked into the control room.

Jodie scrambled to release the freeze frame button, and started the tape again. Embarrassed by the mere inclination that he might have thought she was looking at him, which she was, she wanted to fold into herself and disappear. She had to be a shade of purple right about now, she thought.

He closed the door behind him, and walked over to join her. "What's it look like?" he asked, taking the seat Gavin had vacated.

"Good," Jodie said, in a voice she didn't recognize. She cleared the frog from her throat and tried again. "I mean, great."

"Did you find something wrong?" he asked,

looking up at the screen. "I noticed you had it on freeze frame."

"I—I—" she mumbled inanely, and shook her head while pointing at the screen. "I thought I saw a little something, but it's fine. You know me." She chuckled. "If there's a flaw somewhere I'm bound to catch it." Her attempt at laughter failed miserably and what came out was a nervous giggle.

A slight smile touched Will's full lips, as he leaned back in the chair so far she thought it would crash to the floor. The chair, obviously well worn from Gavin's wider frame, rocked back without falling over.

The tape continued as Will and Jodie sat quietly watching more of the show. She tried, but couldn't concentrate on it any longer. Being in a dim-lit room alone with Will put something other than the show's footage on her mind. Out of the corner of her eye she snuck a peek at him. He sat staring at the television with his eyes slightly squinted. She hadn't noticed it before, but he had a strikingly handsome profile.

As if he sensed her staring, he turned to her and winked flirtatiously. "Did a nice job, didn't we?"

She nodded, and then shook her head. "I personally didn't do that much."

"But who's still here at—" he held up his wrist checking the time "—eight o'clock in the p.m.?" he asked, with arched brows.

"I am," she admitted bashfully. "But, I came in a little late today," she pointed out.

He shook his head, glancing at the screen now. "That's okay, you're here and that shows dedication. I didn't get to earlier, but I want to thank you for helping to make the taping a success."

"Thanks, but you're pretty good at playing host, which made my job easier."

"Stop being modest. I know enough about what you do to know that part of your job is to make me look good. And for that, I thank you."

"Okay, enough with the compliments. Whose idea was it to have the kids in the audience?" She looked up at the tape as the camera panned their young audience.

He grinned and tugged on the cuffs of his shirt. "Sometimes things just work out, like magic," he said, glancing at the screen and watching the kids ask questions.

"I was impressed by their questions, too," Jodie added.

"Yeah, they're smart kids. We prepped for less than thirty minutes. All of those questions were their own ideas. For some of them this was their second time on the show."

"Amazing, how you're good with kids, too," she said, sounding surprised.

He turned away from the television screen, now giving her his full attention. "How come I get the impression you think football is the only thing I know about?"

Her mouth opened in awe.

"I happen to have a degree in communications with a minor in counseling. After I retired from the NFL I went back and finished my degree. And I plan on going for my master's some time in the near future. Are you still amazed?"

Slightly embarrassed, she shrugged, and made a face

that she hoped he wouldn't take the wrong way. "Maybe amazed wasn't the right word. In Atlanta I worked on a lot of shows where most of the hosts hated when teenagers came in for a taping. You never know what will come out of their mouths.

"These kids," she said, pointing at the screen, "seem so at ease with you, and you with them. Where did you learn how to relate to teenagers so well?"

He folded his arms across his chest and smiled. "My dad," he said.

She remembered seeing his father before. They looked a lot alike. Will was a few inches taller, and pounds heavier, than his father.

"Your dad works with teenagers?"

"He used to. I don't know if you remember or not, but he volunteered with the Boys and Girls Club in Clifton. He was the only black male volunteer they had. I think he wanted to mentor all the African American males in the county."

The look on his face was one of admiration and love for his father. Jodie was touched.

"Sounds like he taught you everything he knows."

"Taught? You mean teaches. He works with me from time to time with the foundation. He's a great speaker and the kids respect him."

It must be nice to have a father that everybody looked up to instead of one that embarrassed you most of the time, she thought. She remembered the summer she graduated from high school when Roz threw a Fourth-of-July barbeque. It wasn't like the barbeques she used to throw when Corey was alive, but she'd tried. Lou hadn't shown up all day until the sun was setting. Then he staggered through the gates reeking of alcohol. He made his way to a picnic bench, sat down, and then soiled himself right in front of her graduating class.

"Your students are lucky," she said softly.

"No doubt," Will said in agreement.

On tape, *The Memphis Zone* was wrapping, and the show's theme music filled the small control room. The music made Jodie remember she was supposed to be going out tonight. Somehow Will's presence had made her forget all about Fire and Ice.

"Under the circumstances, I think we most definitely pulled the show off. In fact, it might be one of the best shows to date," Will said.

"I agree," she said.

"I like your hair today," he said, from out of nowhere.

Instinctively, Jodie's hand rose to the back of her head and she remembered she'd curled it that morning. "Thank you."

Will's eyes had taken on a smoldering look in the dim light. She stared into them as he reached out for what she thought was to stroke her hair. Instead, he tucked her hair behind her left ear, and smiled.

"I remember when you used to wear it cut short, tucked just beneath the ear. They used to call that a pageboy, right?"

Unable to speak, she nodded. His hand grazed her cheek, which must have been flushed crimson or purple, leaving behind a warm feeling that stirred things deep inside her.

"Pageboy, or bob, they're the same thing," she finally said. "It grows too fast, so I stopped cutting it. It's easier this way."

Overhead soft jazz music from Gavin's CD selection played Vanessa Williams, "Dreamin'." That's just what Jodie felt, like she was in a dream. One of her desperately seeking Will Duncan dreams, where she came back to town, married him, and they lived happily ever after.

"So why aren't you out making some guy happy tonight?" he asked.

"I could ask you the same thing," she replied.

He shot her a "are you crazy" look and she realized what she'd said. "I mean why aren't you making some woman happy? You know what I meant."

He grinned and busied himself with changing the tape. "Dedication I guess. I'm determined to get this show onto a major network no matter what I have to give up."

"Must be hell on your social life?" she asked.

"What social life? When I'm not working with one of the kids from my foundation, I'm working on the show or writing an article about something pertaining to the show."

"You sound like a self-professed workaholic."

"Not really," he said shaking his head. "I enjoy what I do, so it's not work to me. It's my lifestyle."

"Do you enjoy hosting better than playing football?"

"It's a lot easier on the body, that's for sure."

Amen, brother. Jodie doodled on her tablet and tried not to let him see her checking out his body. Football had been very good to him, Jodie observed. He wasn't one of those fat football players with a big wide neck.

Will was all muscle, which she'd love to test for an ounce of fat.

"Besides," he continued. "I can't play football all my life anyway."

He grabbed another tape and switched it out for the one in the machine.

Quit lusting over the man, she told herself and closed her tablet. *Get out of here before you do something you'll regret later.* She pushed her chair back to stand up.

"Where you going?" he asked, holding his arm out and cutting off her path.

She looked up, dumbfounded. "The tape's over. I've taken all the notes I need to. I'm going home."

"Relax, I want you to show me where you think my timing's off. I put in last week's show." He spun her chair around, waiting for her to take a seat.

Jodie's face went flushed as she lowered herself in the seat and pulled back up to the table. She was close enough to taste his cologne if she leaned over and licked at his neck. A sultry saxophone tune piped through the speakers and it was almost more than she could take.

Will smiled at her as he started the tape. "Ready to school me?" he asked with a wink.

Oh, in so many ways. I could show you how I like to be touched, or how I like to be kissed, or even where my spot is.

Instead of all that, she nodded. Embarrassed by her thoughts, she turned away to conceal a grin that she couldn't control, and pretended to flip through her tablet.

"Are you blushing?" Will asked, leaning into the control panel and looking up at her face.

Oh God, why couldn't she keep her little dirty thoughts in check? Two years of celibacy could do that to a woman she realized. She quickly ripped the smile from her face and turned around.

"I wasn't blushing. I was smiling and thinking that you're such a perfectionist." *Nice save,* she had to compliment herself. "Stone was right about you. If one little thing isn't just right you won't let it go until you've corrected it, will you?"

He leaned back in his seat as the show on the tape began. "Remember, you pointed out this little shortcoming. And trust me, I don't have too many. In fact, this might be the only one. And you, little lady—" he pulled her chair even closer "—are going to help me fix it."

Her chair bumped his, and their bodies were only inches apart. Her heartbeat sped up. She made a mental check to see which bra she'd put on that morning. The white lace one, yeah, her favorite.

On tape, Will was going through his well-rehearsed show introduction. However, Jodie couldn't concentrate on the tape with him sitting so close to her.

"There." He stopped the tape. "Is that what you meant?" he asked.

"Huh?" She'd been daydreaming and missed whatever he saw. She pulled herself together and sat up straight in the chair. "Uh, can you rewind that? I—I didn't quite catch it."

He hit the rewind button. "You okay?" he asked, with his eyes lowered to her lips.

Letting go of the bottom lip she'd squeezed between her teeth she said, "Yeah, I uh, I just kind of zoned out for a minute. I guess I'm getting tired." She hunched up her shoulders to stretch them out. "It's been a long day, you know."

What did she do that for? Will started the tape again, and pushed his chair back slightly before turning to face her.

"Turn around," he instructed.

"Do what?" she asked, looking up into his face, serious now as he grabbed the arm of her chair and spun her away from him.

Jodie tried to get up, but his hands were on her shoulders. His touch was warm and firm as he began to knead the muscles in her shoulders. She wanted to stop him, but it felt so good all she could do was hold her head down and pull her hair to one side.

"You've been working too hard. Your muscles are so tight. I bet this feels good."

"Uh-huh," she moaned, licking her lips. Then she closed her eyes for just a moment to enjoy the stress reliever.

"When you get home tonight…fix yourself a nice warm bath. Add some bath salts or beads or whatever you like, and roll a towel behind your neck. Then put on a little jazz and relax yourself." His voice was almost a whisper.

His hands and his voice worked a rhythm together in order to hypnotize her, rendering her helpless. The bath he'd painted looked so good in her mind's eye, that the only thing missing was him.

When Will's hands moved lower down her back, soft moans escaped her lips in time with the music. Her breathing slowed and everything mellowed out to the soft sounds all around her.

His breathing grew louder and heavier until she could feel it against the nape of her neck. His breath preceded the first soft kiss that caused her breath to catch in her throat. Before she could take a breath, he planted another soft kiss inches lower than the first. A sensation rocked Jodie's body like nothing she'd experienced before. She sucked in her bottom lip to stifle the next moan.

Suddenly, his hands moved away.

She opened her eyes as he slowly turned her chair around to face him. He reached out for her hand, and thinking that was the end of a very special moment between them, she took his hand and they stood up.

He reached out and stroked the side of her face, cupping her chin. In a slow and steady movement, he raised her face to meet his. Before it registered in her mind what was about to happen, he kissed her.

Chapter 12

Will's full lips made contact with Jodie's, kissing and tasting every inch of her mouth before parting her lips with his tongue.

Something in the far recesses of her mind screamed no, but her body didn't hear it and gave in to the kiss. He tilted his head, giving him better access to her mouth while his hand slipped around and up the middle of her back pulling her closer to him. Their tongues danced a circular dance until Jodie became light-headed.

Kissing Will came so natural to her it was like something she'd been born to do. His soft and hot tongue sought out hers in an urgency she matched. His hands moved down to her hipbones and pulled the lower half of her body against his. Together they radiated so much heat the room became a sauna.

Then, needing desperately to catch her breath, Jodie pulled her head away.

He allowed her only seconds to catch her breath, before he brought her face back up to meet his. His thumb glided softly across her bottom lip twice, before he lowered his head and took her mouth again. This time the moans in the room were escaping from his lips. His mouth grew hungrier as his moans grew louder.

His hand caressed the back of her head holding her mouth to his. She kissed him like a new wife whose husband had come home from a war. If she never kissed him again she wanted to make this something to remember for the rest of her life.

The song, "Always and Forever," an old school tune, came through the speaker reminding Jodie of something she used to say about Will. "I'll always be in love with that man." And now here she was, being held in his arms, just like in her dreams.

If he didn't stop kissing her she was going to ignite into flames and rip her clothes off right here in the control room.

Then it hit her like a bucket of cold water: she could never have sex with Will. He was forbidden fruit. Her eyes sprang open and she pressed her palms against his forearms to break away.

She looked up into his smoldering eyes as a flash of confusion crossed his face. "What's wrong?" he asked, maintaining his grip around her body.

She shook her head and pushed harder until he released her.

"Jodie, wait." He reached out for her as she bolted for the door.

Without turning around she said, "I'm sorry, I didn't mean to do that." Then she reached for the doorknob.

He reached out. "Don't apologize," he said, and planted one palm against the door.

She couldn't look at him. She held the doorknob in a death grip, praying he'd move his hand and free her.

Standing directly behind her and practically whispering in her ear he said, "You didn't do anything wrong…I did. And I'm sorry. Stay, I promise it won't happen again."

She nodded and he moved his hand. Then, like a bolt of lightning she was out the door.

The number six, hanging upside down, bounced against the door of motel room sixteen. The boom box inside the room was turned up on high. Next door, someone banged on the wall, but none of the guests in room sixteen could hear them.

Randall, the front desk clerk, answered the second complaint in the last half hour about the noise coming from room sixteen. He'd rented the room to a teenage couple who'd paid him double, because they weren't old enough to rent a room.

The young girl had on a pair of jeans so tight Randall's mouth watered when she turned around. He knew what they were doing in that room, and he only wished he could watch.

However, if he didn't go tell them to quiet it down, someone would call the police and his father would discover his lucrative business of renting to teenagers. Although he didn't see what the big deal was—they had to have sex somewhere. If you lived with your grand-mother, like he did, there was no chance of taking a girl home. He only regretted not having his camera equip-ment already installed in that particular room.

Armed with a flashlight and his three-hundred-pound body, which deterred most people, Randall locked the office door behind him. The motel wasn't in the best part of town, and the last thing he needed was to get robbed again.

He strolled past each room stopping to listen at every door. A lot of the working girls rented rooms by the hour providing him with plenty of listening and viewing pleasure.

Before he reached room sixteen he heard the music bouncing off the walls. The rap music of Three 6 Mafia shook the windows. Randall was a rap fan, he preferred metal bands, but the group was from Memphis and he'd heard the music before.

It sounded like a wild party was going on inside. He tapped his flashlight against the door as hard as he could. "Front desk, open up."

Nothing happened, so he pressed his ear against the door. He heard male and female voices, and more than the two he'd rented the room to.

These kids have to go or I'll be in a world of trouble. He banged on the door this time with his opened palm. "Hey, man, come on let me in," he yelled out, trying to sound like one of their young homeboys.

Still nothing.

He tried it again. "Dude, open up. It's me."

A few seconds later, the door swung open. A tall young black man in nothing but a pair of jeans looked at Randall like he was crazy.

"Man, what do you want?" he asked.

Randall peeked inside the room and his eyes almost popped out of his head. Two young black girls in their underwear reached for the sheet to cover themselves.

The young guy stepped out and pulled the door to block Randall's view. But not before he noticed bottles of beer on top of the dresser, and smelled the strong aroma of marijuana.

When Randall didn't respond, the young guy shoved at his chest. "I said what do you want?"

Randall turned his flashlight on and shined it in the young man's face. "Front desk. You guys gonna have to get out of here."

The volume lowered in the room before the kid swatted the flashlight out of his face and took a step toward Randall. Fear gripped Randall and he took a step back, almost losing his balance. "Hey I don't want any trouble, but I rented this room to two people. It looks like more than two people are in there right now. What are you'all doing in there?" He took another step back, hoping this guy didn't decide to call his buddies and kick Randall's butt.

"We'll keep it down," the kid said and turned to go back inside.

"No, you don't understand," Randall pleaded. "You've got to go, now. I've gotten complaints and somebody's going to call the cops. You need to carry your party somewhere else."

Before the kid could go back inside the room, the swirl of blue-and-red lights caught their attention.

Randall turned around and almost peed his pants. His father was going to kill him.

The kid disappeared inside, but left the door cracked. Wide-eyed, Randall watched as clothes flew everywhere and the whole crew tried to get into the bathroom at once. Damn, why hadn't he installed that camera equipment already?

Minutes later, two police cars sat outside room sixteen where several teenagers lined up outside the motel room. Randall told the officers everything he knew, but swore he had no idea the young man who rented the room was underage.

"He looks older than I do," Randall pleaded with the officers. His father was going to find out about this for sure. Randall had probably spent his last night admiring the beautiful brown-skinned prostitutes that frequented the motel.

Keenan leaned against the motel room window with his head lowered. He recognized one of the policemen and hoped the cop wouldn't remember him.

Officer Weiss singled Keenan and Mike out and had them follow him over to his squad car.

"Aren't you guys on Fairley High School's basketball team?" the officer asked.

Keenan felt the world around him falling apart. If the coach found out about the party his basketball career was over.

"Yes, sir," Michael answered. "We just came by to pick up one of our buddies. We had no clue what was going on inside until we got in there."

"What's your name, son?"

"Michael Adams, sir. And this is my teammate, Keenan Dickerson."

Keenan felt the officer's eyes on him but didn't dare raise his head.

"Where's your car?" Officer Weiss asked.

"Huh?" Michael asked, caught off guard.

"You said you came to pick somebody up. I don't see any bikes parked out here, so where's your car?"

"Uh." Michael nudged Keenan who didn't respond. "Uh, our buddy drove it to the store. He's coming right back."

"Yeah." Officer Weiss sucked in a deep breath and shook his head. "I'm really disappointed, boys. Both of you have a shot at a career in the NBA, but not by pulling stunts like this."

"Sir, like I said we—"

"Yeah, I heard you. You just wandered in there innocently." He turned to Keenan. "Is that right?"

This time Keenan looked up and opened his mouth to answer, but didn't get a chance.

"Weiss." Another police officer walked up. "We've got a couple of empty beer bottles, but that's it."

"No drugs?" Weiss asked.

"Looks like they smoked it all." The officer did a double take on the boys.

"Hey, don't you guys play basketball for somebody?"

Keenan knew they should have taken the party to his house. If they had, he wouldn't be on his way to jail.

"Let me talk to you a second." Officer Weiss took the other officer aside a minute.

When he returned he had a serious look on his face. "You boys want to tell me who supplied the drugs?"

Keenan shrugged, but didn't dare look at the officer.

"How about who bought the beer?" Officer Weiss asked.

When he didn't get a response he continued. "Drugs or not, everybody's going down to the station tonight. Maybe you'll talk down there."

One by one all five of them were placed in the waiting police cars.

A couple of hours later, Keenan sat in the police station, his high completely gone, waiting to see what they were going to do with him. He wasn't giving up any information no matter what they said. He didn't even care if they called his coach right now, he wasn't admitting to anything. All he wanted to do was get out of there and go home where he could sit in his room and smoke a joint in peace.

Will's phone rang several times before he answered it. It was Saturday night and he had a house full of men, all watching the NCAA tournament not wanting to be disturbed.

"Hello." He tried to keep the annoyance out of his voice.

"Will, it's Dave Weiss."

At the sound of his voice, Will knew he wasn't going to see the rest of the game.

"Officer Weiss. This can't be good news." The only time Will heard from Dave Weiss was when one of his kids had gotten themselves into trouble with the law. One of the first kids to complete the Forward Motion program was Dave Weiss's nephew. Since then, the officer had kept an eye out for Will's kids, as Dave called them.

"Actually, I need a favor."

Will took the phone and walked into the kitchen away from the game and the noise. "Sure, what can I do for you?"

"We've got a kid down here that I'm hoping you can help me with."

"Where's down here? The police station?" Will asked, knowing the answer.

"Yeah. Picked him up at a motel with a group having a party. Drugs, drinking, girls, you know what I mean?"

"Yeah, who is he?" Will asked, taking the back stairs up to his room to change clothes.

"His name's Keenan Dickerson. He plays basketball for—"

Surprised, Will stopped on the stairs. "I know who he is," he said, cutting the officer off. "Did you call his parents?"

"Nobody at home. The kid says they're out of town."

"How about his sister?"

There was a silence on the other end.

"Dave, did you try his sister?" Will asked, as he continued up the stairs.

Officer Weiss cleared his throat. "He says he's an only child, and doesn't have any relatives. The kid doesn't want to talk. I tried to reach his coach, but he's out of town, too. Think you can come down and talk to him? I really don't want to place him in a holding cell. And I'd hate for this to leak to the papers."

"Yeah. I'll be there in twenty minutes."

"Thanks, Will."

After Will hung up, he decided to call Jodie. He wasn't sure he should get involved with whatever family problems they had.

He made a trip back downstairs to his home office and found her home and cell phone numbers in his briefcase.

While listening to his buddies enjoying the game, he sat down and dialed her number. She didn't answer either of her cell phones, so he called her apartment. Voice mail picked up and he left a brief message for her to call him whenever she got in. He didn't want to alarm her, so he only said it was important.

He asked Avery to lock up in case he didn't get back before they left, and took off.

At the police station, Officer Weiss ushered Will into a room where a tall skinny Keenan sat looking angry and tired.

Will offered him a bottle of water but Keenan turned his head and let out a heavy sigh. This wasn't going to be easy and Will hadn't expected it to be. Most of the kids Will worked with rejected him at first.

He took the seat on the other side of Keenan and turned it around backwards. He straddled the chair and sat there staring at his best friend's kid brother.

"Do you know who I am?" Will asked, wanting to know just how bad Keenan's parent's had bad-mouthed him.

Keenan nodded, and then looked away.

"You've heard of the Forward Motion Foundation?"

Keenan shook his head.

"Then how do you know me?"

Keenan gave Will a scorching look and crossed his arms. "You're the guy responsible for my brother's death," he said bitterly.

A chill ran up Will's arms as Keenan stared him down.

Chapter 13

By far this had to be the worst Saturday night Jodie had experienced in a long time. She sat across the table from the most boring man in all of Memphis.

John King worked for the IRS but didn't give tax advice. He was divorced with two children, a twelve-year-old boy and a ten-year-old girl. He'd just purchased a new Chevrolet Impala. And last summer he'd vacationed in Tunica, Mississippi. For two whole weeks, he announced proudly.

How did she know so much about him? He wouldn't stop talking about himself. If she'd been interested that would have been nice, but she wasn't. He hadn't asked her one thing about herself, although she could even tell you how much his divorce cost.

"Tracy tells me you're new in town?" he asked,

between what looked like a perfect set of false teeth. The only thing he had going for him.

"Yes, I've been here for about two weeks." She didn't bother to reveal she was originally from Tennessee.

"Then you'll have to let me show you around town. A beautiful lady like you shouldn't be going out unescorted."

Jodie stifled a laugh. If that was a pickup line, John didn't get out much. "Thanks, but I've already taken the tour."

"Then we'll have to make it a movie. Maybe we can catch a matinee tomorrow?"

She shook her head. "Sorry, I've got church tomorrow. Don't you go to church on Sundays?" she asked.

He shrugged and looked around dumbfounded. "I'm afraid I'm a heathen. I haven't been to church in over two years."

"Uh." Jodie shook her head. "That's too bad. I'm looking for a man who's in the church."

"I suppose I could go to church. You know, I ain't got nothing against God," he said laughing. "It's the pimping preachers I can't stand." Then he picked up his drink and stared at a young woman passing with her breasts exploding from her top.

Jodie shook her head. She was going to kill Tracy once she got off the dance floor. This little arrangement was her idea and Jodie would never let her live it down.

Once they were in the car on the way home, Jodie let Tracy have it.

"But, he's a good man, Jodie. He works hard and he's dependable," Tracy pleaded her friend's case.

"I'm not trying to hire the brother," Jodie replied.

"Okay, so he's not William, but he still has potential," Tracy said, giving Jodie a frustrated look.

Jodie gawked at her, openmouthed. "And what's that supposed to mean?"

"Girl, you know you compare every man you meet to Will. I see it in your eyes."

"I do no such thing." Jodie rolled her eyes at her friend and looked out the window.

Tracy shook her head. "Yes, you do. You scrutinize a man's clothes, his shoes and everything else about him. You did that last week when we were down on Beale Street, and then again tonight."

"Okay, what's wrong with wanting a man who makes your stomach quiver and your body tingle all over just by touching your hand." *And when he kisses you, fireworks go off in your head.*

"Damn," Tracy said, in a slow drawl. "You feel all that?"

"No," Jodie lied. "But what's wrong with wanting that?"

"Nothing, but give John a break, he has potential."

"A break! Give me a break," Jodie replied, nearly shouting. "The guy talked about himself so much I could hardly get a word in. And if you see so much potential why didn't you go out with him?"

Tracy cleared her throat. "I did. But he's not my type either," she confessed, putting on her blinker and making a right-hand turn.

Jodie laughed. "Oh, what am I? A charity case? Don't try to hook me up with any of your rejects.

Besides, I've already got my hands full with work and Keenan. I don't even need a man right now."

"Girl, I know you don't want to hear this, but a man is exactly what you need right now. A good man is like a good massage—every hardworking woman needs one."

"The only man I have time for is in the twelfth grade. Which reminds me, I need to check on him." Jodie reached inside her purse for her cell phone.

"Yeah right, I'll remind you of that the next time I spend the night with Lorenzo and you want details."

Jodie scrunched up her nose. "Uh, I've never asked you for details."

"What? You were practically squirming when I told you about our weekend in the Bahamas."

The phone was not in Jodie's purse so she looked around the car. "What do you expect, I haven't had any in over two years."

"What's wrong?" Tracy asked, when Jodie reached under her seat.

"I thought I had my cell phone," she said, opening the glove compartment. "I must have left it at home." She settled back in her seat and threw her hand out. "Where's yours, I want to check on Keenan."

"Who could get a phone in this purse?" Tracy held up her small silver clutch bag. "I left mine at home, I figured you'd have yours. You've got two."

"I wasn't about to bring the one for Gator House, but I usually keep mine on me." Jodie could have kicked herself. She'd planned on calling Keenan every couple of hours since Roz and Lou had left for Jamaica earlier.

"Want to ride by your mom's before we go home?" Tracy asked.

Jodie thought a minute and then shook her head. "Naw, he should be okay. I talked to him before we left, and he was going to watch the NCAA playoffs on TV." She glanced down at her watch. It was after three in the morning. "Besides, he's probably asleep by now." At least she prayed he was.

Jodie walked through the front door of their apartment laughing at Tracy's John King impression.

"Baby, why don't you let me take you on the trip of a lifetime. I got a coupon good for three nights at one of them time-share resorts in Orlando. We can go to SeaWorld, go swimming and check out the night life." She switched to a female voice. "Oh, John, that sounds like so much fun. When are we going?" Then back to a male voice. "Baby, let me talk to my hookup at the airport and get us two buddy passes. You'll never forget this trip."

Jodie bent over holding her stomach, she was laughing so hard.

"John King's the cheapest man I know," Tracy said, closing the front door.

"Oh my God, girl, you're a fool. If he's that bad why were you trying to hook me up with him?" Jodie asked, as she swung her purse and hit Tracy on the arm.

"He works for the IRS now. I thought maybe the brother had learned to come up off a few bucks. Did he even buy you a drink?"

"Yes, he did that much."

"Good. If he hadn't I was gonna lose his number for good. The only reason I keep it is because his cheap butt has good contacts when you need something."

Jodie dropped her purse and car keys on the counter next to the answering machine and slipped out of her high heels. "When and why did you two ever go out anyway?"

Tracy kicked off her heels as well. "Girl, that was a long time ago, and we only went to the movies."

They looked at each other and said in unison, "A matinee."

Tracy fell across the couch laughing while Jodie stood at the counter holding her stomach and laughing.

"Oh man," Tracy pushed herself up from the couch. "At least he was good for a laugh, poor guy. He's going to find a woman who doesn't want anything but a ninety-nine-cent Big Mac for dinner and he'll be in heaven."

"Hey, when money's tight a Big Mac will do," Jodie said.

"Yeah, but to brag about how much he's saving while he's feeding you a Happy Meal is cruel and unusual punishment."

Jodie laughed so hard she was screaming for Tracy to stop.

"Well, I'm glad you had fun," Tracy said. "Especially after standing me up last night."

The smile faded from Jodie's face and her cheeks flushed with embarrassment. She hadn't told Tracy about Will kissing her last night, and decided to keep her mouth shut about it.

"Sorry, but you know this job is kind of unpredictable. I don't know from one moment to the next what might happen." Truer words she'd never spoken, Jodie thought as she grabbed her purse from the counter.

"Well, I'm going to church tomorrow, so I'm gonna hit the sack. You're still going aren't you?" she asked Tracy.

"Yes, ma'am," Tracy replied, as she walked into the kitchen.

The red flash on the answering machine caught Jodie's attention and reminded her that she'd left her cell phone on the charger in her room.

"We've got a message," she pointed out to Tracy, as she continued down the hall to her bedroom.

She tossed her purse and shoes on the bed and walked around to the other side and picked her cell phone up from the charger. No messages.

Three raps at her opened door preceded, "You have a message on the answering machine," Tracy sang in a teasing tone.

Jodie pulled her top over her head. "Is it Keenan?"

"No." Tracy waved a finger back and forth. "Guess again?"

"Tracy, it's three o'clock in the morning, I'm not in a guessing mood."

"Come see," Tracy said, then turned and vanished.

In her skirt and bra Jodie trekked back down the hall to the answering machine. Tracy stood by the machine grinning like a Cheshire cat.

"Oh God, don't tell me it's John?" Jodie hesitated, with her hand poised over the button.

"Uh-uh." Tracy shook her head, and then hit the button herself.

Jodie's eyes widened at the sound of Will's voice.

"Jodie, it's Will. Give me a call when you get in tonight, it's important. Call my cell."

Tracy scrambled for a piece of paper as Jodie listened to him recite his phone number. According to the machine, he'd called at eleven forty-five.

"Here, give him a call." She handed the paper to Jodie.

"I can't call him this late. He'll think I'm crazy." She took the paper from Tracy and set it on the counter.

"He said it was important." Tracy shrugged.

"If it was that important he would have left a message on my Gator House phone, but he didn't. I'll call him back in the morning."

"Okay, suit yourself, but if it were me I'd call him back no matter what time it was. It's Saturday night—he's probably still up."

Jodie shook her head. "Naw, I'll wait until tomorrow." Again she contemplated telling Tracy about the kiss, but changed her mind. Whatever Will wanted could wait until the morning.

Jodie figured she'd slept all of about four hours before she stopped tossing and turning and just climbed out of bed. All night she couldn't stop thinking about Will. What had he called her for? What was so important? When she did doze off, she dreamed about him.

After she showered and dressed for church, she went into the kitchen to make herself an egg-white omelet and to start the coffeemaker.

She picked up the cordless phone and pinched it between her shoulder and ear while she called Keenan.

She must have let the phone ring over ten times before the answering machine picked up. Either Keenan wasn't answering, or he wasn't at home. Instead of leaving a message, she hung up and dialed back. Again it rang and rang until she heard Marion's recorded voice.

"Where in the hell is that boy," she said, and hung up the phone.

The nerves in the back of her neck tightened. Something was wrong. She could feel it. Out of habit she walked across the living room and peeked out the window. Not that she expected to find Keenan out there, but it made her feel better.

Back in the kitchen, she flipped her omelet over and pulled out one of the square black plates Tracy had purchased to spruce up the old dinette set Jodie brought with her.

"Smells good in here," Tracy said, when she walked into the kitchen.

Jodie nodded slightly and poured herself a cup of coffee.

"Worried about Keenan?" Tracy asked.

"He's not answering the phone."

Tracy opened the refrigerator. "Maybe he's gone to Sunday school."

"He doesn't even go to church," Jodie replied. "Not that I know of anyway."

"Well this isn't the first time he's been home by himself is it?"

"I don't think so." Jodie thought for a moment. She really didn't know very much about her family's habits, she'd spent so many years trying to stay away from them.

"I'm sure it isn't. I know your mother has been traveling with Marion over the last couple of years. And Keenan's a big boy, he can take care of himself."

Jodie took her plate and mug and sat at the dining room table.

"He's probably just not answering the phone. Let's swing by on the way to church," Tracy said.

Roz's house wasn't on their way to church, so Jodie appreciated Tracy not minding the diversion. "Thanks, Tracy, it would make me feel better."

Tracy poured herself a cup of coffee and grabbed a donut before going back to her bedroom to finish dressing.

Just as they were walking out the front door, the phone rang. Jodie looked back at Tracy who was hurrying down the hall. She peeked over at the caller ID.

"It says private. Should I grab it?" Tracy asked, reaching for the phone.

"Yes. It might be Keenan." Jodie held her breath waiting to see who it was.

"Hello." Tracy's eyes widened as she looked up at Jodie and motioned her back inside.

Jodie's heart almost stopped. Something had happened to Keenan. Keenan was in jail or something worse.

"One moment." Then Tracy's lips turned up into a gigantic smile. "It's Will."

Relieved, Jodie took a deep breath, but her hand was still shaking when she reached for the phone.

"Hello."

"Why didn't you return my call last night?"

Will's tone of voice caught Jodie off guard. He sounded like a father scolding his daughter. "I didn't get in until late. Why? Is something wrong at the studio?"

"You should have called anyway, I was still up."

She turned and shrugged at Tracy who'd closed the front door and leaned against it waiting for her.

"Okay, I'll be sure to call you back next time. I'm on my way to church. What's so important?"

"Keenan's asleep in my guest room."

"What!" She couldn't believe she'd heard him right. "My little brother Keenan?"

"Yeah. I picked him up last night and didn't want to leave him at home alone in his condition."

"Breathe and sit down. Just breathe and sit down," she repeated. Jodie walked around the living room chair to the couch. Tracy followed her.

"Exactly what condition was that?" She knew the answer, and she hated to hear him say it.

"He was probably high on marijuana, and from what Officer Weiss said, he'd had a few beers."

"*Officer* Weiss!" Now her heart began beating double time in her chest.

Tracy touched Jodie's arm to get her attention. "What is it?" she mouthed.

Jodie just shook her head.

"Relax, Dave Weiss is a friend of mine and he knows about my work with athletes. Seems like a couple of the players had a little party at a motel. Things got loud and somebody called the police. Because they recognized Keenan, and couldn't locate his parents, they called me."

"I don't understand. Did Keenan get arrested? Why didn't somebody call me?" She jumped up from the couch.

"He wasn't arrested. Unfortunately, he told the police he was an only child."

She reached down and snatched her purse from the couch. "Where do you live? I'm coming to get him."

"Look, he's okay now. Go on to church and leave him here. I'll bring him by later on today. He'll be fine."

Not if Roz found out, Jodie thought. They'd have the devil to pay.

"Does he know who you are?" she asked, unaware of whether Will knew exactly what she was referring to.

"Yeah…he knows."

Will's name hadn't come up in Jodie and Keenan's conversations in years. She had no idea how he felt about Will.

"He could have called me," she said.

"For some reason, I don't think he considered that an option."

Jodie had walked a circle around the living room talking to Will. She made her way back to the couch where Tracy sat holding the remote with the television on mute. Jodie flopped down beside her.

"So, go on to church, we'll see you later," Will said.

"Will, I don't know about this, if—"

"Your parents don't have to know he's here unless you tell them. Look, I work with kids like him all the time. Let me talk to him for a little bit."

It was only one afternoon. What could it hurt? Jodie reasoned with herself. Roz hadn't discovered him missing yet and maybe Will would do him some good.

"Okay, but I'll be home from church around one-thirty."

"Great, I'll bring him over before dinner."

She said goodbye and lowered the phone to her lap before letting out a heavy sigh.

"Roz is going to kill you," Tracy said, sitting up.

Jodie leaned back on the couch and closed her eyes. "Not if Keenan doesn't do it first."

Tracy took the phone from Jodie and put it back on the hook. "Come on, we're going to be late. You can tell me everything in the car."

"I don't know everything. Not yet anyway. But you can bet I will before the night's over."

Chapter 14

After Will hung up from Jodie, he looked in the refrigerator to see what he could whip up for himself and Keenan for breakfast. His housekeeper didn't work on Sundays, unfortunately.

In the refrigerator he found some eggs, bacon and a jar of grape jelly. He was rattling around with the skillet when Keenan appeared in the doorway. His eyes were slits barely open as he looked at Will.

"Hungry?" Will asked, placing a plate of bacon into the microwave.

"Yeah, a little," Keenan replied. "So, when do I get to go home?" he asked.

Will shrugged. "Officer Weiss released you into my custody. Your parents aren't home, so I can't let you stay there by yourself."

"I'm not stuck here all weekend, am I?"

Will broke an egg over the skillet. "No, you're not. I called your sister. When she gets home from church I'll take you by there."

The look of surprise that flashed across Keenan's face hadn't gone unnoticed by Will. "Why did you tell the police you were an only child?" Will asked.

Keenan shrugged and shook his head. "I don't know." He walked over and sat on a bar stool facing the island and looked around the kitchen wide-eyed.

"What size is the screen on that TV?" Keenan asked, pointing to the family room.

"Sixty-two inches," Will replied.

"Damn, I bet that's nice to watch the game on, huh?"

"That it is," Will said. "Keenan, why didn't you call Jodie last night?" Will asked, trying to stay on subject. "She would have picked you up and you'd be at home right now."

Keenan chuckled. "Yeah, right. Man, she don't care nothin' 'bout me."

That response shocked Will. "That's not true. Your sister loves you. She talks about you all the time." That was a stretch and Will knew it. Jodie hardly talked to him about anything that he didn't initiate.

Keenan sat up as Will placed a plate of scrambled eggs, bacon and toast in front of him. "You talk to Jodie all the time?" he asked Will with a skeptical look.

"Sure. We work together."

Will hadn't expected the look of surprise in Keenan's eyes. Obviously, he had no idea where Jodie worked.

"She works on *your* show?" Keenan asked, picking up his fork.

Will nodded. "Yeah. Do you ever watch the show?"

"Sometimes. When you have somebody good on."

Will would have to get his opinion on what constituted good. "Jodie didn't tell you she worked on my show?" Will asked, taking a seat at the counter next to Keenan.

Keenan laughed. "Naw, man. That's not the type of thing she'd tell the family, you know."

Will wondered if Jodie was really afraid to tell her parents about the job. Could his name still be cursed in their household after all these years? He hadn't meant to open a can of worms at ten-thirty on a Sunday morning.

"Keenan, if your mother doesn't already know, I'd appreciate you letting Jodie tell her, in her own time."

"Hey, you don't say anything about last night…and I'll keep my mouth shut. 'Cause all hell's gonna break loose when she does find out."

Will considered Keenan's proposition for a minute, realizing if anybody told his parents about last night, it would be the police, or Jodie.

"You've got yourself a deal."

Keenan nodded.

After breakfast Will put the dishes in the dishwasher and straightened up the kitchen while Keenan walked around the house. He'd been more than impressed when they came in last night. By the time he walked back into the kitchen Will was ready to go.

"You live here all by yourself?" Keenan asked.

Will nodded.

"Man, this crib is nice."

"This is what hard work, and a short-lived career in the NFL got me. Play your cards right, and you'll get drafted and before long have your own house bigger than this one. You do want to play in the NBA don't you?"

Keenan laughed like Will had asked the most ridiculous question in the world. "Of course I do."

"Where would you like to go?"

Keenan shrugged. "I don't care. I just want to play ball."

"Don't mess your life up, and you'll get to play ball for a long time." Will walked around the counter and patted Keenan on the shoulder when he saw the "here we go again" look in his eyes.

"Yeah, I'll remember that."

"Come on, I want to take you somewhere." His father should be home from church in a few and ready for their golf game, Will thought.

Keenan followed Will out of the house through the garage.

Leaning against the garage wall were Will's set of golf clubs. He popped the back latch of the SUV and threw the clubs inside. Keenan hadn't said a word, he just watched him.

"You remind me of your brother in some ways," Will said.

"What's that supposed to mean?" Keenan asked defensively.

Will watched Keenan's facial expression change from curious to almost angry.

"Just that I can see a little of him in you. His talent

came naturally. He didn't have to work too hard at it. He enjoyed playing football more than anything else. He was my best friend," Will said, hoping to clear up any negative thoughts Keenan had. "You knew that didn't you?" he continued, as he opened the SUV doors.

Keenan shrugged. "I heard something like that. I don't remember him that well. Only stuff people tell me."

"I remember your mother bringing you to our games. You were more interested in running around under the bleachers than the game."

They climbed in the SUV and closed the doors.

"What were you then? About four or five?"

Again Keenan shrugged. "I guess so."

"Yeah, and look at you now. Corey would be proud of you."

Will started the engine and backed out of the garage.

Keenan gestured back toward the trunk. "Where you takin' this stuff to?"

"Oh, I'm going to play a round of golf."

Keenan snorted and shook his head. "Man, I don't play golf. I'm a ballplayer."

The garage door closed. "Who said you were playing? You're watching. I'm playing."

"So what I'm supposed to do while you're out there trying to be Tiger Woods, sit in the car?"

Will shook his head as he pulled out into the street. "Got somebody I want you to meet. Then I'll take you to Jodie's."

Keenan leaned back into the headrest and let out a heavy sigh. "I wish I'd never left the house last night."

An Important Message from the Publisher

Dear Reader,

Because you've chosen to read one of our fine novels, I'd like to say "thank you"! And, as a special way to say thank you, I'm offering to send you two more Kimani Romance novels and two surprise gifts – absolutely FREE! These books will keep it real with true-to-life African American characters that turn up the heat and sizzle with passion.

Please enjoy the free books and gifts with our compliments...

Linda Gill

Publisher, Kimani Press

Peel off Seal and Place Inside...

FREE GIFT
SEAL
PUBLISHER'S
THANK YOU

We'd like to send you two free books to introduce you to our brand-new line – Kimani Romance™! These novels feature strong, sexy women, and African-American heroes that are charming, loving and true. Our authors fill each page with exceptional dialogue, exciting plot twists, and enough sizzling romance to keep you riveted until the very end!

KIMANI ROMANCE ... LOVE'S ULTIMATE DESTINATION

Two NEW Kimani Romance™ Novels
Two exciting surprise gifts

YES! I have placed my Editor's "thank you" Free Gifts seal in the space provided at right. Please send me 2 FREE books, and my 2 FREE Mystery Gifts. I understand that I am under no obligation to purchase anything further, as explained on the back of this card.

PLACE
FREE GIFTS
SEAL
HERE

DETACH AND MAIL CARD TODAY!

168 XDL EF22

368 XDL EF23

| FIRST NAME | | LAST NAME |

ADDRESS

| APT.# | CITY |

| STATE/PROV. | ZIP/POSTAL CODE |

Thank You!

(K-ROM-01/07)

With a smile on his face Will pulled away from his house to meet his father.

Jodie had changed out of her church clothes, cleaned the apartment, finally cooked dinner and still no Keenan. She drove herself crazy trying to imagine what could have happened at that motel last night. And she thanked God Keenan hadn't been arrested.

Tracy had gone to the movies with Lorenzo, leaving Jodie there talking to herself. When the doorbell rang a few minutes later, she marched from the kitchen to the front door fussing.

She yanked the door open and blurted out, "What took you so long? I've been home for hours."

Will and Keenan stared at her like she'd lost her mind.

After everyone was inside, Jodie found herself sitting across the dining room table from Will, while Keenan used the phone in her bedroom. Will told her everything he knew about the incident.

"I can't believe he'd do something like that," Jodie said. "I hate to admit it, but I haven't actually been a part of his life over the last several years. As a matter of fact, I've only seen him a few times, and attended one or two of his games in the past."

"Yeah, I figured you weren't too close. But he's not a bad kid. He just needs some direction before he winds up on the wrong road."

"That's what I'm here for. I just need to spend more time with him."

"Did you know he was doing drugs?" Will asked.

She slowly nodded in acknowledgement. "Yeah,

that's the main reason I moved to Memphis—to help keep an eye on him. He's the only brother I have left."

Will didn't say anything for a few minutes, and Jodie knew the both of them were thinking about Corey.

"How did you find out?" Will asked, breaking the silence.

She wiped at a lone tear that ran down her cheek. "Roz called me over six months ago, the first time Keenan and Marion had a fight. She was scared Marion would put him out. I think she wanted to ask if he could come live with me. But she never did. I don't think she expected me to move here."

Jodie watched Will's brows crease when he nodded. After working with him for a few weeks now she could tell when he was deep in thought.

"When does your mother return?"

"Tuesday, I think. Communication between us isn't…quite what it should be. They left Friday for four nights. Keenan couldn't even manage one night alone without getting into trouble."

"What do you plan on doing until your mother returns?"

"He's staying right here with me. Now, I don't trust him to stay there alone. Roz never should have left him in the first place. She knew what was going on with him."

Will listened without passing judgment, which irked Jodie. She wanted him to agree with her.

"Will, I'm sorry for all the trouble he caused you, and I really appreciate you picking him up last night."

"It wasn't any trouble at all," Will said. "I enjoyed talking to him. We talked a little about Corey on the golf course today. Or I tried to talk to him. He's real quiet when he wants to be. But I do think he needs to get a handle on this before it gets out of control."

"I agree. I'm planning to get him into counseling. We haven't discussed it yet, but we will tonight."

"Well, if there's anything I can do, don't hesitate to call me. Anytime, day or night."

When they exchanged glances, Jodie couldn't help but think of Friday night and how she'd bolted from the room without saying a word.

"Thank you, Will. I appreciate that."

He pushed his chair back and stood up to leave. "I'm gonna get out of the way and let you and Keenan talk. I will see you at the studio tomorrow, won't I?"

Her face must have blushed crimson red, because he looked as if he could read her thoughts.

When she didn't answer right away he started apologizing.

"Jodie, about Friday night," he said, taking a hesitant step closer to her.

She held her hand up to say he didn't have to explain, but he took her hand in his. Inside, she was dying to know what the kiss meant to him.

Yeah. What about it? Was it the most memorable experience of your life? Did it keep you up for hours that night like it did me?

"I just want to apologize. I feel like I took advantage of you, and it won't happen again. I don't know how to explain it other than to say, that was something I've wanted to do for a long time. I guess I just had to get it out of my system. Will you forgive me?"

What! Forgive him for the best kiss she's ever had in her thirty years on this earth? Was he kidding? She pulled her hand out of his and turned her back, walking into the kitchen. She didn't want him to see her blush.

"You're forgiven. I guess I got caught up in the moment as well. I didn't have to kiss you back." She opened the refrigerator door because she had to have something to do with her hands.

He walked over and stood in the entrance to the cozy kitchen. "But I'm glad you did," he said in a smooth deep voice.

She gripped two bottles of cold water and held one up. "Water?" she asked.

He shook his head.

She set one on the counter, and twisted the top off another. Then she turned the bottle up and took a few sips.

He stood there smiling at her from ear to ear.

"Uh, if anybody's interested, I'm off the phone," Keenan announced from behind them.

Jodie spun round and wondered how long he'd been standing there. She hadn't heard him coming down the hall, and the apartment wasn't that large.

"I guess I'll take off now," Will said, this time turning around and walking towards Keenan. He held out his hand, and after a brief hesitation Keenan took it.

"Keenan, you've got my number, so don't hesitate to use it. Anytime."

Keenan nodded, but didn't look too pleased. Jodie followed Will to the front door to let him out.

Outside the door he repeated to her, "You've got my

number, too. If you need me before Tuesday just call. I think Keenan and I understand one another."

"Thanks, but I can take it from here," she assured him.

Will nodded. "Okay. But if something happens don't be stubborn, pick up the phone. I'm always here for you."

Just like he used to be when Corey wasn't around, she thought. She nodded and said good-night.

The minute she closed the door and turned around Keenan started in on her.

"Come on, you gonna take me home?" he asked.

"Say what?" she asked, with a bitter snort. "You have got to be kidding."

"I can't stay here. I've got school tomorrow."

Frowning, she stormed into the kitchen to heat up dinner. "First we're going to eat, then I'll take you by the house to get some clothes. But, you're sleeping on that couch over there until Tuesday." She pointed at the living room couch that was a few inches shorter than Keenan.

"What!" he practically shouted. "No, I'm not! If you don't take me home I'll just call one of my boys to pick me up."

Although he had over five inches on her, she stepped in front of him as he headed for the phone. "You are going to sit down at that table right now and eat. None of your boys are coming by here tonight, or any other night while you're here. I'm taking you to school."

He turned away from her with knitted brows and his lip curled in disgust.

"Keenan, I'm not letting you walk out of here tonight to get into more trouble. You messed up Saturday night so now you have to pay for it. You're lucky that police officer called Will."

Keenan folded his arms and took a deep breath. His eyes narrowed as he looked down his nose at Jodie.

After a few seconds of silence, she walked back into the kitchen. She turned the stove on, looking at Keenan out of the corner of her eye. If he picked up the phone they were going to fight. He finally dropped his arms and walked into to the living room. His eyes were still blazing, but she could tell he had calmed down.

"Does Roz know you're messing around with him?" he asked.

The spiteful tone in his voice sent a shiver down her spine. "What are you talking about?"

"You know what I'm talking about. Does she know you're screwing the guy who killed Corey?"

Chapter 15

To hear those words coming out of Keenan's mouth shocked and appalled Jodie. "Keenan, you can't believe that. You've just heard Roz say that so much you're repeating it. I know, because I did the same thing for years. But, I know better now."

Neither of them smiled.

"And not that it would be any of your business, but I'm not involved with him in any way. We work at the same studio and that's it." On the same show, she wanted to add, but decided against it.

"Yeah, whatever," came Keenan's reply, as he walked over to sit down in front of the television. "Looked like more than that to me," he said, and picked up the remote control. He turned to one of his favorite sports channels.

"I don't know what you thought you saw, but whatever you do, don't mention it to Roz and get her all stirred up when she comes back."

He nodded and kept looking at the television.

Now she was sure he'd heard more of their conversation than she would have liked. When she raised the lid on one of the pots she noticed her hand trembled slightly. Will's presence in her life in any way seemed to stir up old and new fears.

It took two days for Will to get a call from Coach Young. He'd finally gotten wind of the hotel incident, and wanted to get help for his star players.

"Coach, I'd be happy to work both boys into my program. For obvious reasons I have an interest in Keenan's career."

During an awards luncheon the first year of Forward Motion, Will's acceptance speech included a brief synopsis of his football history and why he'd started the foundation. Coach Young persuaded one of his players with a drug habit to enter the program. The kid kicked his addiction and was later recruited by the Minnesota Vikings.

"I understand," Coach Young commented. "Keenan's a bright young man and one of the best guards I've seen in a long time. On the court he's a model player. But off court, I'm really concerned about him. Right now, I don't need him doing anything to jeopardize his position on the all-star team. I'll talk to his folks and see to it that all the necessary paperwork is filled out."

Will cleared his throat. "I think you need to know that if his mother finds out he's a part of the program, she probably won't give her consent."

"She'll give her consent all right. You let me take care of that," Coach Young assured Will.

Come Saturday morning Will walked into Gold's Gym with his workout bag on his shoulder, and Keenan right behind him. After Will changed clothes he met Keenan by the free weights.

"Show me what you got," Will said, pointing to the weights and looking at a reluctant Keenan.

Keenan straddled the bench and took a deep breath. "Like I said, I don't lift a lot of weights. I run and I do a few push-ups and sit-ups. I've got this little off season conditioning program Coach gave us."

"That's it?" Will asked, adjusting the weight on the pole.

Curious, Keenan looked back over his shoulder at the amount of weight Will chose. "Yeah, that's about it."

"Keenan, a conscientious player never gets out of shape. You should spend your free time doing drills. Smoking and drinking will kill your NBA career before it starts."

Keenan sighed. "I don't do it all the time. Besides, folks say I'll probably be a first round pick if I keep my game up."

Will walked around to face Keenan. "Folks huh? Any of these folks played in the NBA before?"

Keenan snorted and shook his head. "Naw, man. So what though? They know basketball."

"You've got to get in and out of college first. What do you normally do on Saturday mornings?"

With a big smile on this face, Keenan said, "That depends on what I did Friday night."

Ever since Will picked him up at the police station, that was the first smile he'd gotten out of Keenan.

The guy next to them dropped his weight, making a loud clinking noise. Will and Keenan turned to him, and then Will recognized him. Reggie Smith from the Memphis Grizzlies noticed Will at the same time.

"Reggie, what's up?" Will stepped over and shook the man's hand as he rose from the bench with his hand outstretched.

"Hey, Will, what's going on, man." Reggie gripped Will's hand and they tapped shoulders.

"Not much. Just getting a little workout in, you know. Say man, when you gonna come down and be a guest on the show?"

"This season, man. You let me know when you want me and I'm there."

Will glanced over to find Keenan looking up at Reggie in awe.

"Sure thing. Hey, let me introduce you to Keenan Dickerson, starting guard for the Mighty Bulldogs."

Reggie smiled and nodded as he grasped Keenan's hand so hard he nearly fell off the bench. "Dickerson, yeah, you made all-star team this year, didn't you?"

Keenan's eyebrows shot up in surprise as he shyly nodded.

"Man, I better watch out, you might be taking my spot one day," Reggie teased.

A grin bigger than the one he'd displayed earlier spread all over Keenan's face. Right then and there Will understood how to get through to him.

After Reggie left, Keenan laid back on the bench ready to start lifting weights. Before they left the gym, Will had introduced Keenan to two more Grizzly players.

Keenan walked out of the gym a different young man than the one who'd walked in. His shoulders were back and his head was high.

"Man, you come here every Saturday morning?" he asked Will.

"Just about," Will said. "I've got a bench and a few weights in my basement that I use whenever I can't make it to the gym. But I work out to keep my body in the best possible shape."

"Yeah, well, I can't afford a gym membership."

Will slowed and turned to Keenan. "I'll tell you what. I'll make a deal with you. You come work out with me every Saturday and I'll take care of your gym fee."

"That's part of the mentoring program?" Keenan asked.

"Sort of, yeah. There's only one condition."

"I knew it was too good to be true." Keenan hung his head.

"You promise me not to let it slip to Jodie that I'm your mentor."

Keenan stopped, forcing Will to do the same. "That's all I have to do?"

"That's right. You can work out and bulk up that skinny frame of yours."

Keenan looked down at himself, and then back up at Will who'd started laughing and walking toward the SUV.

"You've got yourself a deal," Keenan said, as he reached the SUV. He threw his bag in the backseat.

Will noticed a sly grin on Keenan's face when he fastened his seat belt. Then he realized something.

"You weren't going to tell Jodie anyway, were you?" Will asked.

Keenan smiled and shrugged.

A little con artist just like his brother, Will thought.

It looked like Jeffrey and Will were arguing about something when Jodie walked into Will's office.

"I've got the all-star footage, too, so why can't—"

Will cleared his throat loud enough to bring up a lung, Jodie thought, when she knocked on the door.

"Jodie, come on in. Is everything ready for the shoot this morning?"

With his back to her, Jeffrey picked up several tapes from Will's desk and shoved them into his tape bag.

"I believe so. I've got two freelance camera guys meeting us there." She turned her attention to Jeffrey who slung his bag over his shoulder and picked up some papers from Will's desk. "Jeffrey you're gonna miss this one."

"Yeah, I'll be here shooting a couple of wannabe actors in a series of infomercials that Stone's so jazzed about."

"I'm just thankful he didn't ask me to work on those," Jodie responded with a snort. Then she pointed to Jeffrey's bag. "Were those tapes for this week's show?" she asked.

He patted his bag and held it close to his body before glancing up at Will.

"It's just some old footage I asked him to round up for me for a future show. Nothing for this week," Will said.

"Yeah, it's just some old footage," Jeffrey responded, with a little nervous laugh. "Well, I gotta run. I'll catch you guys later, and good luck today."

"Thanks," Jodie said, as he rushed out.

She hadn't meant to meddle, but the look between the two of them made her feel as if she'd walked into the middle of something she shouldn't have.

"I'm sorry if I disturbed you guys," she said to Will after Jeffrey left.

"No problem." Will grabbed his suit coat from the back of his chair. "We were finished anyway."

She looked at her watch. "Then we'd better hurry—the program starts in less than an hour and I need to give instructions to the camera men."

"I'm right behind you," he said, as they left the office.

Jodie rode with Will over to the Civic Center Plaza where several local high school coaches were being honored for their work in the community. After the program, Will sat down with a few of the coaches for interviews.

The freelance cameramen were there and captured all of the shots Jodie wanted. She left the Civic Center excited and eager to edit the footage.

"Another successful shoot," Will said, when it was all over.

"Yeah, I thought so, too. We got some really good

footage of you and the coaches, and of the coaches with those kids. And did you see their eyes? Some of those kids were so excited they could hardly keep their seats. I hope we captured all that enthusiasm on camera."

Will laughed as he started the engine and pulled off. "You really enjoyed that program, didn't you?" He hadn't heard Jodie talk that much since she'd started working for Gator House.

"I did. It was inspiring. We should think about doing a show like that with your foundation."

"I've been thinking about that myself." Will had made his mind up not to tell Jodie about the special he had planned. But, he could use her opinion on some other ideas.

"I've got another idea I'd like to talk with you about," he continued. "*The Memphis Zone* started off with a one-on-one format consisting mostly of interviews. But with all this new technology floating around, I think we need to update the show format. I thought about something a little more interactive. Something that would lend itself to being streamed or clipped over the Internet."

Jodie had already started nodding her head and smiling. "I like it. That's a great idea. And a great way to reach out to your younger audience."

Instead of taking the turn that would lead them back to the studio, Will kept straight. He knew the minute Jodie walked into that studio she'd find something to take her away from him and he wasn't ready to let her go.

"So where'd this idea come from?" she asked.

"One of the kids I'm working with mentioned something about sending an instant message to another talk show. And I thought why couldn't we do that. I'm on the 'Net a lot myself, as I'm sure most of my audience is."

"You know that ties in with the Internet updates Stone has in mind. The site is kind of stagnant and pretty boring, so he plans on overhauling it."

"Great, then my timing for this is good. I just need to sit down with you and work out the details."

When he turned into the parking lot of Madeline's, Jodie looked over her right shoulder at the restaurant.

"I'm starved, so I thought we'd grab a bite before going back to the studio. And you've got to be hungry by now." He pulled the Rover into a parking spot close to the door.

Jodie looked like she was about to say no, but changed her mind. "Sure, I'm hungry."

They climbed out of the SUV and went inside.

"William Duncan, how the hell are you?" Angela Payton, the proprietor of Madeline's met them at the door.

"Angela, I'm fine." Will reached out to give the woman a friendly hug.

Angela was an eloquent black woman dressed in all white, with a matching white silk head wrap. Her flawless cocoa-brown skin gave her a youthful look. And the diamond studded large hoop earrings Jodie would have killed for.

"Angela, you're getting more beautiful every time I see you," Will commented.

After their embrace Angela pulled back and held Will's face in her hands. "And you're still the most handsome man in all of Memphis. I caught your show last week, and I'm so proud of you."

"Thank you. I'm having a ball up there."

Angela dropped her hands and wrapped one around his waist as she turned to smile at Jodie.

"And who's your friend?"

"I'd like you to meet my new producer, Jodie Dickerson. She joined Gator House Productions a couple of weeks ago."

Angela left Will's side and offered a ring-filled hand to Jodie, who accepted. "It's a pleasure to meet you, Jodie. I hope you won't be a stranger and visit us often."

"Thank you. I'm sure I will."

Behind them stood a young woman with short hair and earrings so long they touched her shoulders. Jodie loved them.

"Neva here will seat you. Have a wonderful meal and I'll talk to you soon. I'm taking off for the rest of the day."

Will and Angela said their goodbyes before Neva escorted them to their seats.

"Follow me please."

They were seated at a booth where Neva went over the specials of the day before leaving them alone.

"Angela's a beautiful woman," Jodie commented.

"She takes good care of herself," Will said. "Her husband used to be my philosophy instructor in college. They were big Tiger fans and used to have the whole team over for dinner after the games."

"Wow, that had to be expensive. They don't do that anymore?"

"Robert died about five years ago. That's when Angela opened Madeline's, named after her mother, with her son. No more dinners for the team at her home. They come here now."

"That's nice though, she's still a big fan?"

"Oh yeah, she's still a fan."

The waiter came over and took their orders, leaving behind glasses of water and warm bread.

"You know this restaurant is nice and everything, but I'll be editing that footage all night now," she commented.

He grabbed a piece of bread. "*We'll* be editing the footage. I won't leave you hanging."

Jodie shook her head. "I don't think we should put ourselves in that situation again. If you know what I mean?"

He nodded. "I know what you mean, but we're going to be working together a lot. If we can't get past this, how are we going to be a success together? It was a kiss," he said with a shrug. "One kiss and it won't ever happen again. Let's move on and act like the professionals we are."

Maybe it was just a kiss to him, but to her it was a lifelong dream fulfilled. One of her fantasies had stepped from beyond the shadows into the light of day.

She nodded in agreement with him. Knowing full well when the lights were low and he was around, there would be nothing professional about her behavior.

Chapter 16

Over lunch, Will tried to catch up on Jodie's life. What had she been doing, and who had she been doing it with.

"Tell me about Atlanta," he asked her.

She shrugged. "What do you want to know?" She looked up and popped a piece of bread into her mouth, licking her index finger in the process. Will tried not to get distracted.

"You started as a production assistant. Did you enjoy your work?"

"I loved it, most of the time anyway. When I wasn't sitting around getting coffee for the producers. I didn't really start getting into anything until I was assigned to work with Mack. He didn't believe in wasting a P.A. on running errands all day long."

"According to Stone he's a great teacher."

"He is. My first week with him he had me working the editing machine. I worked on a series of one-minute spots covering great sports legends. I basically spent my days writing and editing my spots."

"So you did learn a little something about sports?"

"I surfed the 'Net for almost anything I needed. I knew less about sports then than I do now. Although I have to admit I'm learning a lot. I keep my television tuned to ESPN."

"When did you decide you wanted to be a producer?"

"My junior year. I needed a part-time job and my instructor had a contact at Turner Broadcasting. He liked my work, so I got the job. After one day in the studio I was hooked."

"Yeah, I understand that feeling. Right after I recovered from knee surgery and realized I wasn't going back to football I was invited to sit in on a radio show, which led to covering for a buddy of mine that worked on another local sports show when he was sick. That show went off the air when he took over a popular sports show in Baltimore. By then I was hooked and wanted my own show."

The waiter stopped by to see if they needed anything. Will said they were fine, so he disappeared.

"Is that when you met Stone?" Jodie asked.

"Naw, I met him years earlier. He was already into producing his own shows. He left working with his uncle Mack in Baltimore I believe, before settling in Memphis."

"New York," Jodie corrected him. "They worked in

New York together. Mack used to tell us all about his nephew and how he went on to open his own studio. Great story."

"Yeah, he's holding his own. He's carved out a nice niche for himself here in Memphis."

They spent the next thirty minutes talking about the business. Will wanted to know more about Jodie. He knew what she did at work but he wanted to know what she did when she wasn't at work.

"So you don't mind working the late, sporadic hours involved in production?"

"I'm used to it," she replied.

"Hell on your personal life isn't it?"

She laughed. "What personal life? In this line of business you aren't afforded one. I'll admit to less work at Gator House, but I can't believe we're sitting down for this meal knowing we've got footage to edit."

"Relax, it'll get done. Sometimes you have to breathe. How do you spend your spare time when you're not working? Got any hobbies?"

She shrugged. "I haven't had much time for hobbies since moving here. But, I do like to read, and periodically I'll go out."

"Who do you go out with?" he asked, curious to know if she'd started dating anyone in Memphis.

"Tracy, or whoever. Why do you ask?"

He absently scratched the side of his face and shrugged. "Just curious I guess."

"I have friends you know," she said.

"Male or female friends?" he asked, not letting the subject go.

She smiled and bit her bottom lip.

"Ah, it must be a man. I see those big dimples of yours whenever you blush."

"I'm not blushing," she said, holding up her head and tucking her hair behind her ears.

"How come you aren't? The minute I mentioned a man, you started blushing. Who is he?"

"I've been out a time or two, that's all. Nobody special, or that I care to share with you. Like I told you I don't have time for a social life. Besides the job, I spend my spare time trying to help Keenan."

"How's he doing, by the way?" Will asked, knowing full well how things were with Keenan, but Jodie wasn't supposed to know that.

"He's okay. Staying out of trouble for now anyway."

"You know, I didn't tell you this before, but I ran into your mother last year at a fund-raiser for charity. She gave me the coldest look. Something tells me she doesn't like me," he said jokingly.

Jodie waved her hand at him. "She has issues—you're aware of that."

"Yeah, me. I think I'm her issue. You know, I've tried to understand things from her side of the table and I guess if the shoe was on the other foot—"

Jodie stopped him. "You wouldn't act like her for one minute and you know it. Will, she's angry and she can't move on for the life of her."

"I know. She's in pain. I just wanted to sit down and talk to her for a few minutes. Just to let her know what really happened, not what she thinks happened. But she won't hear anything I have to say."

"Will, no matter what you say, Roz is going to believe what she wants to. What's in her head is right, and the rest of the world is wrong. That's the code she lives by."

The waiter reappeared. "Okay, who's got room for dessert?"

They looked at each other, shaking their heads. The waiter left the bill on the table and disappeared. Will didn't want their brief lunch to come to an end.

"I hope you enjoyed your lunch?" he asked.

"I did. The food and the company, I might add."

She smiled at him, and he knew everything would always be good between them. "I enjoyed talking to you, too. See, we need to do more of this. Especially since we'll be working so close together. We need to be in tune with one another."

She gave him an incredulous grin and crossed her arms. "More of this, huh?" she repeated.

"Yes. How about happy hour later this week? You know, we can sit around and talk about the show over a drink."

She burst out laughing. "If I didn't know better, I'd say you were trying to ask me out on the sly."

He shook his head. "Nothing sly about it."

"Will, I'm sure you have women throwing themselves at you. You probably have several girlfriends right now. So, why would you want to go out with me? Your producer."

"You've got it all wrong. I'm a one-woman man, and I've never had several women. Even after my divorce. I asked you out because I enjoy being with you, and I want to get to know you better."

"And you will. We work together every day. Which is one reason we should keep everything professional, like you said earlier."

"Bump what I said, and say you'll go out with me?"

She leaned forward, propping her elbows on the table. "Will, I don't date professional athletes, past or present. Nothing personal, but I've had girlfriends in Atlanta who dated players with the Falcons. The relationships always ended with the woman getting her heart broken."

Will shook his head. "Well, I'm sorry about your friends, but all professional athletes aren't alike. Besides, I'm a television host now. What do you have against them?"

She laughed and shook her head. He had to laugh himself.

"Nothing," she said, with a shrug of her shoulders.

He pulled out his credit card and picked up the bill. "Great, because television hosts don't break hearts," he said with a wink.

After lunch they returned to the studio and edited the footage with the assistance of the show's interns.

Jodie pulled into the driveway of Roz and Marion's immaculately landscaped home. The place hadn't looked this good the last time she was in town. But then, that was over two years ago.

Their childhood home in Clifton had never looked this good. Roz didn't do yard work then, and Jodie doubted she did any today.

Jodie killed the engine, but sat there listening to the

radio for a few minutes. She dreaded going inside that house. She didn't want to enter their little wonderful world where the earlier years of her life didn't exist, and were never talked about anymore. It was as if Roz and Marion had been together all of their lives.

But, she'd been in Memphis for over three weeks now and she hadn't stopped by yet. If for no other reason than to see what life was like for Keenan, she had to visit. Begrudgingly, she opened the car door and stepped out. A stone path led to the front door where a large welcome mat greeted her. She rang the doorbell and took a deep breath.

A few seconds later, the front door swung open. "Here's my middle child," Roz said, loud enough for anyone in the house or on the street to hear.

Jodie hated being referred to that way and didn't know why Roz insisted on calling her that to her face.

"Come on in here. It's about time you came by."

Roz pulled her inside and hugged her as if they hadn't talked a week ago.

"Sorry it took me so long to get over here, but I've been really busy."

"That's what I hear," Roz said, releasing her embrace and giving Jodie the usual scrutinizing from head to toe. She ran a hand through her hair. "I see you made it to the salon."

"Yeah," Jodie said pulling away. She was amazed that a little conditioner and a wrap set could fool Roz.

"Jodie, come on in." A loud husky voice came from down the hall.

Roz stepped aside and Jodie had a full view of

Marion. He was heavier than she remembered. With a fat cigar hanging from his lips, he made a beeline for her, and wrapped his hefty arms around her body.

"What took you so long to get by?" he asked, and after a nanosecond continued. "You know our house is your house. Come by anytime night or day."

Jodie coughed from the disgusting cigar smoke.

"Aw, hell, I forgot about this thing." Marion held the cigar between his fingers and stared down at it. "That's right, you don't smoke do you?" he said, walking into the living room and extinguishing the cigar in an ashtray.

"No, I don't." Funny how Jodie hadn't smelled the stench of smoke when she walked in, but now it was taking up all the air.

"We were in the kitchen getting ready to eat dinner. I hope you're hungry?" Roz said, as she walked down the hall into the large eat-in kitchen.

Jodie followed her, with Marion in tow. In a dress and high heels anyone would have thought Roz was on her way out.

"No, I'm fine. I've already eaten."

"Then have a piece of this rum cake," Marion offered. "I had it shipped back from Jamaica. You haven't had cake until you've had rum cake." He walked over to a cake plate sitting in the middle of the island, and picked up a knife to cut her a thick slice.

"Marion, she don't want no rum cake," Roz scolded him.

"How do you know what she wants? She just finished dinner—she's probably ready for dessert."

"Sure, I'll have a little piece," Jodie said out of spite,

and walked over to take the plate from him. Roz looked at her from the stove mumbling something about one piece would stay on your hips for eternity.

"I had some of this in Negril and I had to order one for the house."

Jodie thanked him and walked over to the kitchen table to sit down. She took a bite and smiled up at Marion who seemed to be waiting for a response. She had to admit it was moist and delicious.

"So what do you think?" Marion asked.

Jodie nodded. "It's good, really good. If I'd known about this I would have had you send me one."

"Get another piece to take home with ya before you go."

"Maybe I'll take a piece for my roommate," Jodie responded, knowing Tracy would love the cake as well.

"Cake is the last thing that girl needs," Roz said. "She's got enough hips and ass for another person. What's she been eating?"

Jodie hated when Roz talked about people. "She's built just like her mother, and I don't think she's that big."

"Well, keep on wolfing down cake like that and you'll look just like her."

Marion walked over to the pantry and got out a few Ziploc bags and set them on the island by the cake plate. "Jodie, cut yourself a few pieces before you leave. I don't need to eat all that cake and obviously your mother's not having any."

"Thank you, Marion."

"I'm going to watch a little television, call me when dinner's ready," he told Roz.

"Marion, don't you go in there and fall asleep in front of that television. You know how hard you are to wake up when you fall asleep before bedtime."

Marion nodded and kept walking. "I'm not going to sleep."

To an outsider, they may have seemed like the typical American family. But, Jodie knew the real deal. Roz was a showpiece. At fifty-three, she walked around the house dressed all the time in case Marion brought business people home for drinks. They entertained a lot and had a party for just about every occasion. This was the life Roz had always wanted.

"Where's Keenan?" Jodie finally asked. He was the real reason she sat through their version of *The Real World.*

"He's up in his room. He just came in from basketball practice."

So far so good, Jodie thought. He obviously hadn't mentioned anything about Will, or Roz would have brought it up by now. Jodie didn't actually think he'd say anything, especially if he didn't want Roz to know about the motel incident.

Jodie finished off her cake and stood up. "I think I'll run up and holler at him."

"He might be asleep. His coach suggested some program that's supposed to help his attitude and he's been grumpy ever since we agreed to enroll him. Like I said, when he's not playing basketball he's asleep."

That's what you think. "Well, I'll wake him up. I need to talk to him."

"Uh-huh." Roz followed Jodie across the kitchen.

"Just don't carry any money with you." Her boisterous voice boomed through the kitchen.

Jodie ignored the wisecrack and walked up the back steps from the kitchen to the second floor. She remembered Keenan's room being the first door on the left. She knocked first, but didn't get an answer. She didn't hear any music or the television going. Another soft tap followed by, "Keenan," produced a quiet response.

"Yeah."

"It's Jodie. Can I come in?" she asked.

"Come on."

She slowly opened the door and found Keenan stretched out on the bed talking on his cell phone.

"Hey, let me hit you back. Yeah…yeah…tomorrow." He closed his flip phone and threw it aside on the bed.

She walked in and eased the door closed behind her. After a quick glance at the video vixens on the screen, she turned to Keenan. "Did I disturb your call?"

He shook his head. "It wasn't nobody."

He sat up and swung his long legs off the side of the bed. Jodie walked around the typical masculine room with posters of LeBron James and Allen Iverson on the sliding closet doors. High in one corner was a Nerf basketball rim, and an orange-and-black foam Nerf ball set on top of his dresser.

"Looks like you didn't mention your weekend adventures to Roz yet," she said, taking a seat at the foot of the bed since there was no chair in the room.

He looked up at her startled. "You didn't say anything did you?"

"No, I didn't. But at some point you're going to have to."

"Why?" His eyes widened innocently.

"Keenan, do you want them to find out from somebody else, before you can tell them?"

He shook his head and stood up. "That won't happen. Who's gonna tell them? Will won't tell, and I know you're not going to tell."

He gave her a knowing smile and Jodie understood one thing. If she mentioned the hotel incident, Roz would know she worked with Will. Keenan held up his hands as if to say, the choice is yours.

Jodie crossed her arms and responded with a lopsided grin. "Are you this clever on the court?"

"Better." He winked and walked over to grab the Nerf ball. From the opposite corner of the room he shot the ball across the room and directly into the rim.

"Aren't you a little old for Nerf ball?"

He shook his head and retrieved the ball from the floor. "Nope. It's the only ball I'm allowed in the house." He pointed at his basketball sitting in a corner next to the television.

"It gives Marion a headache," he said, with a smug smile.

Jodie nodded. She could imagine that, but wouldn't expect Keenan to understand.

"The All-Star Classic's this weekend, you comin'?" he asked, landing another perfect basket.

"Of course I'll be there," she said proudly. The thought of finally getting to see Keenan play excited her. It seemed as if they'd passed that awkward acceptance stage, and this was possibly the best time to bring up a touchy subject.

"Keenan, I was talking to somebody who told me about this counselor that's really good with young adults."

He missed the next basket. The muscles twitched in his jaw.

Jodie continued. "I thought it might be a good idea to make an appointment and try to get down to the bottom of whatever it is that's causing you to experiment with drugs."

He crossed his arms. "It's hereditary. You didn't know that?"

"No, it's not. Who told you that?" It wasn't that she didn't believe it herself, but that wasn't the type of thing to tell an impressionable teenager who'd started experimenting.

He walked back over to the side of the bed and sat down. "Nobody. When's the last time you saw Daddy?"

The question caught her off guard. Had he known about her Clifton drive-by? "It's been a while, why?"

"His birthday's comin' up, you know?"

"Yeah, I know."

Then Keenan lay back on the bed with his hands clasped behind his head. "He's your dad and you never go see him."

Jodie dropped her head as a large dose of guilt crawled under her skin. She lay back on the bed with him staring up at the ceiling. The position reminded her of something they used to do as children. He'd always liked to lie in the middle of the floor looking at the designs in the ceiling.

"Let's go see him," Jodie said.

Chapter 17

Stone paced the front of the conference room as everyone crept in single file looking from face to face trying to figure out what was going on.

Jodie sat next to Leta who drummed her fingernails against the table. "What's going on?" Jodie asked.

"You don't know?" Leta asked, looking surprised.

Jodie shook her head. "No, he hasn't said anything to me."

"Then we're all in for a surprise."

"All right. I know you're all wondering what this little meeting is about," Stone said as he stopped pacing.

"Over the last couple of weeks I've been meeting with someone from Sports Central about *The Memphis Zone*. As you know, Will and I have been working hard to get picked up by a major network."

Faces lit up, and people sat up in their seats. Jodie noticed that the only one not in the room was Will.

"Well, we've passed what I call phase I. Somebody over there is interested in the show."

Manny started the applause first from his position next to the door, then everyone else joined in.

A rush of excitement flowed through Jodie's veins. Syndication would mean so much to Will, and it could only add to her résumé.

"Over the next couple of weeks I want you to assume they're watching every show and give it all you've got. I'm going to sit down with Will and Jodie to create another tape for the network executives. But thanks to everyone in this room, we've got a multitude of great shows to choose from. I just want you to know I appreciate the hard work and long hours you put into the show, and everything else you do for Gator House Productions."

Just as Stone began to elaborate about the tape, the door eased open and Will snuck in. Or, he tried to, but everyone turned and glanced at him. At that very moment, seeing him standing there with his arms crossed leaning down as Manny whispered in his ear, Jodie realized her attraction to him hadn't ceased years ago. She still had the hots for that man.

That she'd secretively wished more than a kiss had gone on in the control room, was something she hadn't even been able to admit to herself before now. She wanted all the things she used to fantasize about. She wanted a steamy hot relationship with Will that was unlike anything she'd ever experienced before.

At the end of the brief meeting she pushed her chair back and stood up to follow the crew out, then remembered Stone wanted to talk to her and Will.

Will had already moved to the table and took a seat.

She sat back down a few seats closer to Stone this time, but still on the opposite side of the table from Will.

After everyone left the room Stone said, "I know you two have a lot on your plates right now, but I need you to pile one more thing on. I want a tape pulled together that highlights the very best of *The Memphis Zone*. You know, something that'll knock their socks off."

Will looked at Jodie and nodded. "Sure, we can pull something together. When do you need it?"

"By the end of next week, at the latest. I'm not looking for a series of random clips, that's what we sent before. I want a show, about a show."

Will leaned forward, elbows on the table, stroking his chin and looked at Jodie. "Between me and you, and a couple of interns, I don't think it'll be a problem. What do you think?"

With both men staring at her she gave a reassuring nod. "Sure, I can squeeze it in if you think the crew can?"

Will chuckled. "You know I've got the best crew in television. Of course they can. We'll start this afternoon."

"Great," Stone replied. He said something else on his way out, which Jodie faintly heard. Her eyes were fixed to Will's staring back at her. Something about him today completely turned her on; not that he didn't normally turn her on, but this was more than that. Today he was giving off some type of male pheromones that were calling her name.

"We've got a week and a half to pull this video together. That's gonna require some late nights," he said, not asking but telling her.

"Yeah, I know. I'm used to it. Aren't you?" she asked smugly.

He arched one brow and smiled.

The minute they walked out of the conference room, Leta grabbed Will and Jodie to go over details for Friday's show with Coach Savage. Will was finally going to devote a show to the Lady Tigers. At the same time, Jodie put the show's production assistant, Anastasia, in charge of pulling together footage for the video.

Before Jodie could go back and check on Anastasia the studio went dark. A power outage in the area brought everything to a standstill. To Jodie's dismay, the crew all agreed to assemble at Will's house to start on the video.

Jodie knew Stone was counting on her to produce this video, so if the crew was going to Will's house, she'd have to go, too.

She trailed Leta to Will's house in Germantown, which looked more like an estate to her. The glow of the setting sun cast an orange backdrop on the redbrick house that sat on what looked like five or more acres of land.

The crew's cars lined up side by side in his driveway. Jeffrey had pulled the Gator House van into the garage next to Will's SUV. Jodie got out of her Cavalier and followed Leta inside through the three-car garage.

They walked through a mudroom which led to a large eat-in galley-style kitchen.

Jodie, Jeffrey, Leta, two production assistants and Will went to work creating a concept for the video. They sat around Will's big-screen television like they were watching a good movie.

Jodie sat on the couch next to Will. He made himself even more comfortable by sitting back into the cushions. In the process, his knee grazed Jodie's thigh. Their closeness was already driving her to distraction, so she shifted in her seat a little to put some distance between them.

In two hours, the outline of the video was established. Jeffrey called for a break. "I'm going for a beer. Anybody else want one?" he asked.

"I'll fix myself a glass of water," Jodie said, and she sprang up from her seat to follow him.

Jeffrey showed her where the glasses were.

"Jodie, I can't remember if I've ever asked, but how do you like working on the show?" Jeffrey asked.

"I love it. I've learned a lot about sports, which gives me stuff to talk to my little brother about."

"He plays basketball for Fairley High School, right?"

"Yep."

"Didn't you have an older brother that used to play basketball, too?" Jeffrey asked, opening his beer.

Jodie didn't really want to talk about Corey. "No, he played football." By now half the crew knew that Jodie and Will were from the same small town, and had to have known each other before she started working there. Even Stone had figured it out.

Jeffrey opened a second beer for Leta. "Did he play around the same time as Will?" he asked.

"Huh?" Jodie asked, over the sound of the icemaker.

"He was older than you so I thought maybe he knew Will."

"Yeah, they played together. They were a couple of years ahead of me."

"Man, what are you doing in here, bottling the beer?" Leta asked when she entered the kitchen.

Thankful for the intrusion, Jodie left them arguing and returned to the family room where the crew was sprawled out on the couch and floor.

"I think we've just about sucked the life out of everybody tonight," Will said.

"But look how much we've got done," Jodie pointed to the outline.

Together they sat down and spent a few minutes making notes on the outline while most of their crew nodded off.

Then Anastasia stood up. "Sorry, guys, but I've gotta go or I'll fall asleep at the wheel."

"Me, too," Leta added, coming out of the kitchen with Jeffrey. "I've been up since five this morning."

Not wanting to be left with Will, Jodie said, "Okay, let's call it a night."

But as it turned out, a few minutes later everyone pulled off but her. Her car wouldn't start.

"Damnit," she cursed under her breath and turned the key again. The Cavalier didn't want to play tonight.

"Darn it, I want to go home," she yelled at her car.

A tap at her driver's side window practically made her jump out of her skin.

"Open the door and let me give it a try," Will said.

Still sitting in his driveway, she didn't move. She could call Tracy or the auto club, or somebody, she thought.

He bent down and tapped on the window again.

Under the glowing light from the side of his garage, his smiling face urged her to open up.

She released her grip on the wheel and opened the door. "I'm sorry, I don't know what's wrong with this thing," she apologized as she climbed out of the car.

"What were you doing, sitting in there praying it would start?"

"Something like that," she mumbled.

He sat down, first moving her seat all the way back giving him leg room. Then he tried to start the car. After two failed attempts, he stopped. "You might need a jump."

He put the car in neutral and with the door propped open, backed it up some. "I'll pull my truck out and give you a jump."

As he walked around the car Jodie glanced from his big Range Rover to her little Cavalier and gasped. "Man, you'll probably blow my motor up with that big thing."

He laughed. "It won't hurt, I promise." Then he opened his door to climb in.

Jodie turned around, got into her car, and began to pray. "Lord, please let my car start. It's late, he's fine and I'm horny. Please don't let me do anything stupid."

After he hooked up the jumper cables and tried it several times, he gave up.

"Your battery's probably dead," he said, closing her hood.

"Probably?" she asked.

"Hey, I'm just a shade tree mechanic, but that's my guess." He put the jumper cables back into his SUV and drove it back into the garage.

Jodie stood beside her car with her arms crossed. "Now what," she whispered to herself. She pulled out her cell phone and flipped it open.

"Come on in," Will said, as he walked around to the back of his truck.

"That's okay, I'm calling Tracy to pick me up."

"Why? I can take you home."

"I wouldn't want to put you out like that. My ratty car's already stuck in your driveway."

"You wouldn't be putting me out. Come on in while I change right quick."

She hesitantly followed, closing her phone. She hated to have Tracy come get her at eleven at night when she had to get up for work in the morning.

Back inside the house, she closed the door behind her and followed the path she'd just come through back into the family room.

The Lakers were playing Minnesota on the big-screen TV as she sat down to wait for him. After a few minutes, her cell phone rang.

"Hello," she answered in a whisper.

"Jodie, where you at?" Tracy asked, sounding concerned.

"Uh, I had to work late."

"I called the studio but you didn't answer. Why are you whispering?" Tracy asked.

"My car won't start so I'm getting a ride home."

"With who?"

"Will," Jodie regretted saying.

"Will Duncan!" Tracy screamed.

"Yes. And don't make a big deal out of it. Like I said we worked late."

"Just you and him?"

The suggestive tone of Tracy's voice made Jodie blush. "No, of course not. The whole crew." If she told Tracy where she was, she knew she'd live to regret it.

"What are you going to do with your car?"

"I guess I'll leave it here until tomorrow. Can I use your auto club card?"

"Sure, girl. I'll leave it on your dresser. If you need me just call and I'll swing back by."

Jodie couldn't have Tracy bring her out here. "I'll be able to take care of it, just don't forget the card."

"I won't, and hey don't rush home tonight. Stop for a drink. Take your time, girl."

"Bye, Tracy."

"Stop for a late-night dinner or something. Girl, you're with the most eligible bachelor in all of Memphis. Lighten up and enjoy yourself."

Will walked into the room. "Sorry, but I had to get out of those dress pants," Will said, as he crossed the family room.

"Was that Will?" Tracy asked. "Where are you?"

"Gotta run. See you in the morning." In a flash, Jodie hit the end button and closed her phone.

"That's okay, I was just sitting here watching the game."

"Who's winning?" he asked, coming around to sit on the couch next to her.

The minute he sat down, she practically bit her bottom lip off. Why in the hell did he have to sit right up under her?

"Uh." She kept waiting for the score to appear on the screen, but it didn't. "The Lakers I think," she said, with a smile.

He nodded.

"I'm sorry to have to put you through this," she said.

"No problem," he said, "Just let me see what the score is."

"Where's the bathroom?" she asked, cursing herself for that last glass of water.

"The other side of the kitchen." He pointed behind him.

"Thank you." She made a quick trip to the bathroom and back. When she walked back into the family room he was standing looking out the patio window. He heard her approach and turned around.

"I forgot to ask if you wanted a tour of the house," he said.

Her eyes widened. "Well, I would but considering the hour…" She shrugged.

"Come on, I'll make it quick." He crossed the family room and started down a side hallway.

Jodie followed him.

He showed off all 4124 square feet of the place, then took her into the basement.

He switched on a light and she followed him down the carpeted steps into a den just as large as the family room upstairs.

Several pictures of him during his football days were

hanging on the walls. Jodie walked over to the mantel above the fireplace and looked at the snapshots. Among the numerous pictures of football teams, she spotted a picture of Corey, and picked it up.

Will walked over behind her.

"That's the only picture of him I have. Other than the group shot." He picked up another picture of the whole team and handed it to her.

Jodie took it and had to squint to find Corey.

"That's not a very good picture," he said. "It kind of got scuffed up in my things over the years."

"You don't have any pictures of you guys together?" she asked.

He shook his head. "I used to have one, but I don't know what happened to it. I looked everywhere for that picture, too."

Jodie thought about a picture she had in her photo album and turned around to look at him.

"You miss him don't you?" she asked.

He smiled. "Yeah. We used to talk a lot. About everything. He was my best friend."

"Yeah, I know how you feel. It doesn't seem like he's been gone as long as he has. And with Keenan playing ball it makes me think of him more."

Will walked up to take the photo from her. They held it together for a moment, looking into each other's eyes.

His face came closer to hers as she released the photo. Without looking around he placed it back on the mantel. She looked down at the group photo in her hand. His hands cupped around hers until she released the photo. When she did he reached over and kissed her gently on the forehead.

She smiled up at him with a warning look.

He held his hands up. "I promised that wouldn't happen again didn't I?"

"Yes, you did."

Then he looked into her eyes and shrugged. "I'm sorry, but I couldn't help myself." He looked up at the spotlight shining on the mantel. "It must be the lighting in here." Then he looked back down at her. "You look so beautiful under it."

She turned away from him, biting her bottom lip. "Is this the end of the tour?" she asked. *Lord, give me the strength to walk away from this man tonight.*

He showed off his home theater equipment, and then took her home.

Chapter 18

Will checked his watch again. Keenan was fifteen minutes late. He had five more minutes to show up or Will would have to notify his coach. The program only worked if the athlete was held responsible for his own actions, and showing up to their weekly meeting on time was Keenan's responsibility.

Avery walked into the office and tossed a rolled-up piece of paper onto Will's desk.

"There he is," he said, pointing his finger like a gun at Will. "I was about to start renting out office space. I didn't think you were conducting any more business out of here."

"I'm supposed to be meeting Keenan Dickerson at seven."

Avery snapped his left arm out to look at his watch. "He's late."

"Yeah, I know that. He's got a few more minutes before I have to report him."

"Let's hope he makes it. I'd hate to see him miss the All-Star Classic."

"I don't think Coach Young would do that whether he missed a meeting or not. He'd probably wait until after the game to punish him."

"How's it going anyway?" Avery asked, as he pulled out the chair across from Will's desk.

"He's doing just fine. Aside from the fact that we're just getting started."

"How's his sister taking it?"

"She doesn't know," Will admitted.

Avery leaned back in his seat, clasped his hands behind his head and shook it slightly. "You're asking for trouble."

Will didn't want to think about what would happen when the Dickersons found out he'd been mentoring Keenan. Hopefully by then, there would be vast improvements in Keenan's behavior, and they would thank him.

"It'll be okay. You waiting on somebody?" Will asked Avery.

"Naw, I just stopped in to get something. I'm beat. I made two school visits today." He leaned over bracing his palms against his thighs as he stood up.

Will looked at his watch again. Seven-twenty. Keenan's time had run out.

Will really didn't want to call his coach, so he decided to ride over to the school and look for him. He stood up with Avery and reached in his pocket for his car keys.

In the doorway stood tall, thin, out-of-breath Keenan Dickerson.

"Sorry I'm late. My ride punked out and I had to find somebody else to run me over here."

Will breathed a sigh of relief, and pulled his hand out of his pocket. "That's okay. Come on in."

Will walked around his desk to shake Keenan's hand. "This is my partner, Avery," he said introducing them.

Avery gripped Keenan's hand.

"Avery Williams, quarterback for the Washington Redskins," Keenan said, with his lips turned up into half a smile.

Avery nodded. "That's right, Will and I played together."

"Cool."

Will hoped Keenan would be as impressed with his new counselor as he was with Avery.

On the ride from Will's office to Butch Robinson's office, Keenan asked question after question about Will's college football days.

"Being an athlete in college is much harder than in high school. It's a high pressure life," Will assured him.

"Yeah I know, I can handle it," Keenan said with a shrug. "My studies are cool."

"I know your grades are good, and that's great, but college athletes' personal lives are watched with an intensity that other students don't have to worry about. Anything you do that reflects poorly on the university, such as that little motel party, will be blasted all over the news the very next morning. And believe me, you'll get suspended or maybe kicked off the team."

Keenan looked at Will with skeptical eyes and shook

his head. "You never partied in college?" His facial expression showed his disbelief.

"Sure I did." Will chose his words carefully. "But, I didn't do anything off-field that would draw media attention." He pulled up to a red light, and turned to Keenan.

"I was fully committed to my team. I had a personal obligation to not let them down in any way. I'm not that kinda guy, and I don't believe you are either."

"I'm a team player, I ain't never let the guys down."

The light changed and Will took off. "Not yet you haven't, but the minute you fail a drug test or miss practice because of drinking or drugs, you become a liability to the team."

"I'm not gonna do that."

"That's why we're working together. To make sure you don't."

Will pulled up to the strip mall where a small but highly respected counseling office sat between a Kinko's and a tax office. He explained the counseling process to Keenan.

"Do I have to talk to this guy?" Keenan asked.

"You don't have to do anything. But, Butch works with student athletes all the time. If you want to talk, he'll listen. What you say to him is between you and him. He won't even discuss it with me."

"Yeah, whatever, but I'm not the one who needs a shrink." Keenan opened the door to the Range Rover and climbed out.

Jodie stopped by CVS to get a birthday card, then swung by Roz's to pick up Keenan. April seventh was

Lou's birthday and she had promised Keenan she'd go with him to see Lou. Now she was thankful she'd made the drive-by. At least she wouldn't be totally shocked by the condition of her birthplace.

They rode all the way to Clifton talking basketball. After watching ESPN at night, and Sports Central at work, Jodie had picked up a thing or two. Brother and sister were bonding, and Jodie loved it.

Then the conversation died as they pulled up in front of the house. The same Ford Focus sat in the driveway, and if possible, the house looked worse than it had a few weeks ago. The dilapidated state made Jodie's heart ache.

Once at the door Keenan rang the bell. Jodie saw the curtain move and knew Lou had been looking for them. Keenan had told her that he always managed to at least bring him a card for his birthday every year.

The front door finally swung open and a young woman who looked much older, smiled at them.

"Hi, Keenan, come on in." She held the screen door open.

"Hey, Cee Cee, is the old man here?" Keenan asked, as he walked in.

"Yeah, he's here. He's in there watching television as usual." Cee Cee's curious eyes moved from Keenan to Jodie.

Jodie slowly walked in behind him, gripping the birthday card in her hand. The house felt like a strange place to her. The screen door was dirty and had a big hole in it.

Keenan looked back over his shoulder. "This is Jodie, my sister." He continued into the house.

Cee Cee smiled at Jodie and held out her hand. "Hi, Jodie, it's nice to finally meet you. Lou talks about you all the time."

Jodie took Cee Cee's thin but well manicured hand and shook it. "Hi, it's nice to finally meet you, too."

As Jodie passed Cee Cee she realized the woman wasn't as young as she initially thought. She just looked young. Her hands and the lines around her mouth as she smiled portrayed a much older woman.

The house had been totally redecorated. Gone were the drapes that Roz had custom made for the living room windows. Vertical blinds hung in their place. The living room was clean but understated with only a couch, coffee table, and one Queen Anne style chair.

She passed through the country kitchen decorated with cows everywhere. On the towels, the throw rug, and even the border going around the room. Next to the kitchen was a small den.

"Happy birthday, Daddy."

Jodie heard Keenan ahead of her as he entered the room.

"Keenan." Lou's voice sounded pleasantly surprised. "Come on in here, boy. It's good to see you."

In the doorway Jodie watched as Lou stood up from his easy chair and gave Keenan a big hug. The sight almost brought tears to her eyes. She walked into the room holding out her card.

"Happy birthday, Lou," she said, standing behind him.

He released one arm at a time from around Keenan's shoulders and slowly turned his upper body around in her direction. He moved as if he had back problems. He blinked a few times before turning all the way around holding Keenan's card in his left hand.

"Jodie?" he asked, as if he wasn't sure it was her.

"Yeah, it's me," she said. Where had that nervous chuckle in her voice come from?

"I know it's you. I ain't that far gone that I don't know my own daughter. I'm just surprised is all. You came on my birthday." He stood there grinning at her.

Since he wasn't making a move to come get the card, Jodie walked up to him and handed him the card. "Yeah, surprise, and happy birthday." She laughed and held out her card.

He reached out for the card, but pulled her into his arms giving her a big hug like he'd done Keenan. She could smell the liquor on him. He didn't look as if he'd been drinking, but the smell was probably embedded into everything he owned. His body was thinner than she remembered, and weak. A large lump grew in her throat.

After Lou let go of her, Jodie joined Keenan on the love seat cattycorner to Lou's easy chair while Lou sat back down and opened his cards. His face flushed with happiness and his eyes danced with joy as he read the cards aloud. Suddenly, Jodie felt horrible about not having a gift to go along with the card.

"Cee Cee, get the kids something to drink," Lou said.

Jodie turned her head to find Cee Cee standing in the doorway with her arms crossed. "Sure, what you all want?"

"Got any Pepsi?" Keenan asked.

"Water's fine for me," Jodie said.

"Coming right up." Cee Cee turned back into the kitchen.

Lou set his cards on the fold-out table next to his chair where the remote control and the TV guide sat. "This is real nice of you all. Thank you for the cards, they're beautiful."

The television was the same old General Electric floor model they had when Jodie lived there. On top of it sat a VCR and a few tapes. There weren't any more seats in the room, so when Cee Cee returned with their drinks she walked over and sat on the arm of Lou's easy chair.

Jodie was aware of Lou's eyes on her as she surveyed the room. He grinned at her and shook his head.

"My baby girl," he finally said.

Jodie smiled back and tried to think of something clever to say. The differences between his and Roz's life were dramatic, and Jodie felt sorry for him.

"You in Memphis for a visit?" he asked.

"Not this time. I've moved back."

"Really," he said, with a surprised look on his face.

"You watching this?" Keenan asked, pointing at the television and the nature show Lou had been watching.

"Here, help yourself." Lou held out the remote control.

Keenan took it and started surfing the channels.

"You staying with Roz?" Lou asked.

"Oh, no. I've got an apartment with Tracy."

Lou laughed a little before he started coughing, and Cee Cee left the room as if he knew what was coming.

"I don't blame you for not wanting to stay with her. I haven't seen that woman in years, but I'd bet she hasn't changed. She's still a bitch on wheels, trying to manipulate everybody around her to get what she wants."

Here we go again, Jodie thought. She hated to hear them talk about each other. She already knew her parents' flaws inside and out.

Lou leaned back in his chair until the footrest popped out and he reclined. "I know I couldn't take her treating me like one of her children. Barking orders at me when I was a grown damned man. She wanted to control everything. After Corey died she got worse. It'd been different if I thought for one minute she loved me, but she never did."

"Lou, she loved you," Jodie said, hoping to make him feel better. The sparkle was going out of his eyes and his face morphed into something sad and pitiful.

"All Roz wanted was a ticket out of town, and she thought I was that ticket. When my job transfer fell through, she gave up on us." He turned to Jodie. "You guys are the only good thing to come out of that marriage."

A restless sigh came from Keenan. Jodie could only imagine how many times he'd had to hear this. No wonder he didn't come to visit Lou that much either. And she didn't blame Cee Cee for leaving the room. Jodie wanted to do the same thing herself.

"So, you don't get ESPN?" Keenan asked.

"We only have basic cable," Cee Cee responded, from her spot in the doorway.

Jodie thought she had left, but apparently she'd heard everything.

"Turn to channel four," Lou said. "They show the games sometimes."

"Mind if I use the restroom?" Jodie asked.

Lou leaned forward and lowered his footrest. "Naw, baby, this is just as much your house as mine. You know where the bathroom is. Go ahead."

Jodie stood and walked past a smiling Cee Cee to get to the bathroom. What she really wanted to do was see the house. She wanted to see what they'd done to her old room. The bathroom was down a long hallway past her old room, and Corey's old room. The same room he shared with Keenan once he moved out of their parents' room.

After she used the bathroom, she came down the hall and stopped at her old room. She didn't see anybody so she opened the door and peeked in. The room was pretty. Scarcely furnished like the rest of the house, but draped in light blue and white curtains and trimmings. The queen-size bed had a white bedspread with colorful decorative pillows piled on top. A picture of wildflowers hung above the bed.

"That's the guest room," Cee Cee said, coming down the hall.

Embarrassed for snooping, Jodie pulled the door closed. "Sorry, I couldn't help but look and see what you'd done with the room."

"You're welcome to come and visit anytime you want. We've got the room. It's where my mother stays when she comes over."

"You're not from around here?" Jodie asked.

"No, I'm from Little Rock, Arkansas. That's where my family lives."

"How on earth did you wind up in Clifton?" Jodie asked.

Cee Cee smiled and shrugged. "It's a long story. Sometimes you'll follow a man to the end of the earth, if you know what I mean."

Jodie nodded that she understood.

They walked back into the kitchen where Cee Cee offered Jodie something to eat. Jodie could hear Keenan and Lou in the den talking about basketball.

"Thank you, but I'm really not hungry." Jodie was dying to ask Cee Cee about Lou's weight loss. He was getting older, but he wasn't that old.

"Lou looks a little thin. Is he taking care of himself?" Jodie asked.

Cee Cee gave Jodie a despairing look and shook her head. "He's drinking more. All he does is watch television and drink. I keep telling him he's gonna waste away, but he won't listen to me. The more I talk about it the more he drinks, so I just shut up."

Cee Cee walked over to the glass-top kitchen table and sat down. She opened a package of cookies and offered Jodie one.

Jodie accepted the cookie and sat across from her in one of the stained cloth chairs with bent metal legs.

"He used to take breaks from drinking so much," Jodie said, not so much to Cee Cee as to herself. "He would stop for a little while and just when you thought maybe he'd given it up, he'd stagger in one night reeking of alcohol."

"Well, he doesn't take breaks anymore. But he's still a wonderful man. He's good to me, you know."

Jodie ate her cookie and looked away. No, she didn't know. She didn't even understand how Cee Cee could stand to stay with him.

On the ride home Keenan was jazzed about one thing. Lou had promised to come to the all-star game next week. Jodie hated to admit it, but she knew her little brother was about to get his heart broken.

Chapter 19

The week leading up to the Memphis All-Star Classic was by far the best week Jodie had had since moving to Memphis. Roz was so busy with all the media attention Keenan was getting, Jodie hadn't heard from her once.

At the studio, she'd found time to work on the video Stone wanted and almost completed it. Then Stone turned around and gave her the green light for a new segment of *The Memphis Zone* she'd been working on with Leta.

She'd even stopped avoiding Will to discover they worked extremely well together.

After work Friday, the Gator House crew occupied the back table at Clicks with wings and beer for everyone. Except Jodie, who didn't drink and had grown tired of their wings.

"Who wants another round," Jeffrey asked, waving the waiter over.

"No more for me," Leta said. "We've still got to put the finishing touches on that tape tonight in case you forgot."

"Why can't we work on it tomorrow?" another crew member at the end of the table asked.

"I'm not working tomorrow, Saturday's my daughter's birthday," another crew member stated.

"We've got to finish it tonight," Jeffrey said. "Tomorrow's the all-star game, and I'm going," he said, and left for the bar when a waiter didn't show up.

Several of the crew members looked at Jodie. "You know I'll be there. My brother's playing."

"Guys, there's not that much left to do. And Jodie and I can actually finish it up. You enjoy your weekend," Will said.

Jodie looked at Will, who sat next to her, in surprise. "When did you finish the tape?" she asked.

"I didn't," he whispered in her ear. "Only a few decisions need to be made and you and I can do that. If we get the whole crew involved we'll be working on it all night. We can go to my house and knock it out in a few hours. What do you say?"

She thought about the last time she was at his house.

"Then you have the whole weekend to enjoy the game and play. All I need is your final approval on a few clips." He looked at his watch. "We can be at my house in thirty minutes and finished before eleven."

Jodie looked into his eyes, seeing something in them that blocked all common sense, preventing her from reasoning like she should have. She nodded as a little voice inside her head whispered, "don't go home with that man." But she ignored it, and picked up her purse.

Outside, Jodie stopped Jeffrey in one last-ditch effort to stop herself.

"Jeffrey, are you sure you don't want to have one last look at the tape to check the sound quality or anything?"

"Naw, I've seen it. I'm gonna run by Vicki's tonight. You know, see if my son's up and maybe talk to her for a little while, if she'll listen."

Jeffrey had been trying to get back with his ex-wife ever since Jodie started working at Gator House.

"Well, good luck with that."

"Thanks." He turned to Will who'd opened the driver's side door of the Rover. "Dude."

Will held his head up. "What's up?"

"We're gonna talk real soon, about…you know, right?"

Will nodded and Jodie had a suspicious feeling Jeffrey was talking about her. "Okay, that sounded like some code talk to me. What's that all about?" she asked, pointing from Jeffrey to Will.

Jeffrey slowly walked away. "Nothing. It's a guy thing."

"Uh-huh, I'm betting it's a guy thing about a girl." She narrowed her eyes at Jeffrey who smiled back at her and shrugged. He turned around, waved, and continued to his van.

"You riding with me?" Will asked.

She'd parked her Cavalier two cars down from his Range Rover. "No, I can follow you. I don't really want to leave my car down here." She pulled out her car keys. "Can we stop and get something to eat first?"

"I've got something at the house. Come on." He jumped into the SUV and closed the door.

She climbed in and started her car. How did he know she'd want what he had to eat? She pulled out of Clicks and followed the SUV.

In the last couple of weeks something had happened between them. They'd managed to develop a very good working relationship aside from the obvious attraction they had for one another. She'd even kept her fantasies about him at bay, most of the time anyway.

Will adjusted his rearview mirror and slowed down so he wouldn't lose Jodie. In the month that she'd been at the studio he'd found himself more and more attracted to her. He thought about her night and day, but most of all, he thought about what would happen if he was ever close enough to kiss her again.

Thirty minutes later, he pulled into his driveway and raised the garage door. He watched Jodie pull up behind him and get out of her car. He didn't have a plan for the evening. He hadn't thought about her coming home with him until the words came out of his mouth. Thank goodness his housekeeper always left him dinner on Friday nights.

He climbed out of the Range Rover as Jodie came up alongside him.

Jodie glanced at her watch. "How long do you think this will take?"

"Not long," he replied, and walked over to unlock the door. "Why, you got a hot date tonight?"

"If I did I wouldn't be here."

"You just might," he responded. Spunky, smart-alecky, she was everything he remembered her being, and exactly how he'd liked her. Feisty women turned him on, but no one more than Jodie.

He walked through the mudroom into the kitchen and tossed his keys on the counter.

"Make yourself at home," he said, and opened the refrigerator for a bottle of water.

She looked nervous as she set her purse on the island and pulled out a bar stool to sit down.

"Want some water?" he asked.

She shook her head. "I'm okay."

He turned up the bottle, thirsty and a little nervous himself. If she was anyone else he wouldn't have needed to drink the whole sixteen ounces of water in a couple of gulps. He tossed the empty water bottle in the garbage can and turned around to her getting up off the stool.

"I'm gonna go wash my hands so I can help you cook dinner. Looks like you aren't too eager to start, and if we don't get started I'll be here all night. And that's not what I had planned this evening."

"Oh, we don't have to cook anything." He walked over to the refrigerator and opened the door. Sitting on the top shelf was a Pyrex dish with Rita's mouthwatering lasagna inside. He grabbed the dish, set it on the counter, and then turned to Jodie.

"All you have to do is help me fix a salad and open a bottle of wine. Dinner's been waiting on you all evening," he said, leaning against the counter.

She tried not to blush, and he wanted to walk over and take her into his arms—to hell with dinner. Lasagna wasn't what he was hungry for right now.

"Yeah, right," she said, and turned down the hall.

Will washed his hands in the kitchen sink and looked in the refrigerator for something to make a salad with. On the bottom shelf was a bag of prepared salad mix. He was going to have to give Rita a raise. Next, he pulled out a bottle of wine and set it on the counter.

"I don't drink," Jodie said, when she reentered the room.

"I'm not a big wine drinker myself," he confessed. "But you'll have to have at least one glass with me." He searched in the drawer for an opener.

Jodie walked around the counter and picked up the bag of salad mix. "Where's your colander? I'll rinse the salad."

"My what?" he asked, as he pulled two wineglasses down from the cabinet.

"You know, the thing you use to rinse spaghetti with. You do have one don't you?"

"Oh, that thing." He walked over next to her and opened the cabinet above her head. "I just didn't know that's what you called it." She took a step back when he reached over her for the colander.

Instead of setting it on the counter, he held it out to her. She accepted it, but he didn't let go. Their eyes met and his mouth went dry. He licked his lips and tugged playfully on the colander. She smiled back at him. He stopped playing and gave in before he did something he wouldn't be able to stop. He walked away to get plates, while she opened the salad bag and rinsed the mixture under cold running water.

He wanted to stick his head under that water.

"So when do I get to see this masterpiece you've completed?" she asked.

"Right after we eat, I'll pop the tape in." He nodded and proceeded to put the lasagna on their plates. "Robbie put a little jazz from Norman Brown and Candy Dulfer to it."

"Do you have a bowl for this?" she asked, finished with rinsing the salad.

"Sure." He returned to the cabinet and pulled out a salad bowl and handed it to her. "You know what I don't have, though?" He snapped his fingers.

"What's that?"

"Garlic bread."

"If you've got some bread, butter, and garlic powder, I can make some garlic toast." She snapped the top on the salad and placed it in the refrigerator.

"Maybe I should have had you cook me something tonight instead," he said pointing to the butter inside the refrigerator door. "The bread and garlic powder's in the pantry down there." He pointed at the wood-paneled door past the end of the pantry.

"Making garlic toast is hardly considered cooking," she said with a chuckle and found the pantry.

"That's better than I can do. My poor housekeeper felt sorry for me since every time she cleaned my refrigerator it was empty. So she started cooking for me, too."

"You have a housekeeper and a cook?" she asked, spreading butter and garlic powder on cut slices of bread.

He shook his head. "She doesn't consider herself a cook, so I can't call her that. She's a housekeeper who throws together a meal every now and then. It's not like she cooks for me every day. She only comes in twice a week."

"Only, huh. Must be rough." She chuckled sarcastically.

"I usually have a lot of guys over and we tend to make a mess." He put the plates in the microwave and proceeded to open the wine bottle. She found the toaster oven and set the bread inside. While she waited on everything to heat up, she sat back on the bar stool and accepted the glass of wine as he poured it.

"I don't drink you know, so I'm only going to have a few sips," she said.

"That's okay. I just hope you like it." He poured himself a glass and joined her at the bar. She had her legs crossed and her red polished toes peeked from below her pants leg, making him want to take her sandals off and caress her feet.

"Tell me something," he said after clearing his throat. "How come you used to spend your day avoiding me around the studio?"

She hesitated a moment, then shrugged and picked up her glass, taking another sip. "I don't know. It just doesn't look right for us to spend so much time together, under the circumstances."

"It doesn't look right to who?" he asked, wishing he were the rim of that wine glass that her lips so elegantly sipped from.

She set her glass down, and gestured absently. "People, you know."

He had an idea exactly who she meant. "Do you mean your mother?" Her gaze locked with his. He knew her mother had to be behind the reason she didn't want Keenan to tell her family she worked with him.

Before she could answer, the microwave buzzed.

She stepped off the bar stool, and he reached out and grabbed her arm. "Jodie, your mother doesn't work at Gator House. And even if she did, I wouldn't care. I like spending time with you, at or away from work. I can feel a connection between us and I think you feel the same thing."

He let go of her arm and she walked over to pull the toast from the toaster, then put in two more pieces.

"You're gonna make me burn the toast," she said without answering him.

Will followed her and pulled the plates from the microwave, and then the salad, and salad dressing from the refrigerator. She added the pieces of warm toast to the plates.

He managed to get some salad on each plate, but when she reached for her plate, he took her hand. She looked up, startled, and he found himself backing her against the counter, lacing his fingers between hers. He couldn't stop himself. He stood a few inches over her looking down into her eyes and smelling the subtle but feminine scent of her perfume. She opened her mouth to protest, but he covered those lush lips with his mouth. She didn't resist.

Hot flames shot through Jodie as he kissed her softly once, and then again, this time opening his mouth a little. His warm, soft lips parted hers and her knees started to buckle while his tongue inched its way into her mouth. His other hand slid along her back holding her up.

Is this why she'd agreed to come here? Jodie asked herself. She knew being alone with Will was a dangerous position to put herself in; yet the moment he mentioned going to his house, she said okay. His head tilted, giving him better access to her mouth, and she stopped thinking about anything other than having his tongue in her mouth.

Her head started spinning as his tongue danced with hers in a slow sensual move that made her whole body tingle from the exquisite pleasure. He brought her hand up and placed it behind his neck, releasing her fingers. While he planted soft wet kisses across her lips she caressed his neck.

His mouth slowly moved away from hers and he looked down, breathing heavily with starving eyes as he met her gaze.

"Wow, that wine must have gone to my head," she said, for lack of something better to say and feeling a little embarrassed that she'd let him kiss her again.

He smiled and licked his lips in that way that drove her crazy.

"You only had two sips," he said in a husky voice.

"Yeah well...that must have been some potent wine."

"It's not the wine," he whispered in her ear right before he kissed it. Then he took her other hand in his and placed it around his neck.

"No," she said between ragged breaths and bit her bottom lip. At six-six he stood over her, his body pressed firmly against her breasts, which she couldn't count on to hide her feelings for him. "What is it then?" she asked, as an inferno inside her began to swell. He'd managed to turn the kitchen into a raging furnace.

"Desire," he said, and kissed her forehead. "Passion," he added, kissing the tip of her nose.

"What have you been doing, reading romance novels?" she asked, with a nervous laugh as she shifted her body slightly at the feel of his hard manhood pressed against her pelvic bone.

"No, I've been craving you," he whispered.

The toaster oven buzzed and Jodie jumped in his arms, but her hands remained clasped behind his neck.

Slowly, he released her and she adjusted her top and spun around. "I'm starved," she said, reaching for her plate. *God, I can't control myself around this man.*

"So am I," he said in her ear, as he pressed his body against hers.

His hands caressed her shoulders and slid down the sides of her arms as he whispered in her ear, "Jodie, I don't want lasagna."

Her hands trembled as she pulled the bread from the toaster. "What do you want then?" she asked, knowing the answer to that question. He wanted the same thing she wanted.

"This," he said, and with one arm around her waist turned her around to face him.

He looked down at her, his face hard and his eyes filled with a lust for her that excited her to no end. She watched him reach for, and then undo the first button on her blouse. Her whole body trembled until she stopped him at the second button.

Jodie whispered, "We shouldn't do this."

Chapter 20

"Why not?" he asked, lowering his mouth to her neck.

Oh God, please make him stop. I can't think. "Because…because, it'll complicate things," she said, listening to her own hoarse, ragged voice.

"I can handle it. How about you?"

His soft lips traveled down her neck, leaving kiss after kiss along her sizzling flesh. She bit her lower lip and shook her head. "I can't. You don't understand. I'm…I'm going through a lot of things right now."

"If you're talking about Keenan, I don't think you'll have to worry about him, he's getting his act together."

"How do you know?" She grasped his fingers after he attempted to reach for the third button.

He started to say something, but then hesitated and

cleared his throat. "After a visit to the police station, I think he's scared straight."

"I hope you're right. But, he's not exactly what I was talking about."

Will took a step back. "Then what is it? Talk to me. Let me help you work it out."

She took a deep breath and turned around to the now lukewarm plates on the counter. "I thought you were going to feed me?" she asked.

She could hear his disappointed sigh behind her, and she understood his pain. She wanted nothing more than to have old fashioned, hot, sweaty, satisfying sex with him right now. Just like she'd dreamed of doing so many nights in the past. But getting involved with him would only complicate things on the job, and with her family.

He kissed the top of her head, and she couldn't resist leaning back into him. His arms came around her and pulled her closer against his body. With one hand she reached out toward her plate. She fought her body for control. Common sense told her to grab that plate and sit down and eat, but her body had something else in mind. It wanted to feel Will's skin, to see what was pressed against her lower back and have him caress every inch of her starving body.

"I guess we'd better eat before it gets cold?" she said.

His arm reached out across the counter after her hand. He laced his fingers in between hers and brought her hand back to her side.

This time when he turned her around, she willingly

raised her arms and wrapped them around his neck. He'd awakened something deep within her that heeded to his call. She wanted this man right now more than anything else on this earth.

Will slowly unbuttoned the rest of the buttons on her blouse and pulled it open. Her breasts smashed against his chest as his arms went behind her and pushed the plates out of the way. He hoisted her up on the counter.

"Nice," he said, running a finger along the edge of her lacy bra. Then he kissed the flesh of her cleavage.

His warm mouth set her ablaze. As he pulled her blouse down from her shoulders she repeated to herself, *This is the man I've wanted all my life, this is the one.* A blissful feeling engulfed her and she blushed uncontrollably until his mouth met hers again and his tongue went on a searching expedition that she never wanted to end. This kiss was more aggressive and hypnotizing than the one before.

His hand gently cupped her breasts through the white lace. She arched her back praying he'd release her breasts from their prison, and he did just that.

Not a word was spoken between them. Will freed her breasts and her nipples perked up waiting for him.

As he rolled her nipples between his fingers his mouth found hers again and kissed her with such force her head backed into the cabinet. He caressed her breasts with the warmth of his hands releasing a gush of excitement from her that came out in a low moan.

In one quick movement, his mouth left her lips and closed over her nipple. His mouth was hot and wet as he sucked one breast, while caressing the other with his hand. Jodie arched her back, and he left one breast for the other. She moaned as his tongue flickered over her nipples, alternating between sucking and licking.

She could hardly catch her breath as he stopped long enough to take her bra and blouse all the way off. He tossed them behind him on the island. Then he turned back to her and smiled.

"What?" she said, feeling a little embarrassed to be sitting on his kitchen counter bare-breasted.

He reached out and touched her nipples. "You're beautiful," he said in a husky voice.

She shivered in response, and her nipples hardened.

"Would you be terribly upset if we didn't eat right now?" he asked.

With her panties soaked, and an irresistible urge to rip his clothes off, she shook her head.

"Good."

He lowered his head and feasted on her breast again, causing her body to almost explode. Then before she could catch her breath, he lifted her from the counter and carried her in his arms out of the kitchen, up the stairs, and into his bedroom.

With her pulse racing, she kept her arms firmly wrapped around his neck until he set her down on the edge of the bed. Then she let her arms slide from around him to her sides. All too aware that she had on nothing but a thong, a pair of butt-hugging slacks and some sandals, she crossed her arms over her breasts.

Will bent down on one knee and her eyes widened. He took her sandal into the palm of his hand and worked the strap until it was undone.

"You don't look comfortable," he said, in a casual tone, even though he'd just carried her up a flight of stairs. "Let's get these off." He massaged her foot a little before sitting it down and picking up the other foot.

Her eyelids started to flutter, but before she could relax into the gentle massaging of her toes, he stopped. He rose from his kneeling position and reached out a hand to her. She stood up with her bare feet sinking into the plush carpet. When he reached for the button on the side of her pants, she reached down and held her hand over his.

He stopped and looked down at her. "What's wrong? Change your mind?"

She hadn't changed her mind at all, but she wasn't about to do anything reckless. "Will, I don't carry condoms around in my bag or anything, so—"

"Don't worry. I've got plenty," he said, placing his other hand atop hers to continue working the button.

"Wait a minute. What—have you got a drawer full of condoms?" she asked, pushing his hand away.

Will stopped and took a deep steady breath. He took Jodie's hands in his and brought them to his mouth, kissing the back of her hands. Then he wrapped his arms around her waist. "Don't get the wrong impression. I don't have a drawer full of anything. But I've got tonight covered. That's all I'm saying."

"So you planned tonight?"

He cocked his head to the side and drew his brows together. "No. I just like to be prepared, and the minute I laid eyes on you I wanted you."

"And I'm supposed to believe that?"

He took her hand and they walked across the room

into the master bathroom. Jodie hadn't seen anything like it before. The room was all white and beige with a splash of dark brown. He had double sinks that looked like bowls sitting on top of the counter.

He pulled open a drawer and produced a sealed package of condoms.

"New pack?" she asked.

"Your pack," he said. "I haven't been with anybody in a long time. And I don't run through boxes of condoms." He moved closer to her, pulling her into his body.

"Now," he said, giving her a kiss on the forehead. "I hope you haven't changed your mind?" Before she could answer he captured her mouth in a long arousing kiss.

The bathroom spun around as Jodie closed her eyes and helped Will wiggle her slacks over her hips. His hands caressed her rear end and gave her a gentle massage that caused her body to ache with desire. She moved her legs farther apart, unable to stop herself. His fingers slid under the string that was her thong and methodically eased it down over her hips until it landed on top of her pants.

He released her hips and took a step back. For a few seconds he didn't say anything, he just smiled. Then he reached down and helped her out of her pants.

"You're as beautiful as I imagined you would be."

Filled with an uninhibited desire to be with this man, she bit her bottom lip and tried to stifle a smile. In a raspy voice she almost didn't recognize she said, "But am I going to be the only one in their birthday suit? Or, do I get to see what I've been dreaming about for years?"

A broad grin spread across his face. "You've been dreaming about me, huh?"

She shrugged and held onto her bottom lip. "Maybe once or twice."

"What did you dream about?" he asked, pulling his shirt over his head.

"This," she said, taking a step forward and placing the palms of her hands on his warm chest. He pulled her closer and she ran her tongue across his nipple, eliciting a loud moan from him.

Then he picked her up and she wrapped her legs around his waist. "Come on, let me show you what I've been dreaming about."

Chapter 21

The usher took one look at Jodie's ticket and instructed her to go down one more level and check with the next usher. To Jodie's surprise, her seat for the Memphis All-Star Game was second row courtside. The usher took her as far as he could, and then pointed to her seat. Thanks to Marion's connections her seat was next to Roz's. Oh joy-joy she said, as she excused herself past several other people on the second row.

The minute Jodie sat down Roz turned and stared at her like she didn't know who she was. "You forgot to wear blue," she said rather annoyed.

"What?" Jodie looked down at her green outfit.

"Keenan's on the blue team, you were supposed to wear blue. I reminded you when you came by to pick up the ticket," Roz pointed out in her navy-and-white blouse with white slacks.

Jodie shrugged. "Guess I forgot."

Roz shook her head and glanced around at the crowd.

Jodie settled back into her seat and crossed her legs. Next to her were two empty seats. Earlier in the week Roz had told her Lou and Cee Cee would be sitting next to her if they showed up. Which Jodie doubted.

"Where's Marion?" Jodie finally asked Roz as she smiled and waved politely at a couple looking back at her.

"Those are a couple of Marion's supporters." She dropped the fake smile and turned to Jodie. "He's walking around here somewhere with that damned cigar hanging from his mouth trying to look important."

Unbelievable, Jodie thought. Roz's enthusiasm and support for Marion's career turned on and off like a light switch.

"Oh, look, there's Keenan." Roz waved as the teams made their way to the floor.

Jodie stood and cheered with the rest of the stadium and heard a group of young girls several seats away screaming Keenan's name. She turned her attention to the floor and beamed as her little brother's name was called and he ran onto the floor.

"Where is Marion?" Roz fussed looking behind them. "He's going to miss the tip-off."

Jodie was proud of Keenan. During Corey's football days she'd been too young to appreciate his game. All she wanted to do was go to the games with her friends and wait for Will to notice her. This afternoon, the game was all about Keenan.

After all the introductions Roz began waving her hand frantically to catch Keenan's attention. Her waves couldn't compete with the screams of some of Keenan's young friends.

Finally, Keenan looked up into the stands and waved at the young girls, who screamed louder. He blushed and shook his head.

"Look at those girls," Roz hissed. "That's the kind of trash we need to keep Keenan away from. It's girls like that that will ruin his NBA career."

Jodie laughed. "They're kids."

Roz held up her chin and pursed her lips. "I had Corey at sixteen. I was a kid, too."

Marion finally took the seat next to Roz and waved down at Jodie. "I see you made it."

"Wouldn't have missed it for the world," she replied.

"Good, good. I know Keenan will be glad you came."

Marion and Roz talked about the various people he'd run into while getting something to drink. Which Jodie assumed he drank already since he came back empty-handed.

She finally caught Keenan's eye when he looked their way. He raised his chin and smiled at her. That felt good. Then he pointed to the empty seats next to her and all she could do was shrug her shoulders. He dropped his smile and dribbled the ball behind his back and made his way back to the bench. Her chest pained as if she'd been stabbed. Keenan had personally asked

Lou to come to the game, and even had Marion send him two tickets. Jodie didn't think he would show, but had hoped he'd prove her wrong.

Minutes later, the game was underway and Jodie sat there mesmerized by Keenan's skills. This wasn't the playground where she'd last seen him play ball. This was big-time high school ball and Keenan played like the star he was. She couldn't believe he was even the same quiet guy that she saw moping around. On the court he was in charge, bringing the ball down court and setting up the plays. He hit a three-pointer and the young girls in front of Jodie went into hysterics.

When the girls finally sat down Jodie spotted Will. He and another man were ushered down to their first-row, courtside seats. Her heartbeat quickened. Dressed casually, he took his seat, reaching out to shake hands with several people around him who either recognized him, or he knew.

All she could do was think about last night. She knew he'd be here, but hadn't expected to see him. She tried to turn her attention back to the game, but found herself repeatedly looking in the opposite direction at Will. Then as if he'd sensed her looking at him, he turned his head and looked directly at her.

Their eyes locked and they spoke to each other in a language only they knew. Then he smiled at her. She gushed from the inside thinking about the sex they'd had the night before. A blissful feeling found its way to her lips as she blushed and nodded at him.

They turned back to the game, but Jodie found it hard to concentrate knowing Will was sitting within viewing distance. Mentally, she relived last night, the best night of her life, over and over again in her mind.

At the halftime buzzer, Jodie left Roz and Marion arguing over the game while she went to the restroom. When she walked out she saw Will through the crowd of people coming and going. He stood across from the ladies' room talking to the same guy he'd come in with. He spotted her and waved her over.

After last night, Jodie wasn't sure what to say to him. She zigzagged through the people trying to get to the concession stand or restroom before the second half.

"Hey, how you doing?" he asked as she approached.

She smiled. "I'm good."

"Jodie, I want you to meet somebody." He turned and patted the man on the shoulder.

"This is my business partner, Avery Williams."

She held out her hand to Will's business partner who was fairly handsome and built like a Mack truck.

"It's nice to finally meet you," he said, shaking her hand.

Jodie smiled politely as he gripped her hand, pushing her rings into her flesh. "Same here," she replied, wondering what Will had told her about him.

"So, how do you like working at Gator House?" he asked as Will turned and greeted a young man who walked over to say hello.

"I like it a lot," she admitted.

"Even working for this pompous perfectionist here?" he asked, pointing at Will's back.

"He's not that bad, as long as you don't criticize him," she said playfully.

Avery laughed and shook his head. "You've got him figured out all right."

"What's so funny?" Will asked joining them.

"Nothing." Avery shook his head and chuckled. "Hey, I see somebody I need to get with. I'll let you two chat and catch you back inside." He left them alone.

Before Jodie could open her mouth Will asked, "Why didn't you call me this morning?"

"You didn't call me either," she pointed out.

He looked over her head and spoke to a group of young black men when they passed.

"Is that how it works? You…we have sex and I'm supposed to call you all excited the next day?"

"What are you talking about?" he asked.

"Your fingers don't look broken. Why didn't you call me?" she asked, in a defensive tone.

Will looked stunned. He blinked like he'd never thought of calling a woman after sex. Now Jodie wished she'd given more thought to going to look at that tape last night.

"Because I asked you to give me a buzz to wake me up. I was kind of wiped out when I went to bed you know," he said with a smile.

She shrugged. "Sorry, I was busy."

"All day?"

"Mostly, yes."

They were silent and somebody backed into their space and apologized while standing to the right of them.

Will opened his mouth to respond, but froze. A look came over his face that Jodie had never seen before. She turned to see what he was looking at and saw Roz standing outside the ladies' room giving him a hard, dirty look.

Her gaze turned from Will to Jodie, and a sickening feeling curled Jodie's stomach. Roz rolled her eyes and continued into the restroom.

"I'm sorry," Jodie said turning to face Will.

"Don't worry about it." He gestured vaguely but there was a slight crack to his voice. "I know she still hasn't forgiven me."

"Corey was her world," Jodie began. "And I don't think she'll ever get over him being gone. She can't seem to bury him like everybody else has. She just needed to blame somebody. And I'm so sorry it was you." Not sure why she felt compelled to defend Roz, Jodie did.

The look in Will's eyes as he stared at her was one of loss and loneliness. He looked as if he'd been in his own hell over Corey's death.

"I don't blame her," he said looking away. "I can only imagine it's not easy losing a son." Then he turned back to Jodie. "Just like it's not easy losing your best friend. And before you say anything, I know I was able to go on and play football, Corey wasn't."

He was reminding her of the pain she'd felt when she saw him at the wedding reception. All she thought of was the wealth and fame he'd attained that Corey could have possibly attained if he'd been alive today. She didn't want to go there again. Not after last night anyway.

"Will, I'd better go back to my seat before the game starts." *Or, before Roz comes out of the restroom.*

"What are you doing after the game?" he asked.

"I'm not sure, why?"

"I'd like to see you."

The sadness was slowly leaving his face replaced with a questioning curious look.

She'd turned her body so she could see Roz the minute she exited the restroom and she hadn't come out yet. Jodie talked fast. "I might go by the house and see Keenan for a few minutes if he goes home after the game."

Will laughed. "I doubt that he will. Win or lose tonight those guys are going to party."

"Yeah, well you're probably right."

"So can I see you?"

His face was one big smile now, and she welcomed the joy back. "Sure, what do you want to do?"

Neither one responded for several seconds. He just looked at her, licked his lips and smiled. She had to look away so he wouldn't see her blushing. If he was thinking the same thing she was thinking, and she was certain he was, she knew exactly what she wanted to do.

"I love it when you blush," he whispered in her ear.

She whipped her head around and tried her best to stop grinning like a fool.

"There's those big dimples I'm so fond of. How about I come pick you up after the game and we can decide what we want to do then? It's Saturday night so we've got plenty of choices."

She could hear the buzzer inside the stadium announcing the start of the second half.

"Sounds good. I'll see you tonight."

Jodie left Will standing there grinning at her as she

reentered the stadium. All the way to her seat she kept asking herself, "What the hell am I doing?" Sleeping with Will again would only complicate everything in her life. But after last night, how could she say no.

When she took her seat Roz was already sitting down. Jodie hadn't seen her exit the restroom and was surprised. That meant she'd seen her still talking to Will when she came out. Big deal, she told herself. They were adults and she was having a conversation. Roz would have to get over it.

The second half started without Roz saying a word to her. Jodie could see Roz was deliberately not looking in her direction. She watched the game, talked to Marion, and rooted around in her purse for something she never found. She was pissed.

Jodie looked past Roz to speak to Marion. "Marion, how many points does Keenan have right now?"

"He started this half off with seventeen. He'll end the game with over twenty points easily."

"Wow," she said sitting back.

"I know who you were talking to out there," Roz said, looking straight ahead.

Jodie bit her bottom lip to keep from laughing. Roz pouted like a child who hadn't gotten her way. "I'm sure you do," Jodie said in response.

"You've been gone a long time, but in this family, we don't converse with the enemy."

Jodie couldn't help but laugh this time. "The enemy!" she said. She knew Roz didn't like Will, but to call him the enemy, was like something out of a spy movie.

With a straight back and eyes blazing, Roz turned to

Jodie. "He practically killed your brother. He should be in prison today instead of allowed to walk around a free man doing whatever he pleases."

Her voice grew louder. "I don't ever want to see you speaking to him again," she demanded.

The icy, strained tone of Roz's voice caught the attention of a few people sitting around them. She stared at Jodie as if waiting for an answer, but Jodie didn't respond. She couldn't. Watching the veins in Roz's neck and the stricken expression on her face made Jodie realize something. Roz would never be able to forgive Will for the accident. And there was nothing Jodie could do about that.

Marion reached over and took Roz's hand and yelled something about the game. Everyone around them stood as the announcer said Keenan Dickerson was at the free throw line. Roz turned back to the game.

Jodie wanted to scream. She wanted to let Roz know she wasn't sixteen anymore and she couldn't tell her who to associate with. But under the circumstances, she kept her mouth shut. She wanted to get up and run as far away from Roz as she could. Just like she'd done when she went off to college. But, she reminded herself that tonight wasn't about Roz, it was about Keenan. She was here in support of him. She wouldn't leave until the game was over no matter what Roz said.

The second half ended with the Memphis All-Star Blue team winning. The coach and the team jumped around the floor in a frenzy of excitement. Everyone looked ecstatic except Keenan.

"Jodie, come on by the house, we're throwing a little celebration party tonight," Marion said as he stood up.

"For Keenan and his friends?" Jodie asked, surprised.

"Yeah." Marion perched his cigar back between his lips. "For anybody who wants to come by. So come on by."

Roz never said a word. But Jodie didn't need her to, she already knew what she was doing after the game.

Keenan jumped into the passenger side of Michael's car and handed his MVP trophy over the seat back to Jay.

"You the man tonight," Jay said to Keenan. "Taking home the MVP award and scoring twenty-nine points."

"And did you see the honeys screaming in the stands?" Michael added.

"Yeah, that too," Jay said.

Keenan listened to his friends, but didn't feel the same enthusiasm they did. He'd had a good game and now he wanted to get out of there.

"Where we headed first?" Michael asked, as they left the stadium.

"Stop by my house so I can take the trophy inside," Keenan said.

"Naw man," Jay pleaded. "Let's ride around with it. Take it to the party with us. Dog, you need to show this off."

Keenan twisted in his seat to face Jay. "For what? So some knucklehead can break it. Man, I'm taking that home and put it with all the rest of them, and then we can hit the streets."

When they reached the house all the lights were on and several cars were parked in the driveway and out front.

"Hey man, your folks having a party?" Michael asked, trying to find a place to park.

"Yeah, it's supposed to be for me, but they invited all their old stuffy friends."

"I bet they got some beer in there," Jay said.

"Yeah, but you know my folks, we better not act like we want any. Come on, let's run up to my room while I change."

Michael parked the car and the three of them made it into the house and up to Keenan's room after Roz made Keenan and Michael parade through the living room so everyone could congratulate them.

"Man, your father's a trip," Jay said, flopping down on Keenan's bed.

"He's not my father," Keenan said, pulling a change of clothes from his closet.

"I mean your stepfather. He throws you a party but doesn't invite any of the team or any girls over. What's up with that?"

"He's a politician," Michael added. "The party's not really for Keenan, it's for show. You know how they do."

"Yeah." Jay nodded, but didn't look as if he really understood.

Keenan changed clothes while Michael called several people on his cell phone and they talked about where the party was tonight.

In less than thirty minutes the boys descended the stairs on their way out.

Roz was in the entryway talking to a few guests who had just arrived. Keenan stopped when he heard what she was saying.

"You know that good-for-nothing Lou could have come to the game. Marion paid good money for those two tickets. But did Lou sober up enough to come watch his only son play in the biggest game of his life? Hell naw!"

Jay and Michael stood behind Keenan on the steps.

Roz closed the front door and turned around, startled to see Keenan and his friend. "Keenan, where you going?"

He hurried down the stairs. "Out with my friends."

"Don't you'all leave yet. Your uncle Marvin just got here. Come on in and say hello."

Keenan didn't say anything to anyone. He opened the front door and stormed past Roz. Michael and Jay followed him, saying good-night as they cleared the door.

Michael started the car, turned up the radio, and they drove away.

"Keenan, don't sweat it," Jay finally said after a few minutes. "I never even met my old man. At least you know who yours is."

Michael shook his head. "Man, Jay, thanks for those insightful words." He chuckled. "You always got something to say to make a guy feel better."

"What? It's true, man. I never met the dude."

"Drop me off at ya boy Chris's house. I'll meet you'all at the party later."

Michael gave Keenan a curious look. "Chris the guy you get your weed from?"

"Yeah, I'm gonna get a little something for the party."

"Shoot, man, I got that covered." Jay leaned forward and rested his forearms on the edges of the front seats. "You know I copped a sack before the game. We're set, baby," he said in a high-pitched voice.

"I don't want no weed. Just drop me off at Chris's."

"Aw, Keenan, don't do nothing stupid man," Michael warned.

Keenan ignored Michael and thought about the hundred-dollar bill he had in his pocket. Lou had eased it to him when he and Jodie went down for his birthday. Keenan didn't care about the money anymore. He didn't care about Lou anymore either.

Chapter 22

Will shot upright on the couch as he held his cell phone to his ear.

"What's wrong?" he asked anxiously, glancing at Jodie before getting up from the couch.

The pained expression on his face told Jodie their night was over before it began. After the game she'd gone home and showered and changed. He picked her up an hour later. After a drink at Zanzibar's they rode to his house, where she hoped for a repeat of last night.

All she could think about was the new sexy bra and panty set she'd purchased earlier at the mall. If anyone had told her a couple weeks ago that tonight she'd be sitting on Will Duncan's couch eager to strip out of her clothes, she never would have believed them. She'd dreamed about it, sure, but she had no idea it would ever happen.

"Where are you?" Will picked up a pen from the coffee table and flicked it, looking at Jodie.

She reached in her purse and pulled out a small tablet and handed it to him.

"Thanks," he whispered to her and walked over to the opposite couch and sat back down. He bent down and started writing.

Not a good sign, she thought.

"Stay where you are. I've got to make a run first, but I'm on my way." He flipped his phone closed and looked over at her, taking a deep breath.

"Something wrong?" she asked.

He gave her a strange look like he was contemplating telling her about the phone call, but instead looked away. "One of the kids I mentor is in trouble." He glanced over at her chewing on his bottom lip.

"I hope it's nothing serious?"

He nodded and stood up. "I think it is. I'm sorry, but I've gotta go pick him up." He handed her tablet back to her.

"Where is he?" she asked, reaching for her purse.

"Stranded out on the street in a bad neighborhood."

"Do you want me to ride with you?" she asked, standing up. She wasn't sure what she could do but she wanted to offer to help.

"No!"

He answered so abruptly it startled her. "Okay...well."

He walked around the coffee table and pulled her into his arms. "I'll run you home first, but thanks for understanding. Sometimes I'm the only one these kids have, so I have to be there for them."

"No, I understand. It's no problem really."

He eased back, and tilted her head up by the chin. He looked longingly into her eyes before kissing her softly on the lips.

Jodie closed her eyes and thought about what would have or possibly could have happened if the phone hadn't rung.

"What are you doing tomorrow?" he asked.

She absently shook her head, unable to think about anything other than tonight. "Uh, I've got a few things to do for work, but other than that nothing that I can think of right now."

He released her and held her hand as he walked toward the kitchen. She followed him knowing they were on their way out.

"Then why don't I call you and we can get together and do something? I want to see you again before Monday morning. We need to talk." They cleared the kitchen, the mudroom, and walked out into the garage.

She wasn't sure how she felt about being rushed out like some one-night stand he didn't want to see again.

He walked her to the passenger side of his SUV and held the door open. Before she could climb in, he stepped in front of her and reached in to kiss her again. This time he tilted his head giving him full access to her mouth and planted on her the softest most seductive kiss she'd ever experienced with her mouth closed.

And as if that wasn't good enough, he slowly parted her lips with his tongue and almost lost himself in the moment.

"Umm, why tonight," he whispered in her ear as he pulled himself away from her.

His eyelids were heavy as he gazed at her with so much desire in his eyes it couldn't be mistaken. She knew at that moment nothing between them would be the same again. They would definitely have to sit down and talk before going to work Monday.

He finally tore himself away from her and closed the car door once she climbed in.

Jodie followed him with her eyes around to the driver's door cursing the kid on the phone under her breath.

Keenan stood outside J.D.'s Lounge looking up and down the street. He wasn't old enough to go inside the lounge, but he knew several of the guys hanging around outside. They shook his hand, patted him on the back, and offered him a drink in celebration of the game.

A police car turned the corner and cruised along the street. Several men hurried inside the lounge while a few others stared the police down as if daring them to stop.

Keenan's heartbeat raced even faster than it was already. For a minute he thought he saw the car speed up, and he wanted to take off running. Then he realized he was only tripping and stood his ground. The car cruised by, letting the officer on the passenger's side check out everybody on the sidewalk.

Keenan's skin itched all over and he had to bite his lip to keep still and not draw attention to himself. He felt his eyes slowly closing and pulled them back open. The last thing he needed was to get locked up tonight. He might not be so lucky this time.

The cruiser drove on past the club and Keenan leaned against the building taking a deep breath and wiping the sweat from the side of his face. As soon as the coast was clear, he paced back and forth in front of the club again unable to stand still. He'd messed up this time and he knew it. He just wanted to go somewhere and sleep it off. Everybody he knew was out partying or unwilling to come down to J.D.'s to pick him up. Everybody except Will.

The door to the lounge flung open and a man was thrown out stumbling into Keenan. The man smelled like a liquor bottle and a pack of cigarettes. Keenan pushed the foul-smelling old man away and wiped at his nose.

Will hurried to pick up Keenan after not getting an answer on the kid's cell phone. He called repeatedly but the voice mail kept picking up. Not telling Jodie Keenan was in trouble would come back to bite him he was sure, but doing so would mean letting her know he was Keenan's mentor. He chose to make that decision after picking Keenan up. On the phone he sounded high or drunk, Will couldn't tell.

As Will turned the corner and pulled up to J.D.'s Lounge his headlights shined on a man straddling the curb. He staggered from the street back up to the sidewalk flailing his arms in the process. From the back Will couldn't make out the man's age or even tell if it was Keenan or not. But if he wasn't careful someone would hit him before the night was over. Will stopped the SUV and unbuckled his seat belt.

Someone tapped on the passenger side window. He turned to see Keenan peering through the window at him.

Will unlocked the door and Keenan climbed in and closed the door. He didn't even look like the same young man who just under eight hours ago received the MVP trophy from the all-star game. What had happened to him in such a short time?

Keenan's head hung low and he shook it as he struggled to put his seat belt on. "Man, I messed up."

Will didn't speak, but turned on the interior lights. Keenan shielded his eyes and turned to look out the window.

"Look at me," Will said, in a voice sterner than he'd meant to.

Keenan's head slowly came back around and he looked at Will. "I messed up."

"You said that already." Will was more disappointed than he wanted to admit. He reached across the seat and took Keenan's chin in his hand, holding his head up to look at his eyes. His eyelids fluttered as Keenan tried to open them wider.

"What are you high on?" Will asked, letting go of him and turning off the light.

Keenan lowered his head as if it weighed a ton.

Will could hear him mumbling something under his breath, but not loud enough for Will to make out. He started the engine and pulled off.

As he drove away, Keenan's head shot up and he frantically looked back over his shoulder in the direction of the lounge. "Man, they're back there."

Will glanced back but knew he wouldn't see anything other than the same drunk staggering in front of the lounge. "Who's back there?"

"My boys. I left my boys back there," he explained in an agitated manner.

"No, they left you. Remember, that's why you called me."

"Boy oh boy, I messed up. Can we stop and get something to drink?" Keenan asked, wiping at something on his face over and over again.

Will slowed down, pulled the SUV over, and stopped. "We're not going anywhere until you tell me what you're on. What's wrong, winning the game and getting the MVP trophy wasn't good enough for you?"

With his index finger Keenan repeatedly tapped at his temple like he was trying to get something out of his head. "Man, you just don't know what it's like. The pressure."

"You're wrong. I know exactly what it's like. When I was in high school Corey and I alternated receiving the MVP trophy. Pressure is a part of high school sports. If you want to compete you have to push yourself. Your brother taught me that."

Squirming in his seat now, Keenan pointed at Will and shouted, "See, there you go! Everything has to be about Corey. Corey did this. Corey was good at that. I can't be no damned Corey, man. I'm sick of it. I'm Keenan," he literally screamed.

The outburst was like a release for him. Immediately afterward, he leaned against the headrest and slouched down in his seat.

What a toll Corey's death had taken on everyone around him. Will started the car and continued to a destination unknown.

"Hey, I'm sorry. I won't talk about him again if it bothers you."

Living with Roz had to be hard on Keenan. Corey was her pride and joy and Will was certain she compared Keenan to Corey every chance she had.

They rode along in silence for a few minutes. Keenan couldn't seem to find a comfortable spot in his seat. He twitched and stretched as if he'd been confined in a small box. He looked sick so Will drove in the right-hand lane just in case he needed to pull over quick.

"Are you going to tell me what you took tonight so I can determine if I need to carry you to the hospital or not?"

Keenan shook his head vigorously. "I don't need to go to the hospital. I just need to sleep it off. Don't take me to no hospital." He sat up peering out the front window with a panic-stricken look on his face.

"What is it you need to sleep off?" Will kept his tone even and tried not to look as worried as he was. He wanted to be here for Keenan, but didn't want to be blamed if he'd done something to harm himself.

"We smoked some weed, that's all. But that was some powerful stuff. Man, I don't feel right. Then my boys wanted to go down on Beale Street. I'm too messed up to go down there, I just want to go home."

Will decided to head to Jodie's as he glanced down at Keenan's legs shaking like he had to use the bathroom. If he took Keenan home in his condition, Roz would probably have the police come lock Will up for something.

Keenan was under the influence of something other than marijuana, but Will didn't know what.

"Are you okay?" Will asked, wanting to stop the car before Keenan threw up.

Keenan mumbled something and rolled the window down.

Will made a quick right and pulled alongside the curb. The minute the SUV stopped the passenger door swung open and Keenan stumbled out onto the sidewalk and threw up.

When he climbed back in the car Will handed him a paper towel.

"Can I get some water now?" Keenan asked, breathing heavily.

Will drove to the nearest gas station and went in for two bottles of water. When he returned Keenan had slouched down in the seat again as if he were hiding from someone behind the tinted windows.

"So what happened after the game?" Will asked.

After opening the door and rinsing out his mouth, Keenan held the cold bottle against his forehead. "Marion had a stupid party. He just wanted to look big in front of his uptown friends. Tell them how proud he is of his stepson, when he can't even tell me that to my face. So, I booked."

"Where did you go?"

"To a friend's place."

"What friend?"

"Man, you ask too many questions." Keenan returned to looking over his shoulder.

Will knew exactly where he had to take Keenan this time, to Jodie's place.

Chapter 23

Jodie peeked out her bedroom window and saw Will's Range Rover parked next to her Cavalier.

"Oh no, oh no," she repeated as she hurried into the bathroom and yanked the rollers from her hair. A few more minutes and she would have been sound asleep.

The doorbell rang again and she pulled her robe off and grabbed a pair of sweatpants hanging on the back of the bathroom door.

She ran her hands through her hair as she walked down the hallway and thought, "If he thinks he can drop that kid off somewhere and swing by here for a booty call I'm going to have to straighten him out. I don't do booty calls."

She pulled the door open as the doorbell rang for the third time.

Will stood on the other side with a serious look on his face. She immediately knew something was wrong.

"I'm sorry, I know you were probably asleep, but—"

Before he could say another word, Jodie gasped at the sight of what looked like an inebriated Keenan walking up behind him. *Oh God, no.*

"Jodie, yeah. She's my sister." Keenan passed Will, elbowing him in the side. "I told you this is where she lives." He pushed the door open wider and walked in. "Hey, Jodie."

Her heart sank. Keenan had gotten into trouble with the police again.

"What happened?" she asked Will, as he walked in behind Keenan.

"I thought it was best I brought him here instead of taking him home in that condition."

"Another run-in with the police?" Jodie asked.

"No. He called and asked me to pick him up."

Keenan had made his way into the kitchen. "Man, you don't have any cold water?" he asked, looking in the refrigerator.

Jodie's jaw dropped. "That's who was on the phone?" she asked in a whisper.

Will nodded.

"Where was he?"

Keenan slammed the refrigerator door. "I need something to drink, man."

Will followed Jodie into the dining room. "Somewhere he had no business being."

She turned around. "Why didn't you tell me it was

him?" she asked, keeping her voice low. "I could have rode with you. He's *my* brother."

"Because he's trying to get me to straighten up and fly right." Keenan stood at attention and saluted Will.

She'd hoped he hadn't heard that.

"Isn't that right, Mr. Duncan?" Keenan laughed and started opening cabinets.

"Keenan, what have we been talking about every week?" Will asked.

Jodie's head quickly turned from Will to Keenan. What were they talking about?

Keenan held onto the cabinet door, but lowered his head. "Having respect for myself."

"So tell me what's happening with you right now?" Will walked around Jodie and stood in the entrance to the cozy kitchen.

Keenan opened and closed the cabinet door with a thud. "Man, I said I messed up. I just wanted everybody to leave me alone, damn."

The conversation between them had Jodie at a loss. She felt like the odd man out in her own place.

"So you went and got high? We've talked about that. Is that any way to solve your problems?" Will continued.

Keenan had given up on finding a glass so Jodie walked into the kitchen, pulled one from the cabinet and filled it with ice and water. The men walked out of the kitchen while she was in there.

Will pulled out the seat across from Keenan. "After a day like today you should be proud of yourself. Why would you want to dull that experience by getting high?"

"I just wanted to be left alone."

Jodie sat the glass of water in front of him. She knew what his problem was; she had predicted it. "Keenan, I'm sorry Lou didn't make it to the game. I'm sure he had a good reason for not showing up. Maybe what's-her-name got sick."

At the mention of Lou's name Keenan's whole body tensed. He turned up the glass of water and finished it in a few gulps. "I don't care nothing 'bout him coming. If it was important to him he would have been there." He shrugged. "Or if I was Corey he'd a been there for sure."

"That's not true." Jodie spoke up in Lou's defense.

"Then tell me why he couldn't come watch his only son play in an all-star game? He never comes to my games, just like you." Keenan stood up and knocked the chair behind him to the floor in the process.

"Keenan, Lou's an alcoholic. He hasn't stopped drinking since you guys left Clifton over ten years ago, and you know that."

"So what, he drinks, a lot of people drink. There were people drinking at the game." He walked out of the dining room and into the living room.

Jodie was right behind him. "Keenan, stop acting like a child. You grew up with that man. You remember him getting drunk and not coming home for days. He hasn't changed, so you might as well quit expecting things from him that he can't give you."

Keenan's face glistened with sweat as he wiped it with the end of his shirt.

Jodie had never seen Keenan behave the way he was tonight. He ranted back and forth across the living room complaining about everything from being compared to Corey, to feeling unwanted in his mom's house. He couldn't wait to go to college and never come back, just like her. Their arguing continued until Keenan became belligerent.

Will finally stepped in. "Keenan," he firmly called his name to get his attention. "Don't talk to your sister like that. The number two rule of Forward Motion is respect for others. And I don't care what you're on right now, I won't let you talk to Jodie like that."

Will walked over and placed a comforting hand on Jodie's back. "Right now you've got two choices. You can lay down and sleep it off, or I can take you home right now."

It didn't take long for Keenan to go and pass out across Jodie's bed.

"Is that what drugs do to you?" she asked.

Will nodded and pulled her closer to him on the couch. "He said he smoked some weed, but I think he's had something else. Maybe that joint was laced with a little PCP, or he got a hold of some crystal meth."

"Oh, God, I heard about that stuff."

"Yeah, it's highly addictive."

She tucked one foot underneath her and snuggled up to him. "How can we tell if he's on that or not?"

"Insomnia's one way. I knew a guy who held two full-time jobs while on that stuff. He worked all the time to support his habit. We had no clue he was using until it started eating away at him. It tears you down."

She took a long deep breath and buried her face in her hands. "I don't want to lose him to drugs."

"He doesn't want to get strung out like that either. That's why he called me. Whatever he took scared him."

"Think we should carry him to the hospital?"

Will shook his head. "Let's just sit tight for a little while."

She thanked God Will wasn't about to leave her there alone with Keenan. She wasn't afraid of him, but she'd heard horror stories about what people did while strung out on drugs. If Keenan woke up crazy and out of his mind she needed Will to help her.

"When he doesn't come in tonight Roz is going to flip out. I'll call and let her know he's sleeping over here. I'll be right back." Jodie took the phone into the bathroom and made the quick and painful call.

When she returned Will sat on the couch with his head back and his eyes closed. "Why were you reciting those Forward Motion rules to Keenan?" Jodie asked, after remembering him doing so.

Will opened his eyes and took a deep breath. "Jodie, I'm Keenan's mentor. He's part of my Forward Motion program."

Her jaw dropped. "When did this happen?" she asked.

"A couple of weeks ago."

"And you weren't going to tell me?" she asked. *How could he do something like that?*

"I've just started working with him about—"

"Whose idea was that?" She couldn't believe Roz would let Keenan work with Will.

"Coach Young called me after the motel incident."

"Does Roz know?"

"She knows he's in a program and he's getting help, yes. But, she doesn't know I'm his mentor. And Jodie, she doesn't have to know. The program does a lot of good things to help athletes just like Keenan. And I'm making progress with him."

She gave him a startled gasp and pointed toward her bedroom. "Is that what you call progress? He's high as a kite."

"I know what he did tonight set him back a bit, but the most important thing is for him to trust that he can talk to me about anything when he needs to."

"He needs a professional counselor. You're not a counselor."

"Each student in our program is paired with a mentor and a counselor. Keenan's started his counseling session already."

Jodie's jaw dropped again. "He's already seeing a counselor?"

Will nodded.

She'd been trying to get Keenan to talk to her and all along he'd been spending time with Will talking to him.

"Why are you doing this?" she asked.

"I feel like I owe it to him."

Jodie looked into Will's sad face, and didn't know how to respond to that.

"Do you know what Roz is gonna do when she finds out?"

"Keenan told me. All hell's going to break loose. But you see, unlike you, I'm not scared of her. There's nothing she can say, or do to me at this point in my life to hurt me."

"I'm not scared of her either, she just…she's just my mother."

Jodie and Will shared a knowing smile as they realized she had called Roz her mother.

"Forget about us, and think about Keenan. He's the one who has to live with her."

"I am thinking about Keenan. Jodie, he's dealing with a lot right now, and he needs to know somebody will be there for him no matter what."

She stood up with her hands on her hips. "I've tried to do that. But he called you tonight instead of me. In just a couple of weeks you've gotten further along with him than I have."

Will stood up and wrapped his arms around her neck and looked into her eyes. "Give him some time to get used to you being back in his life. I believe Keenan feels abandoned, by you and his father."

"Did he tell you that?" she asked, teary-eyed.

"He didn't have to."

Jodie laid her head against Will's chest. Her eyes stung, she was so tired and sleepy, but more than anything she was outdone.

"How long has Keenan been asleep?" Will asked.

"I don't know." Jodie pulled back out of his arms. "What time do you have?"

He looked at his wristwatch. "It's three-forty."

"He went to lay down at about two. You mean we've been talking for almost two hours?"

"Looks like it, but Keenan's still asleep, that's a good sign."

"Or we think he is," she said. "I'll go check."

Jodie walked down to her bedroom and cracked the door open. She heard Keenan snoring, as he lay sprawled across the middle of her bed. Gently, she pulled the door closed and returned to the living room.

Will sat on the couch with his head back and his eyes closed again. Jodie sat beside him. He reached his arm out and pulled her closer. She snuggled up next to him and lay her head against his chest.

He turned and kissed her on the forehead. Then, she fell asleep.

Chapter 24

The bright sun coming through the vertical blinds on Sunday morning woke Jodie. Neither she nor Will had moved in the few hours they'd slept. She lay still for a few minutes listening to him breathe, and feeling the rise and fall of his chest. She wanted to wake him and together they could go climb in her bed. But, Keenan was in there. Instead, she eased his arm from around her shoulder, which caused him to stir a bit, and lifted her sore body from the couch.

She eased down the hall to peek into her bedroom. Keenan lay curled up on one side of the bed snoring like a freight train. After closing the door she went across the hall into the bathroom to shower and get dressed.

As she showered she thought about everything that was happening around her. She'd had sex with the enemy, as far as Roz was concerned anyway. But she didn't care what Roz thought anymore. She wanted Will, even if nothing could ever be between them other than what they had right now, great sex. He obviously wanted her, so she was going to live this fantasy out to the end.

She left the bathroom and checked on Keenan again. He was waking up.

"How do you feel?" she asked, walking into the bedroom. She was still angry with him but glad he hadn't done anything worse like overdosed.

He rolled over on his back. "Like I got hit by a train."

She walked over and opened the blinds. "Yeah, that's about what you look like. Why don't you go get cleaned up? I left a washcloth and a new toothbrush on the sink."

He turned his head away from the bright light and asked, "What did Will say when he left last night?"

"He's still here," Jodie said, as Keenan sat up on the side of the bed.

Keenan looked back at her in surprise. "No shit!"

She nodded.

"Then I guess you know about the mentoring thing?" He wiped the sleep from his eyes and yawned.

"Yeah, I know. I also know about the counselor you never mentioned." She walked around his side of the bed and grabbed a jogging suit from her closet.

"He told you about that?" he asked, sounding surprised. "What else did he tell you?"

"Oh, relax boy, he didn't tell me anything you guys talk about. He just explained the program to me." She threw her jogging suit on the bed. "Now go get cleaned up. I'll fix breakfast and then we need to talk."

He walked out but stopped in the doorway and turned around. "Are you two doing more than working together?" he asked.

"What do you mean?" she asked, trying to look surprised.

"You know what I mean. Is he your man?"

"No," she answered maybe too quickly.

"Yeah, right." He turned and walked across the hall to the bathroom.

Jodie closed her bedroom door and stood with a hand on her hip. What had she done? Did Keenan pick up on something between her and Will? And if he picked up on it, would everybody be able to do the same? She shook her head. "Complications, I don't need any more complications," she mumbled as she changed into her jogging suit.

A few minutes later, she headed back down the hall to cook breakfast. Will was watching television when she entered the living room.

"You're woke," she said cheerfully, hoping and praying he hadn't heard what Keenan asked her. The apartments weren't that big; nor were the walls that thick.

Will stretched his arms over his head and yawned. "Yeah, and my back and neck are killing me. I slept sitting up all night?"

"If you call three or four hours of sleep all night, then yes, you did. So did I. And my body doesn't feel any better."

"Want a massage?" he asked, and winked at her.

She shook her head and went into the kitchen to see

what she had for breakfast, but not before biting her bottom lip to keep from blushing.

"You don't know what you're missing."

"You're probably right," she called out from the kitchen. *Lord, I know he's right.* "What do you want for breakfast?"

"Whatever you're having. How's Keenan?"

"He said he feels like a truck hit him, but he's okay."

Jodie started cooking breakfast and a little while later Keenan came out of the bathroom and Will went in. Jodie wanted to walk over and talk to him so bad, but she feared he'd storm out of the place and they'd never find out what happened to him last night. So, she cooked in silence fighting back the urge to talk.

She was about to put bread in the toaster when the doorbell rang. She glanced up at the clock on the kitchen wall; it was eight o'clock in the morning. She wasn't expecting anybody and Tracy had stayed all night with Lorenzo. Plus, she had a key and wouldn't ring the bell. But then if she saw Will's SUV parked out front, she just might, Jodie thought.

She pushed the toast level down and went to open the door. Without looking out the peephole she turned the knob and pulled the door open.

Dressed for church in a matching pink suit and hat, Roz forced her way in past Jodie. "Where's Keenan?" she demanded.

At the mention of his name, Keenan sat up on the couch. "How did she know I was here?" he asked, looking at Jodie.

Jodie cursed under her breath and glared at Roz. "I

said I would bring him home in the morning, you didn't have to come over here."

"It's morning!" Roz spat out.

Glancing down the hall, Jodie hoped and prayed Will wouldn't come out of the bathroom just yet.

With a quick snap of her head Roz turned her attention to Keenan. "Why didn't you come home last night? What's wrong with you? Have you been getting high again?" She fired off one question after another at Keenan, who held a tight-lipped expression.

Keenan stood up and cut his eyes at Jodie. "Thanks."

"Young man, as long as you are living in my house, and under my roof, you *will* come home *every* night. You're not out on your own yet."

"Yeah, well that's not too far away."

Roz waved a hand toward his bare feet. "Grab your things, I'm taking you home."

He was slow to move, but stopped when he met Will in the hallway.

Roz and Jodie turned and saw him at the same time.

"Damn." Jodie's heart sank. A sickening wave of terror welled in her belly at the realization that Roz was about to say something horrible. She wouldn't be able to help herself. Will didn't look afraid or startled. He merely patted Keenan on the shoulder as they passed.

"Good morning, Mrs. Roberts," he said in a nice professional voice.

Jodie thought Roz's eyes would pop from their sockets. Then her lips tightened, practically disappearing, as she stared hard and long at Will.

He continued into the small living room that definitely wasn't big enough for the both of them. Fearful he would offer his hand to Roz and get it bitten off, Jodie stepped between them.

"Before you say something you'll regret later, you should thank Will for—"

"Thank him for what?" Roz roared.

"He may have saved Keenan's life last night," Jodie pronounced, before realizing the significance in her choice of words.

"Jodie." Will reached out for her arm and tried to stop her.

"How?" Roz asked, looking as if she were about to explode. "The man's a killer. He drove that car off the road and right into a tree killing my son." Her eyes began to well with tears as the veins in her neck swelled.

"He killed him before he had a chance to grow into a man. Before he could show the world just how talented he was. Corey was supposed to be a professional football player."

The crazed look in Roz's eyes scared Jodie. Roz was out of control. Jodie tried to get a word in, but Roz wouldn't stop. Will reached down and squeezed Jodie's hand.

With her arms folded protectively in front of her, Roz turned away from them and walked across the living room. "I sat in that hospital room and held my baby's hand until he left this world. And that never should have happened." She reached the patio door and spun around. "And he knows it never should have happened." She pointed at Will. "That's how I know he killed my baby."

Jodie let go of Will's hand and started across the room as Roz started to cry. She shook her head as Jodie approached.

"Mrs. Roberts, you're right. I am partially to blame for the accident. And I'm sorry," Will said.

Jodie snapped her head around toward Will. "What are you talking about? It was an accident," she declared.

He nodded. "Yeah, but I was the driver. I'm the one who drove off that road into the tree."

"Will, you swerved to miss an oncoming car." Jodie didn't understand what he was trying to do. "That car came into your lane, you had no choice."

Keenan came storming through the living room past everyone. "I'm sick of hearing about Corey," he screamed, and yanked open the front door. "He's dead, just leave it alone." He slammed the door behind him.

Dead silence filled the room for a few seconds.

Will walked out the door behind him.

As soon as he left Roz spoke up. "I don't want him anywhere near my son, do you hear me?" Roz narrowed her now dry eyes at Jodie.

"You're a witch, you know that?" Jodie could hardly stand the sight of this woman who called herself her mother. "I can't believe you would say those things to his face. Not that they made good dinner conversation when we were growing up. But by now I would have thought you'd outgrown trying to hurt people."

"The man killed your brother! What part of that don't you understand?" Roz exploded.

"It was an accident!" Jodie screamed back. "You can't blame him for that. For over fifteen years you've told anybody who would listen how Will killed Corey. But it's not true. You can't do that to that man."

"Well, you seem to be more worried about him than what he did to your family." Roz narrowed her eyes and gave Jodie a disgusted look. "You must be sleeping with him. Is that how you cherish your dead brother's memory, by having sex with that man?"

Jodie squeezed her fist at her side to keep from slapping Roz. "I've done nothing to tarnish Corey's memory. Will was his best friend."

"And now he's yours. Is that what you're telling me?"

"No, I was only trying to explain that he helped Keenan last night, but you wouldn't let me finish."

"Well, we don't need his help anymore. He's done quite enough for this family." Roz turned to leave. She stopped at the open door and looked back over her shoulder. "And I'm not a witch. I'm a mother who does whatever she has to, to protect her family." She slammed the door on her way out.

Jodie ran over and yanked the door open. She stepped out and looked into the parking space where Will's SUV had been parked. It was empty.

It took three days for him to fess up, but Keenan finally admitted to Roz that William Duncan was his mentor. Roz wanted to die. When Marion and Coach Young told her about a program that would better Keenan's chances of getting a scholarship she was so happy she didn't check the program out like she should have.

She sat at the kitchen table smoking a cigarette

when Marion walked in. He was late again. When he saw her sitting there by herself, he curiously glanced around the room.

"What's wrong?" he asked.

She took a long sweet draw from the cigarette and blew it out at a slow steady pace, to calm her nerves.

Marion threw his car keys on the kitchen table and shrugged out of his suit coat. The same suit she'd bought for him less than three months ago, that was already getting tight.

"You just gonna sit there, or would you like to let me know what's going on now?" he asked, then turned away.

She snuffed out her cigarette in the ashtray and blew the last bit of smoke out the side of her mouth. "You lied to me," she finally said.

Marion had walked over to the refrigerator, and held the door open staring at her. "Woman, what are you talking about? I've never lied to you about anything."

"What kind of program is it that you and Coach Young talked me into putting Keenan in?"

Marion shrugged. "A mentoring program I guess, why?"

"Do you know who he's working with?"

After grabbing a bottle of beer and closing the door, Marion sighed tiredly holding the bottle to the back of his neck. "No, I don't, but I'm sure you're about to tell me. Do I need to sit down?"

She crossed her arms and looked at her little potbellied husband. Marion was a great provider, but he'd never treated Keenan like his own son.

"Yes, come sit down. I want to tell you a story."

"Is this going to take a long time? Because I have a stack of paperwork I need to do before bed."

She pulled out the chair next to hers, and patted the seat. "No, it won't. I want you to understand who's been mentoring our son."

In as calm a fashion as she could, Roz told Marion about the day her firstborn left this world. For the umpteenth time she went into detail explaining the who, what, when, where and why of the automobile accident. She pointed out that William Duncan took her baby's life.

"The same William Duncan that has been mentoring Keenan for the last couple of weeks."

Marion looked like he did when he was staring into the faces of the poor in his district, and Roz hated that patronizing look.

"Baby." He reached across the table and took her hand in his. "I thought the police report said that was an accident?"

She snatched her hand back. "You never saw the police report," she snapped. "Besides, I don't care what it said. I want Keenan out of that program. I don't want him working with that man."

Marion took a deep breath and ran his hand across his face. "Coach Young spoke very highly of the program. Maybe we can give it—"

"No! I'm not going to give him time to kill another one of my sons. We don't need his help. Keenan is going to get a scholarship anyway. The phones been ringing off the hook with recruiters calling."

"Roz." Marion reached out and took her hand again.

"Let's talk about this in the morning after I've had some sleep, and you've had time to think about it." He stood up. "The mentor wasn't working on improving Keenan's basketball skills."

"I've thought it over," Roz replied, reaching for her pack of cigarettes. "I'm taking him out of that program tomorrow."

Marion took a deep breath and squared his shoulders. "In this house we make those kind of decisions together. Now we'll talk about this in the morning. I've got work to do." He picked up his suit jacket and walked through the kitchen into his study.

Roz watched him leave as she held up a slightly trembling hand and lit another cigarette. The vein in her temple throbbed as she took the first long drag and held her breath. She closed her eyes and exhaled slowly until the trembling stopped.

Seconds later, she walked over and picked up the cordless phone sitting in the center of the kitchen island. She punched in Jodie's number and waited until the answering machine turned on. At the sound of the beep, she cleared her throat and left her middle child a message.

Chapter 25

Lying naked with her head on Will's chest listening to the strong thump of his heartbeat was exactly where Jodie wanted to be right now. She'd just experienced the most satisfying thirty minutes of her life. After their first time, she didn't think sex between them could be any better, but every night this week he'd proved her wrong. So she lay there with a silly smile on her face thinking about how long she'd waited for a moment like this with him.

"What are you thinking about?" she asked him.

"Nothing really. What were you thinking about?" he asked, as he caressed her bottom.

"If Stone could see us now I wonder what he'd say."

Will chuckled, shaking the bed slightly. "He'd say, I knew it."

Jodie propped up on one elbow and looked into his eyes. "You're kidding?"

He shook his head and squeezed her butt cheeks. "Sorry, baby, but I think he knows already."

"How do you know for sure? Did he say something?"

He turned to look at Jodie, smiling, and reached out to move her hair away from her face. "No, but trust me he knows how I feel about you. It's just something a man picks up on."

She positioned her chin on his chest a few inches from his nipple and asked, "How's that?"

He reached around to affectionately pinch her nose between his fingers. "Like I've found something I've been searching for all my life. Before you walked into that studio I had the show, and the Foundation to look forward to, but something was still missing. Now—" he shifted so he could look directly into her eyes.

"I look forward to seeing you every morning. Spending the whole day, and whenever possible, the night with you. I love it when you smile. It makes my day. When you're happy, I'm happy. When you're sad, I'm sad."

He didn't speak for the next couple of seconds, but continued to stare longingly into her eyes. Jodie swallowed the constricting lump in her throat.

Her eyes widened. "Wow, Stone can sense all that?"

Will threw his head back laughing.

She hadn't expected anything that came out of his mouth so she didn't know what to say. The possibility of him caring that much for her was beyond her wildest dreams. What she had with Will was great sex, but that was it.

His laughter died down and he must have noticed the confused look on her face because he reached over and kissed her on the forehead.

"Don't worry about it. We don't have to tell anybody until you're ready."

"Maybe there isn't anything to tell."

He lay back on his pillow and took a deep breath. "What's that supposed to mean?"

"Will, I enjoy being with you. And I'm not going to lie. The sex is great. I just don't know if we should take this any further."

He nodded. "Mind if I ask why not?"

"You know why. Our lives would be hell. I couldn't put you through that."

"Jodie, let me tell you a little story. My parents got married when they were nineteen years old, against my grandfather's wishes. He wanted a college-educated man for my mother. My father worked for his father in a grocery store in upstate New York. After they were married my grandfather wouldn't speak to them until my oldest brother Kenny was born. He eventually got over her marrying him and now calls my dad son."

"Yeah, but how old is your grandfather?"

"Somewhere in his eighties now, but he gets around like a sixty-year-old man."

Jodie rolled over on top of Will and straddled him. She looked down into his beautiful black eyes and smiled. "I don't think she'll be calling you son anytime soon."

He reached out for her thighs and pushed her down his body until she felt something hard against her bottom. Then he grabbed her waist and lifted her up and onto his growing erection. Pleased, she smiled down at him.

"What I was getting at," he said, as he briefly closed his eyes and positioned her right where he wanted her, "is that she'll get over it."

"Never in a million years," Jodie responded.

She started to gently rock her body back and forth over his rising mound as he lay there with his eyes closed and a smile on his face.

"You know I used to try and please other people all the time. Not wanting to ruffle any feathers. Then you come along and now I'm willing to ruffle some feathers."

She stopped and his eyes sprang open. "A football player afraid to ruffle feathers?"

"Who said I was afraid? I didn't because emotionally I knew it would cost me too much. But if being with you means dealing with this thing head-on, then that's what I gotta do. You see, I need more than just great sex from you. And believe me, the sex is great," he said, with a smile.

She laughed and started the gentle rocking again while his big hands gripped her waist and guided her. He was enormous now and ready for round two.

"What do you want from me, Jodie?" he asked, as his hands moved up to caress her breasts.

She knew what she needed from him—love. Only she didn't know if she was capable of handling it right now.

She leaned forward and whispered, "I want you to make love to me."

He licked those beautiful full lips of his and smiled.

* * *

After an uneventful Sunday, where Jodie slept most of the day away, she was well rested and ready for Monday morning. With her cup of caffe latte in hand she pulled open the big red door of Gator House Productions with a smile on her face. It was amazing what new lighting and furniture had done for the reception area. She was getting used to the new duds now.

"Buenos dias." Manny greeted her in his new Hispanic accent.

"What happened to the Italian?" she asked. Last week he even had her saying *ciao* to everyone.

"That was too hard to learn," Manny said, with a wave of his hand. "Besides, the second language of the United States is going to be Spanish anyway."

"Oh, it is?"

"Honey I went to Miami last year and thought I was in Mexico somewhere. Being bilingual is a necessity there, and out west. And I have no intentions of hanging around Memphis all my life."

"The acting lessons are your ticket out of here, huh?" She remembered him saying that on more than one occasion.

"Si," he said, as his face lit up.

She held up her cup to him. "Good luck." She turned to open the door to the inner offices when Manny stood up.

"Oh, I almost forgot. Jeffrey came in early this morning to drop off some stuff. He has a meeting this morning with his lawyer. He's trying to get joint custody of his son, you know."

"Man, she's really going to divorce him, isn't she?"

"Honey, that woman had her another man a long time ago. Jeffrey should have taken his ass home more often. I don't know why these men spend all their time at work and then wonder why their women are having affairs."

"Neither do I, Manny." She pulled the door open.

"Anyway," Manny continued. "Jeffrey said the bio and some other things about this week's guests are on his desk. I would have retrieved it for you, but, honey, I'm not setting foot in his office. Something might crawl out from under that mess and bite me."

She laughed at the animated gestures. "Oh, it's not that bad."

"What! Honey, Mr. Stone won't even go in there."

"I'll stop in and pick it up," she said, still laughing. "Have a good morning." She shook her head as she walked away.

"I always do," he yelled out. "Uh—*Adios, hasta luego.*"

She threw her hand up and waved. "Whatever, Manny," she whispered under her breath.

Jeffrey's office was on the way to her office, so she stopped there first. On top of his desk was a mound of paper and folders scattered everywhere. Coffee stains covered half the folders, and a napkin with a half-eaten sandwich sat on top of another. She understood what Manny meant now.

She found a spot on the desk to set her coffee down, and then put her purse in his chair, while she rummaged through the folders. Most of the manila folders had names scribbled on their tabs, but one particular stack had a *Memphis Zone* paperweight on top.

The red folders had always contained guests' information. She moved the paperweight aside and took the red folder from the stack.

"Living dangerously aren't you?"

Jodie looked up and smiled at Leta standing in the doorway. "I guess you could say I'm adventurous."

"You most certainly are. Not many people have the balls to venture into Jeffrey's cave."

Jodie tucked the folder under her arm and set the paperweight back on top. "I had to risk it. I needed the information on this week's guests and Jeffrey had an appointment this morning."

"His attorney, yeah I know. Manny's told everybody."

Jodie shook her head, picked up her coffee and purse, and walked out.

"You can't have any secrets around here," Leta said as she walked with Jodie down the hall. "Not if meddling Manny gets wind of it anyway. He can't keep anything to himself for more than an hour."

Jodie glanced over at Leta. Was she talking about her and Will? Did she know about them? Or was Jodie being too paranoid?

Leta smiled at her. "So be careful what you say to him, unless of course you want it to get out. Not everybody needs to know your business, if you know what I mean." She stopped talking once they reached her office.

Jodie searched Leta's face for any sign that she knew

about her and Will, but she didn't think she detected anything. "Thanks for the warning. I thought Manny was cool."

"Oh, he is. He's just got a big mouth."

If Leta had suspected something Jodie was glad she at least had the decency not to say anything.

Instead of going to her own office, Jodie kept walking down the hall until she stood outside of Will's office. The door was closed. His door was never closed.

She knocked.

"Come in."

She glanced up and down the little hallway first, and then eased the door open. "Knock, knock," she said.

Will stopped writing and closed the folder in front of him. He sat up grinning as she walked in.

She pushed the door up behind her, but didn't close it all the way. "You know, you don't have to close your door around here," she said, with a mocking smile. "We're a pretty close-knit group."

He laughed. "Cute."

She walked over and took a seat across from his desk. Then moved the folder from under her arm to her lap, while balancing her coffee and purse. "What you up to this morning?" she asked, relaxing back into the chair.

"Just making some notes. Nothing really. I closed my door to keep Manny out. I lose my train of thought every time he comes in and I have to start all over."

"Then I'm disturbing you?" she said, sitting up.

"You never disturb me," he assured her with a wicked grin. "I always have time for you."

Okay, he was making her blush again, and this morning she wanted to keep her mind on work. "I'm about to go over everything for this week's guests. Just wondered if there's anything I should know before I get started?"

He thought a moment and shook his head. "Nothing in particular that I can think of. We can cover all the details in the staff meeting as usual."

"Great," she said standing up.

"You know, Keenan stood me up Saturday and I haven't heard from him yet."

"Will, I'm not sure, but I think Roz took him out of the program." She wanted to tell him about the nasty-gram Roz left on her voice mail the other day, but to do so would have been too embarrassing.

He leaned back in his seat and glanced up at the ceiling. "I was afraid of that, but I'd hoped Coach Young would have been able to talk her out of it."

"She's stubborn. You can't talk her out of anything once her mind's made up."

"Hmm, sounds like somebody else I know," he said.

Jodie's eyes widened. "I know you aren't talking about me?"

"Of course not," he assured her, shaking his head. He stood up and came around his desk.

She playfully rolled her eyes at him. "Because I know I'm not stubborn."

"Not at all," he said, taking the folder from her hand and sitting it on his desk. He backed up against the desk and pulled her closer, positioning her between his legs, and kissed her on the forehead.

"Meet me at Zanzibar's tonight after work?"

"I'll be here pretty late tonight," she said.

"That's okay." He bent down and kissed the tip of her nose. "I'll wait for you."

"What if I'm here until eleven o'clock tonight?"

"Don't be." His head moved lower until his lips met hers.

His lips parted hers and his tongue quickly entered her mouth on an exploring expedition. Jodie's head swam from the unexpected dose of excitement this morning. She loved his mouth, and she loved being kissed by him. He put his whole body, mind and soul into every kiss. His hands caressed her back and tugged her blouse from the waistband of her slacks. Then his warm hands slid up her back causing her whole body to shiver in response.

She heard herself moan as she opened her mouth wider wanting, and needing more of him. She spread her legs wider as he positioned his thigh between them.

Then there was a knock at the door. Jodie jumped back and pulled herself away from Will. Frowning, he let out a deep sigh and stood up. After grabbing her coffee and purse, she glanced up at him.

Another knock at the door, harder and faster this time.

"Come in," Will called out, still sitting against his desk.

The door opened and Larry Stone walked in with a troubled look on his face. The way his gaze darted from Jodie to Will, and back to Jodie again, made her face flush.

"Will, if you've got a minute I want to talk to you about something." Stone turned from Will, giving Jodie a sidelong glance.

"You two weren't in the middle of anything, were you?" he asked her.

Nervous as hell, she shook her head and reached out for the folder on the edge of Will's desk. "No, I was just leaving." She walked toward the door. "Will, uh, we can talk about the show later, after I read this." She held up the red folder.

"Sure thing," he said, smiling like he'd scored a touchdown.

She turned around and walked out of the office closing the door behind her.

Stone watched Jodie's back as she left, and then turned, raising one eyebrow in a questioning slant toward Will. "What's going on between you two?"

Will pushed away from his desk and walked back to his seat. Unless he cleared things up right now, they could get progressively worse. He took a deep breath. "Stone, have a seat."

"Oh, no. It's never good whenever you ask me to have a seat." As he said that, he sat down.

Will didn't know where to start. "I need to tell you something I should have told you over a month ago."

"What's that?" Stone asked, leaning back in his chair scratching his head.

"I'm not sure where to begin," Will said, as he leaned forward, laced his fingers together and placed both elbows on his desk. He took another deep breath to collect his thoughts.

Stone clasped his hands behind his head. "I'm all ears," he said.

Will shrugged and held his hands up gesturing

helplessly. "I guess I'll start at the beginning." He sat back comfortably. "You know I graduated from Clifton High School."

Stone nodded, encouraging Will to continue.

"Well, what you don't know is…" Will recalled how he and Jodie met and how their working relationship had turned into something much more than he intended it to.

Chapter 26

Jodie hurried down the hall and rushed into her office, closing the door behind her. *Oh my God!* She held a hand over her mouth wondering if Stone and Will were talking about them. No doubt Stone realized he'd caught them doing something they shouldn't have been doing. Will was right, he knew something was up.

She walked over and set everything down on her desk, which only looked a fraction better than Jeffrey's, she concluded. Embarrassed by the mess, and unable to concentrate on anything other than what had just happened, she decided to clean up a little before sitting down.

When she bent over to open a bottom drawer she felt a slight breeze on her back. Immediately she stood straight up and reached behind her back touching where Will had pulled her blouse out.

Oh God, I'm going to lose my job.

After nervously cleaning and sorting everything in her office, she sat down to read her e-mail. Stone hadn't come in or called her into his office yet, so she tried to relax.

It didn't take long to plow through the few pieces of mail she had. Then she pulled over the red folder and flipped it open. This week's guest was supposed to be a local sports analyst, but there was nothing in the folder about him.

Instead, Jodie found herself looking at a copy of an article about the Clifton High Wildcats. Stunned, she read the article that highlighted the unstoppable talents of Corey Dickerson, captain of the fighting wildcats, and William Duncan his cocaptain.

Memories of huddling under a blanket on the bleachers watching Corey running down the field resurfaced in her mind. She flipped the article over to find several more from various newspapers on Corey. What was Jeffrey doing with these, she wondered.

She turned the article over and found separate five-by-sevens of Corey and Will. Her eyes moistened and she blinked to hold back the tears. Where had Jeffrey gotten the pictures?

On another sheet of paper were handwritten notes about Corey's career, and the accident that took his life. Reading the notes caused Jodie's stomach to tighten into a ball. She couldn't stop until she'd read the whole thing. By then, the tears were rolling down her cheek and she reached for a tissue.

After a soft tap, the door to her office slowly opened.

Jeffrey walked in holding another red folder. He immediately noticed she'd been crying.

"Jodie, I uh, I think I have the folder here you were looking for." He held it up as he walked in.

She wiped the tears from her eyes, and held up the picture of Corey. "Where did you get this?" she asked, sniffling.

He closed the door behind him. "I was afraid you'd picked up that folder," he confessed.

"What is all this, Jeffrey? You've been doing research on my brother? What for?"

"It's supposed to be a surprise," he replied as he walked over to her desk. "I've been working a special project for Will. But now I've blown the whole surprise." He ran a hand over his head and took a deep breath, blowing out hard.

"See what all this divorce mess is doing to me. I can't even think straight anymore. I meant to take that folder with me today, instead of this one." He tossed the red folder he'd walked in with onto her desk.

Jodie wiped her tears away, and she wanted answers. "What do you mean it's a surprise?" she asked skeptically.

"Will has a special season finale planned. I'm not supposed to discuss it with anyone. Can we swap?" Jeffrey asked, reaching for her folder.

Jodie slowly closed the folder and handed it to him. "Jeffrey, I need to know about this special. If it's going to air on *The Memphis Zone,* I think you'd better tell me what's planned."

Jeffrey took another deep breath and sat down. "I don't know. Will's going to kill me."

"And I won't?" she asked, hoping to scare him into talking.

"Promise you won't tell Will?"

"Give me all the details, and I'll let you know whether I need to address Will or not. What he has planned affects me, and my family. I need to know about it."

Jeffrey nodded. "You're right." He sat back and told Jodie as much as he knew.

Afterwards, she didn't know what to say.

"Let's not mention to anyone that I saw that folder, or you told me anything."

"You serious?" Jeffrey asked.

Jodie nodded. "I won't say anything. Not yet anyway."

After what happened between Roz and Will, Jodie wondered if he'd lost his mind.

In one week it looked as if Will lost Keenan and Jodie. Keenan missed their regular Wednesday mentoring session and Jodie called in ill the same day. Something had went down, but he didn't know what.

He tried Jodie's home phone all day, and left messages on both cell phones. She had to be getting the messages, but she never called back.

Frustrated, he rode by her apartment Thursday evening. He didn't see her car parked out front, but walked up and rang the bell anyway.

Tracy answered the door. "Hey, Will, what's going on?"

"Hi, Tracy, is Jodie home?"

"No, she hasn't been here all day."

He nodded and thought for a second. "You think she's over at her mother's?"

Tracy chuckled. "I doubt it. You know the two of them aren't speaking right now. Jodie avoids that house like the plague."

"Well, she's called in sick for the past two days." He gave Tracy a questioning glance. "If she was sick she'd be in bed, right?"

Tracy shrugged and held the door open wider. "Hey Jodie's my girl, and if she says she's sick, she's sick. But she's not here. You're welcome to come in and see for yourself."

He shook his head. "I believe you. Well, when she comes in tell her I stopped by, and that I've left her several messages."

"I sure will."

"Thanks." Will turned to walk away.

Tracy started closing the door, and then pulled it back open. "Will," she called out.

He stopped on the first step and turned around. "Yeah."

"Jodie's not sick. She's just hurt."

"What happened to her?" he asked, fearful she'd been in an accident.

Tracy pressed her palm against her chest. "She's hurt here. I don't know what happened between you two, and that's none of my business. But my girl's been moping around this place for the last two days in a deep funk."

He leaned against the railing, confused. "Nothing's happened between us. I don't get it."

"Something's happened. She won't tell me what it

is, but I know Jodie, and her feelings are hurt. Did you say something to piss her off?"

He shook his head. "No."

"Then you know how we women are, maybe it's something you didn't say or do."

He snorted. "Jodie's not like that. If I did something wrong, or didn't do something, as you say, she'd be quick to let me know. Naw, that's not it. But, can you do me a favor?" he asked.

"Call you when she comes in?" she guessed.

"If you don't mind? Call my cell phone. The number's on your caller ID."

"Yeah, I know." She twisted her lips as if she was giving it some thought. "She'll be mad at me."

"She'll get over it."

"Um, I suppose I could hit redial by mistake and ring your number."

"That's good enough. Thanks. I'll owe you one."

"Good. I'ma remember and hold you to that."

He nodded and turned to leave. "No problem."

Will went home and spent the rest of the night working on the season finale show. His phone never rang.

Manny passed the doughnuts Friday morning, as everyone sat around the conference table discussing last-minute changes to the show.

Then the door squeaked as Jodie walked in. She looked hot as hell in a low-cut blue-and-white dress. Will wanted to leap from his seat at the sight of her, but remained cool, sitting with his hands folded in front of him.

The only available seat in the room was directly across from him. She walked in and sat down.

"Sorry I'm late," she said.

"Hope you're feeling better?" Stone asked.

"I am. Thanks."

"Good, because we had a last-minute cancellation and Will's revised the script." Stone slid the revised script to Jodie.

Will watched her nod to everyone at the table until she glanced in his direction. A brief, "Hey, Will," and then she lowered her head to the script.

She set her coffee cup down and took the doughnut box when it came her way. This was the first time he'd even seen her accept a doughnut.

"Okay, the sports analyst we've secured to replace Walter Jewel is Ron Kowalski. Ron's a whiz at high school sports and should be able to step right in," Stone reported.

During the meeting Will racked his brain trying to figure out what he'd said or done to Jodie. When she walked out of his office Tuesday morning everything was cool between them. What happened after that, he had no idea.

At the conclusion of the meeting Will walked around the table where Stone and Jodie stood talking.

"Well, I'm glad you're back with us. This guy didn't know what to do while you were out," Stone said, pointing to Will as he approached.

"I took care of a couple of issues by phone and—"

"You never returned my call," Will spoke up.

Jodie turned and looked up at Will. "Excuse me, Larry, but can I speak to Will alone a moment?"

Stone's brows shot up. "Sure. I'll be in my office if either of you need me."

Will waited until the door closed and sat on the edge of the conference table. "How come you can call everybody else back, but you can't call me?"

"Will, we need to talk."

He held his arms out. "I'm all yours. What's up?"

She set her script and tablet down on the table. "I've been doing a lot of thinking, and this thing we've started, it's not going to work."

This thing! He crossed his arms and snickered. "It's not, huh?"

She threw her head back and sighed. "No. And I hope there won't be any hard feelings if we just continue our working relationship and not try to complicate matters."

He wanted to bust out laughing in her face. Who was she kidding? He could see in her eyes that she didn't believe a word she was saying. "Is that why you called in sick the last two days?"

She quickly shook her head. "I really didn't feel well, so I took the time off. Stone was cool with it."

"That's because he thought you were really sick."

She glanced all around the room looking everywhere but directly into his eyes. "Well, I'm back now, and I just want to get to work." She picked up the script. "Is there anything in here I need to be made aware of?"

He stood up. "No, not really."

She nodded and held her hand out to him. "Friends?"

He took her hand reluctantly, unable to believe she was blowing him off like this.

"You know we'll always be friends."

They worked the rest of the day managing to avoid one another by using interns and P.A.'s to deliver messages back and forth.

After the show wrapped, instead of going to Click's with the rest of the crew, Will went home.

Chapter 27

Outside the rumble of a strong storm and heavy rain pelting against the window helped Jodie to sleep like a baby. She woke once to use the bathroom, then crawled back in bed hoping to return to her erotic pleasant dreams.

Hours later, ripped from a sound sleep in the middle of a dream she sprang up in bed and in a panic reached for the phone on the nightstand. Then remembered that by choice, she didn't have a phone in her bedroom.

"Jodie."

"What? Yeah?" She threw back the cover. "Who is it?" she asked, groping for her house shoes.

"Jodie, telephone. Hurry up, it's an emergency."

Half disoriented she recognized Tracy's voice. She pulled her house shoes on and ran over to open the closet door. Wrong door.

By then, Tracy had entered the bedroom and shoved the phone at her. "Here, I think it's Roz."

Jodie closed the closet door and reached for the phone. She shook her head to wake herself up. "What time is it?" she asked.

"After two a.m. Answer it," Tracy urged.

Jodie sat down on the side of her bed hoping Roz wasn't about to deliver another nasty-gram, especially at this hour.

"Hello," she said, after taking a long deep breath. After a few seconds, her eyes widened and she jumped up.

Tracy was still standing there with her arms crossed protectively over her chest. But she dropped them the moment Jodie stood up.

"What hospital is he in?" Jodie asked, as her heart slammed against her chest.

Tracy's hand flew over her mouth.

"What were they doing?" Jodie ran back over to her closet and pulled out a pair of jeans and a top.

"Okay, okay, I'm on my way." She hung up and tossed the phone on the bed.

"What happened?" Tracy quickly asked.

"Keenan was in a car accident. He's in the hospital." She talked and stripped at the same time, changing clothes.

"Is he okay?"

Jodie shrugged. "I don't know. Roz was crying so I couldn't make out everything she said."

"Let me get dressed, I'll drive you." Tracy hurried out of the bedroom and down the hall.

Jodie's pounding heart rang in her ears as she ran into the bathroom to brush her teeth and wash her face. All she could think about was Corey and the afternoon the call came that he'd been in an accident. By the time she reached the hospital he was dead.

Roz had to be about to lose her mind, Jodie thought. The anniversary of Corey's death was a few weeks away and on everybody's mind.

"I'm ready." Tracy stood in the doorway in a jogging suit and baseball cap with her purse on her shoulder.

Running her fingers through her hair, Jodie grabbed her purse and they left for the hospital.

The rain had stopped but the roads were slick. According to the DJ on the radio, car accidents were happening all over Memphis.

Jodie and Tracy ran down the hospital corridor looking around wildly until they found Marion and Roz huddled together in a waiting room. Marion held Roz in his arms as she sniffled into his shirt.

"How's Keenan?" Jodie asked, as she approached them.

Roz raised her head, looking at Jodie with bloodshot, tearstained eyes. "He's in critical condition." Her face fell back onto her husband's chest.

Tracy took a seat and crossed her legs. Jodie sat down next to her. Her stomach was one big knot and she could feel her heart pumping spastically.

A Mexican family at the other end of the waiting room were laughing and joking about something. Jodie watched them thinking whoever they were here to see couldn't be in too bad a condition. She listened to them talk and wondered what they were saying. Manny would know, she thought.

Jodie turned her attention back to Roz. "Who was he with?" she asked.

Marion answered. "We don't know the other young men. The driver was pinned in the car. He's in critical condition too. The boys in the backseat have a few bumps and bruises, but they're all right."

"Was Keenan wearing his seat belt?" she asked.

Roz started crying softly.

"Yeah, all of them had their seat belts on," Marion volunteered.

"Thank God," she said.

They sat there in silence for a few moments watching the Mexican family at the other end chase two little girls around the waiting room. The door to the waiting room opened and a police officer walked in. The two little Mexican girls ran up to him grabbing at his leg. He smiled as their mother walked over and spanked their bottoms until they let go.

Once he was free, the officer continued across the room headed right for them. Jodie sat up straight. This couldn't be good news.

"Mr. and Mrs. Roberts?" he addressed Marion and Roz.

"Yes," Marion spoke up.

"I'm Officer Dave Weiss. I wanted to talk to you a moment about your son."

"What?" Roz asked, nearly jumping from her seat. "Don't tell me you want to lock him up. He's in critical condition for God's sake." She started crying again.

Officer Weiss held out a hand and lowered himself into the seat next to Roz's. "No, ma'am."

"What's this about, Officer?" Marion asked.

"I was one of the officers at the accident scene. We found marijuana and alcohol in the car. I don't know who had what, but I believe all four boys were intoxicated and high."

Roz continued to cry.

"How do you know if Keenan had anything if he's in critical condition?" Marion asked.

"There were lit joints in the car and opened bottles of alcohol spilled all over."

Marion lowered his head and wiped his hand across his forehead. "I don't know what else to do for that boy," he said.

Jodie sat listening to all this as Officer Weiss glanced at her and Tracy, smiled, then turned back to Roz and Marion. Keenan was in big trouble this time.

"I wanted to speak with you because I recognized your son. Several weeks ago we busted up a couple of young folks having a motel party. Keenan was one of them."

Marion and Roz looked at the officer for a couple of seconds and shifted in their seats. Officer Weiss was going to tell them about the motel incident and calling Will. Jodie stood up and excused herself, pretending she had to make an important call.

The officer started to fill them in as Jodie left the waiting room. Outside in the hall, she flipped open her cell phone and dialed Will. She wasn't calling him for herself, she was calling him for Keenan. He needed to be in Will's program, no matter what Roz said.

Will answered on the fourth ring. "Hello," he said, in a deep groggy voice.

"Will, it's Jodie. I'm sorry for calling so late, but Keenan was in an accident, and I'm at the hospital, and this police officer just walked in, and—"

"Whoa, whoa, slow down. Wait a minute."

She stopped and took a shaky deep breath and walked over to another waiting room to pace the floor.

"Okay, start over. What happened and where are you?"

"I'm at Baptist Memorial Hospital. Keenan was in a car accident. Now he's in critical condition."

"Are you all right?"

"Yes…no…I mean I'm a nervous wreck. And now there's a policeman in the waiting room talking to Marion and Roz. He said his name is Officer Weiss, and he's telling them about the motel incident."

"Great," Will said sarcastically.

"He's about to bring your name up if he hasn't already. I don't know what I'm going to tell them."

"Don't worry, I'm on my way down there."

"No, I didn't mean to pull you back into this. I just wanted you to know because Roz has threatened to sue you. I'll…I'll say something."

"Jodie, I'm not going to let you push me away again. I'm on my way."

She hung up, dropped the phone in her lap, and covered her face with her hands. No doubt the officer had told them about calling Will and Roz had put two and two together that Jodie knew all about it, but hadn't told them. She dreaded walking back into that waiting room.

The minute she took her hands down she spotted Lou and Cee Cee rushing down the hall. Behind him was her aunt Lucille whom she hadn't seen in years. She'd actually thought Lucille moved away from the area.

"Jodie, how's Keenan?" Lou asked, as he reached her.

She stood up. "He's in critical condition, that's all I know right now. Everybody's in the waiting room down the hall." She pointed in the direction of the last waiting room.

"Okay, come on." Lou took Cee Cee's hand and hurried her down the hall with him.

Lucille stayed behind with Jodie. Dressed in a bright colored muumuu to camouflage her over-two-hundred-pound body, Lucille held her arms out to hug Jodie. "How you holding up, kid?" she asked.

Jodie smiled and attempted to hug Lucille back. "I'm okay."

Lucille looked at Jodie with downcast features, shaking her head. "It's a shame ain't it? Almost the same time his brother died. I been thinking about Corey all week, too."

That did it. Jodie sat down and the tears poured from her eyes. Lucille took the seat next to her and pulled Jodie into her breast. They cried together.

Several minutes later, the doctor walked into the waiting room where Jodie and Lucille had joined everyone else, but stayed on one end of the waiting room. Where the Mexican family had left. Tracy sat across from them.

The doctor informed them that Keenan had a fractured skull, and a couple of cracked ribs, but he would recover. He asked Roz and Lou to come with him. Keenan was coming around and asked for them. Ahead of Lou, Roz followed the doctor out.

"He's out of the woods, that's great," Tracy said.

"Yeah, but wait until he gets a load of Roz and Lou in there at the same time, he'll probably go into heart failure," Jodie remarked.

"But Lou's here," Tracy added. "That should make Keenan feel better."

Jodie smiled at her. "Yeah, you're right. It will."

The door to the waiting room opened and Will walked in.

Jodie leapt from her seat and practically ran into his arms. He hugged her and kissed her on the cheek.

"Are you okay?" he asked.

She nodded. On the phone she'd told him not to come, but now she realized how much she wanted and needed him in her life.

"Will, I'm sorry." She started to cry again.

"Don't worry about it. I've already forgiven you. I just wanted to be here for you."

Everyone in the room knew who Will was. Jodie pulled him over to sit next to her.

Lucille crossed her legs and turned in the direction away from them. Marion, on his cell phone now, noticed Will but kept talking. Cee Cee sat on the other side of Lucille looking nervous. Tracy was the only one in the room who spoke to Will.

While they waited, Jodie told him everything the doctor said about Keenan. Officer Weiss had left the room, but was probably still somewhere in the hospital.

After a few minutes Will said, "Let's go get some coffee or something."

The minute they walked out of the waiting room they came face to face with Roz and Lou. Will's arm was around Jodie and he squeezed her tighter the second she started to pull away. She didn't want to cause a scene in the hospital, and she knew Roz lived to perform scenes.

The four of them looked at each other for a few seconds, each one seeming afraid to break the ice.

"Mr. Dickerson, Mrs. Roberts, how's Keenan?" Will asked.

Jodie had one arm around Will's waist, and she held on tighter instead of moving away. She needed him more than anything right now.

"He's going to live," Roz said.

"I'll keep praying for him," Will said, and seemed to catch Roz off guard. She didn't have a nasty comeback.

"The doctor says he's lucky," Lou said. "He's going to pull through, but the driver wasn't so lucky. He passed away a little while ago. His family is in another waiting room on the other side there." Lou pointed down the hall.

Tears welled up in Jodie's eyes again. "Who was he?"

Lou shrugged. "Don't know. He didn't go to school with Keenan. He's a couple years older. The police say he's a known drug dealer."

Jodie's heart went out to his family. "The guy couldn't have been that much older than Keenan," she said.

"I don't think he was," Lou replied. "The police said he was speeding. Possibly racing with another car."

Long-faced, and with her arms crossed protectively over her chest, Roz continued to stare at Will.

"I need to go check on my husband," Roz finally said, starting to walk away.

"Mrs. Roberts, if you have a few more minutes I'd like to talk to you about something?" Will asked.

Jodie looked up at him, wondering what was on his mind.

"You too, Mr. Dickerson, if you have a moment."

Roz and Lou exchanged glances for a few seconds before looking away.

"What's this about?" Lou asked.

"Sir, if we can have a seat over here." Will pointed to a small seating area a few feet away. "It's about Corey," he finally said, after neither of them moved.

The four of them sat down as a young woman hooked to an IV machine walked slowly down the hall.

"I've been wanting to have this conversation with the two of you for a long time," Will started off saying. "I just never had the chance." His gaze strayed to Roz. "Mrs. Roberts, you say I'm responsible for your son's death, and I agree I'm partly to blame, but not for the reason you think."

Lou listened intently while Roz raised her chin and stared off into the ceiling.

Jodie squeezed Will's hand to let him know she was right there with him no matter what.

"I was accused of being drunk and driving off the road. That's not true. I hold myself partly responsible because I wasn't supposed to be driving my brother's car that night. When I asked if I could use it, he said no. I waited until he got on the phone with his girlfriend and swiped the keys. I picked up Corey and Mark from the schoolyard and they'd started drinking, but they weren't drunk. Contrary to what you'd been told, nobody was."

Lou cleared his throat and stood up, offering his hand to Will. "Young man, thank you for being here."

Will stood and accepted it.

Jodie crossed over to comfort Roz who'd begun crying again.

Three weeks later, Jodie was outside with a garbage bag cleaning out her backseat when a car pulled up and Keenan got out. He took his time exiting, not quite one hundred percent since the accident.

"What you doing? Getting ready to sell the Cavalier?" Keenan asked, as he walked up to her looking inside with a smile on his face.

"No. I'm just cleaning some of the junk out of there. All this clutter is getting on my nerves. I can't find anything."

He held his hand up to shield the sun. "Yeah, I bet ya Jimmy Hoffa's back there somewhere." A balled-up piece of paper hit him in the head.

"Don't talk about my baby like that. This car has gotten me around faithfully for the last five years. It's like a Timex, it takes a licking and keeps on ticking."

He laughed.

"Where you coming from?" she asked.

"Forward Motion. Will said to tell you he'll call you later."

"Cool. You still going to Clifton for a couple of weeks?"

"Yeah, Daddy said he's gonna come get me next week. Hang out in my old stomping grounds for a few weeks, you know."

She set the garbage bag full of miscellaneous pieces of paper down and picked up a Swiss broom. "He practically moved into your hospital room didn't he?"

"Shoot, Daddy and Marion both were there almost every day. A brother couldn't even rest."

Jodie shot him a quick glance. "Aw, come on, you know you loved all the attention."

"I tell you what. I didn't love all the pain. That's my last time in anybody's hospital. The food was nasty and they wake you up every few hours so you couldn't sleep good if you wanted to."

"You and Marion getting along pretty good now?"

Keenan shrugged. "He's all right. He's renting me a limo this weekend for the prom."

"A limo! Eww, look at you. Going to the prom in style."

He laughed. "They're just scared for me to drive or ride with some of my buddies. They think I don't know what's up. But that's cool."

"Well, I'm happy you're doing better and you look good," she said, as she uprighted the passenger seat.

He held his arms out. "Drug and alcohol free. I feel good. What do ya' say we go grab a smoothie? You know I'll be going off for the summer and you won't get to bug me about spending time with you."

She pointed at the portable vacuum cleaner setting close to the car. "Stop talking and start working. Get that side for me and I'll be ready to go."

"I just got out of the hospital, and you putting me to work?"

She waved a hand at him and smiled. "That was three weeks ago. Come on now, so I can get another punch in my frequent visitor card."

He picked up the vacuum and pulled a card from his pocket. "No, I'm gonna get another punch in my card."

Chapter 28

"Cue the lights and roll tape," Stone said, as the camera moved in for a close-up of Will's face.

"Ladies and gentlemen, today's show addresses an issue near and dear to my heart. As you know, I have a passion for high school sports, and the welfare of young athletes. Two years ago I started the Forward Motion Foundation whose mission is to mentor young athletes dealing with various drug, alcohol or personal related problems. To date, we have helped over thirty Memphis area athletes overcome various problems to go on and play professional sports, or pursue their careers of choice. I want to dedicate today's show to the memory of my best friend, Corey Dickerson, quarterback for the Clifton High Wildcats, who died one month before his high school graduation.

"Our guest today is Dr. Phil Joyner, a local psychologist who treats addiction in young athletes…."

From her seat offstage, Jodie blinked to stop the tears from rolling down her cheeks.

"Are you okay?" Manny whispered, standing next to her. He patted her on the back.

"I'm fine. I just know how hard this show is to do for Will." She wiped a tear from her face.

"He's been working on this for a long time. You weren't supposed to know about it."

She turned to Manny. "You knew, too?" she asked.

"Honey, everybody knew but you. Ain't nothing going on around here that I don't know about, anyway. But they had the damnedest time keeping everything from you. I almost let it slip a time or two myself."

"Shh," Stone hushed them.

Jodie didn't let on like she knew anything. She kept her mouth shut and waited for the end of the film.

The camera switched to taped interviews of students who'd gone through Will's Forward Motion Foundation, and on to careers as professional athletes. Jodie recognized DeJohn Robinson. He'd started off smoking marijuana and then graduated to cocaine. He kicked his habit and went on to start a program mentoring young men in Miami, where he played basketball for the Miami Heat. After the tape, Will and Dr. Joyner discussed treatment methods and how to get help for athletes dealing with all the pressures of organized sports.

At the end of the show as the credits rolled, smiling faces from the Forward Motion and other featured Memphis-area foundations flashed across the screen.

The last picture was one of Corey and Will kneeling together on the football field, with their arms around each other, smiling into the camera.

Below the picture in white letters appeared, Dedicated to the memory of Corey Louis Dickerson 1972-1988.

You could hear a pin drop in the studio as Will stared at the screen a little longer.

Numb from the impact the film had on her, Jodie couldn't move. She'd known this would be an emotional day for her, but she hadn't expected to cry all through the show. Another round of tears filled her eyes.

Will finally turned away from the screen and shook hands with the doctor, as they walked off the set. After the doctor left, Will walked toward Jodie and their eyes met. He wiped at his nose a couple of times and she wiped at her tearstained face. His eyes were misty and he looked exhausted.

"That was a nice surprise," he said, once he reached her. "Where did you find that picture?"

"I've always had it. I stole it from Roz when I left for college. I never wanted to forget him...or you."

Will pulled Jodie into his arms and kissed her gently on the forehead in front of everybody walking around the set. When he pulled back, she looked up into his eyes, and tiptoed to kiss him on the lips.

"I love you, William Duncan," she whispered.

He frowned and shook his head. "I don't know. A relationship between you and me might be too complicated."

She smiled and hit him on the arm. "I'm not afraid of complications, are you?"

He winked at her and licked his lips. "I love you, too, Jodie." He bent his head and kissed her.

At the touch of his mouth, her world stopped and she closed her eyes. His tongue thrust deep into her mouth and she thought she'd explode. They clung to each other as the room started spinning.

She wanted him so bad she forgot where she was, until the sound of applause around them grew louder and louder. They came up for air to find the entire crew of *The Memphis Zone* surrounding them, clapping and whistling.

Jodie leaned her head against Will's chest. "I guess they approve," she said smiling.

He kissed the top of her head. "Baby, I don't care who does or doesn't approve. Everybody's gonna know about us."

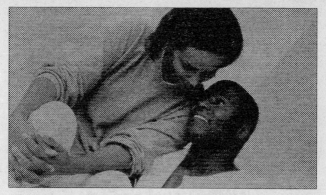

Celebrate Valentine's Day with this collection of heart-stirring stories...

Love in Bloom

"These three authors have banded together to create some excellent reading."
—*Romantic Times BOOKreviews*

FRANCINE CRAFT,
LINDA HUDSON-SMITH,
JANICE SIMS

Three beloved Arabesque authors bring romance alive in these captivating Valentine tales of first love, second chances and promises fulfilled.

Available the first week of January wherever books are sold.

ARABESQUE®

www.kimanipress.com

KPLIB0620107

To realize true love, sometimes you have to weather the storm.

Bestselling author

Melanie Schuster

Before the Storm

When Maya Simpson married Julian Deveraux,
the eldest son of the powerful Deveraux clan,
she thought they would be together forever.
But when overwhelming social pressures convinced
her of her husband's infidelity, she filed for divorce
and left—unaware that she was pregnant.

Now, four years later, they meet once again. Will their
reunion bring the family together or tear them apart?

*"Schuster's superb storytelling ability is
exhibited in fine fashion."*
—*Romantic Times BOOKreviews* on
UNTIL THE END OF TIME

**BEFORE THE STORM will be available the first week
of January wherever books are sold.**

KIMANI PRESS™
www.kimanipress.com   KPMS0020107

**An emotional story about experiencing love
the second time around...**

Sweet Memphis Crush

BRIDGET ANDERSON

Desperate to save her fourteen-year-old brother
from addiction, Jodie Dickerson moves back to
Memphis, Tennessee—just a stone's throw from her
dysfunctional family. She soon runs into sports-show
host William Duncan—the same gorgeous guy she
fell for years ago, right before he crashed a car that
killed Jodie's older brother. Can Jodie ever find
forgiveness so she and Will can realize their love?

"Anderson's wonderfully written romance is one
that readers are certain to appreciate and enjoy."
—*Booklist*

**Available the first week of January
wherever books are sold.**

ARABESQUE®

www.kimanipress.com   KPBA0030107